T0004302

TRAINER'S REVENGE

TRAINER'S REVENGE

• JAMES CATES •

TATE PUBLISHING
AND ENTERPRISES, LLC

Trainer's Revenge
Copyright © 2016 by James Cates. All rights reserved.

No part of this publication may be reproduced, stored in a retrieval system or transmitted in any way by any means, electronic, mechanical, photocopy, recording or otherwise without the prior permission of the author except as provided by USA copyright law.

This novel is a work of fiction. Names, descriptions, entities, and incidents included in the story are products of the author's imagination. Any resemblance to actual persons, events, and entities is entirely coincidental.

The opinions expressed by the author are not necessarily those of Tate Publishing, LLC.

Published by Tate Publishing & Enterprises, LLC
127 E. Trade Center Terrace | Mustang, Oklahoma 73064 USA
1.888.361.9473 | www.tatepublishing.com

Tate Publishing is committed to excellence in the publishing industry. The company reflects the philosophy established by the founders, based on Psalm 68:11,
"The Lord gave the word and great was the company of those who published it."

Book design copyright © 2016 by Tate Publishing, LLC. All rights reserved.
Cover design by Joana Quilantang
Interior design by Shieldon Alcasid

Published in the United States of America

ISBN: 978-1-68270-183-6
Fiction / Christian / Fantasy
15.10.24

Contents

FOREWORD

Trainer's Revenge is book two of three. To get the full understanding of some of the situations presented in this book, it is recommended that you read *Trainer* first.

1 Samuel's Sting

Three-month-old Samuel peddled his tiny feet and hands as Bill struggled to secure the diaper. Bill chattered to the baby, leaning down until the baby focused on his face, looking as if he completely understood Bill's words. Bill selected a sleeper with frogs sprinkled across the fabric and froggy feet and a pullover diaper shirt with newborn-sized trains. As he tugged the shirt over the baby's head, he noticed something at the back of his neck. Bill changed Samuel's baby diaper, talking to him. In the process of dressing Samuel, he noticed what he knew as the mark of Trainer. He remembered the mark from the description of what his looked like. This one was different. He saw the scorpion embedded on top of the old mark that was described to him.

He stopped dressing Samuel as tears pooled in his eyes. "Guys, you've got to see this! We're not finished fighting yet!"

Fred asked , "What's up, Bill?"

The prayer squad moved toward Bill and Samuel. Fred noticed the mark on the boy's shoulder first. Once the others noticed, they stared, not knowing what to think. Bill looked up at the group. "Now what?"

"Now we pray," Fred replied. "Harry, John, could you two join me in the middle with Bill and Samuel? I would like the rest of you to form a circle around us."

Once everyone was in place, Fred started praying. "Lord, we thank you for Bill and all he brings to the prayer squad. We praise You for the blessings young Samuel brings to us as well. We come together agreeing on behalf of young Samuel that You would remove the beast from within him. Your authority is established by the power of Your name and the blood You shed on the cross. We call the authority You have to influence the life of Samuel in a way that You and only You can receive the glory. Show Bill how to teach and train Samuel in Your ways. Give him understanding in Your way. Guide and direct his paths. Lord, hold him and his son in Your hands. Place Your mighty hedge of protection around them."

Harry continued, "You are the king of all kings, and no power above or below the earth or in the heavens can stand against You. May Your will reign supreme in Bill's and Samuel's lives. Give Bill the peace to know that You are directing his and his son's paths. In Your holy name, we pray. Amen."

"Bill, you had to choose to follow Christ. God is showing me that Samuel will have the same choice to make. You are still his father and can influence his decision, but you have to allow him to make it on his own."

Fred and Harry rested their hands on his shoulder as the other prayer squad members prayed.

Adley and Aaron rested beside Samuel, watching and waiting. They saw the concern on Bill's face and hoped for the prayers to come up. Soon after the thought, more began to come and then stopped cold. With only a short delay, the group gathered around them and began to pray.

Aaron could see Trainer fidgeting inside looking and trying to sort what was happening. Adley was already preparing the defense to keep Trainer from harming Samuel. Aaron knew that God's work would go on in this child's life and that the prayers going up would keep them strong.

2 Rebeca

Rebeca had met Bill at his wife's funeral. She had spoken often with Saundra when she was alive and knew Saundra's wish to make contact with Bill. She didn't want to have the feelings she was having, but her heart was determined. She answered Bill's call and arrived at his house to help him with thank-you notes. She soon realized there was more to this than thank-you notes.

"Do you think it is right for me to have the feelings I have for you this soon?" Bill asked.

"I wish I could tell you it is right and fall into your arms right now. My heart pleads for you, but I know it will not be in your best interest. Bill, help me help you. Do you think you have mourned Saundra?"

"I continue to mourn her every day. I break down every night and cry because the bed is empty beside me. I don't know if I will ever stop mourning her."

"It sounds to me like you still need more time to heal from your loss of Saundra." Rebeca held back tears, her heart and mind warring against each other.

Bill's countenance dropped. "Do you want to leave?"

She couldn't believe Bill's words. "No, Bill, I don't want to leave and will not tell you that. I want to wrap my arms around you and never let you go. I want you to be the man in my life. If I tell you that, will you think I am being too forward?"

"Bill, I want to be here as long as you need me. I need someone to help me deal with her loss too. I still cry at night too."

"Thank you." Tears bedded in his eyes.

She took his hands. "Don't be afraid to cry in front of me. Just make a deal with me. With every tear you cry, release some of the pain and replace it with a happy memory."

"That sounds like a deal. Do you want to talk about Saundra?"

"Yes, I would like that."

"I thought about what you said last night. Did Saundra send you to me to help?"

"You know Saundra well. Her love for you extended beyond her life. Yes, she wanted me to make sure that you were taken care of after she passed on."

"Do you think she knew what would happen when you came to help me?"

"She knew what I would do. She didn't know what you would do. She wanted me to make sure you didn't shut down after her death."

"Are you also a devoted Christian like Saundra was?"

"Yes, Bill, we prayed many times for you to receive Christ as your personal Lord and Savior."

"What do you think Saundra would want me to do? I feel like I couldn't ever forget Saundra."

Rebeca knew this part of the conversation was going to come up. "I know she would. She wanted you to live on and knew it would take help from someone else. She wouldn't want you to forget her but instead to honor her with your life."

"Do you think I'm weak because I cry because of this hurt and loss?"

"Bill, tears don't make you weak. Tears make you human, and that is more important than a fake strength that will collapse when the pressure gets great. You are strong to me because you care. That is what really counts anyway."

"I think we need to take it slow for a while. It's been three months since Saundra died. The loss of Saundra still hurts."

"Of course, you will find time, and help from God is what you need now."

She hugged him, and his arms wrapped around her. "I will wait as long you need me to. I know you're hurt and promise to be here for you when you need me."

3 The Wall

Peter drummed his fingers on the armrest of the captain's chair as the van approached Patty's house. The chatter of the other passengers around him faded into nothingness as he stared out the window at Patty's door, holding his breath. The first time they'd picked up Patty, he was certain his heart had stopped. In the weeks that followed, he could no longer deny the feelings she brought out in him. It made Bible study night his favorite evening of the week.

Tonight, he planned to tell her.

The van stopped in front of her house, and she emerged from the door; he knew Richard was chiding in a teasing way. He quickly sprang from his seat and opened the door for her. Once she was settled in the van, he expressed his desire to date her, and she freely returned his expression with joy. As they picked up more members, the van filled up and rendered any serious conversation impossible. It wasn't until they arrived at the Bible study that they could really talk.

They snacked on the food and talked about many things. Most importantly, they set a time and day to go on an official date. Everything had gone well overall, and the time came to pick her up in his car for the date.

His normal escort was replaced with a slightly older, sky blue pickup truck. He parked the truck by the curb in front of the house and placed his hand on the horn, but thought better of it and got out to knock on the door instead. From the other side of the door, he heard Richard's and Patty's voices in indistinct chatter and knew she was getting ribbed again. He wasn't even sure his knock had been heard above the din, but presently, Patty appeared and closed the door behind her.

"Let's go before he gets anything else out."

"My lady," Peter said as he opened her door.

"Thank you." She stepped into the truck.

He slid into the driver's seat, fired the engine to life, and steered toward the stop sign at the end of the street. "Do you have any preferences as to where you want to go?"

"No, but let's go someplace where they have good desserts."

"I know just the place. Real good food and sweet desserts for the craving taste buds to enjoy."

"Um, that is making me hungry. This isn't real far away, is it?"

"Oh, no. Just far enough to get the conversation started, and then we'll be there."

"What is on your mind for conversation?"

"I thought we could start with talking about you."

"Me?" Patty wasn't sure she wanted to be the topic of discussion.

"I think you have a more interesting life than I do."

"I think not, but I'll start out, and then we can talk about you."

"Okay."

"What do you want to know about me?"

"Everything."

"Where do you want me to start?"

"Tell me how you met the prayer squad and Jesus."

Peter smiled. "Well, at least, that starts easy. I met John about three years ago. He'd just joined this group called the prayer squad. I had just lost my job and was possibly going to lose my home. I wasn't against God. After all, he is the ruler of the world, but I never knew God personally and wasn't sure I really wanted to. I ignored his invitation to receive Christ as my savior, but started going to his farm on Thursday nights to join in what John called a celebration.

"I met Fred and Harry at my first Thursday night celebration. I hung around John more. He seemed to fit better with me than the others. For the next year, I met them every Thursday night because it was fun. They started something different the next Easter. Friday night, they met and talked about how they met Jesus and read Matthew's account on what Jesus did for them on that Good Friday. That never left my mind. It played like a broken record until I read it and reread it for myself. Each time I read the account, I started a chapter sooner and read another chapter behind it. John invited me to his church one Sunday. I went to see what they said about this. When I got there, I discovered more about Jesus's resurrection. During the invitation, John and I walked down to the front to talk to the pastor. He showed me more verses, answered more questions until I accepted Christ as my savior that day."

"You joined the prayer squad that day?"

"No; a year after that, I joined the prayer squad. I attended John's church for another year and the Thursday night celebration. After that, John asked me to join the prayer squad."

"How long have you been part of the prayer squad?"

"Just a little over a year now. I've learned more from Fred than I have from the pastor at the church. I have more opportunities to ask questions when I am a little confused in the small group than when I am at church. "Are you confused often, Peter?"

"At first, I was confused all the time. They were patient with me and answered a lot of questions. Recently, I have been able to figure out most things."

"It sounds like you have grown a lot in the last couple of years."

"I hope so."

Bill allowed Rebeca to hold him for a long time. As they separated, he heard her ask, "Are you all right?"

"Yes, I'm fine. The prayer squad is meeting to pray tonight, and I would like to go. Do you have anything else to do?"

"You are going to pray to God?"

"Yes, I have had a busy two weeks since the funeral. All that busyness led me to a moment in which I had to choose between Jesus and death. Jesus saved me from the similar fate of my entire father's line before me."

"You're a Christian now?"

"Yes, Trainer no longer possesses or controls me. The Holy Spirit of God Almighty does that now."

She wrapped her arms around him and said, "Saundra and I have been praying for that for so long. She wanted to be alive when you accepted Christ. You can bet she celebrated with the angels in heaven though."

"I'm sure she did. Do you want to join me? We can eat supper there. It will be a man's supper. You may want to bring some women's food along with you."

"I would love to go with you. May I raid your kitchen to see if there are enough women's food ingredients to make something?"

"The kitchen is yours. Do you want me to help?"

"Sure, you know where the stuff is in there."

She scanned the refrigerator and found limited possibilities after throwing away several ingredients that had already gone bad. "Do you have any noodles or pasta of any kind?"

"In the pantry. Saundra has a lot of stuff in there I don't know what to do with."

"The pantry was a woman's dream; women's food. She pulled out a bag of noodles, some peas, a fresh jar of mayonnaise, and some canned tuna. While the noodles boiled in a pot, she mixed the remaining ingredients together. Within fifteen minutes, she had a pasta salad that rivaled any Bill had tasted and enough to feed an army. "See, quick salads are great-tasting too. You should try it."

He scooped a small sample up with a spoon and nibbled on it, savoring the flavor. "Mmm, very good. This is really good. You may be elected to make this more often."

"I hope so. When do we need to leave to get there?"

"We can leave anytime now. Time sure travels fast when you're having fun."

"Are you sure I would be welcome?"

"Good food is bribery enough. I'm sure I can get you in the door."

"Good, let's get going."

After seating Rebeca in the Benz, Bill rounded the car and sighed as he made himself comfortable in the driver's seat. He could remember all too clearly the event leading to the hospital stay. That didn't change the fact that he liked that car. Since then, he sold the truck and driven his Benz with pride.

Avoiding looking at Saundra's Benz, he backed out of the garage and aimed the car in the direction of the house on Power Lane. "You know, this is the first time that the prayer squad meeting is being held in this house."

"Oh, why is that?"

"Fred bought the house from me a few weeks ago. The deal was final a couple of weeks before he even entered the house."

"This is the house that Saundra talked about as Trainer's house."

"Yes." Bill went silent for a time before continuing, "From what I learned. The prayer squad had a real fight over that house. I was with them when they went to take the house away from Trainer. That was a sight to see."

"Trainer made it difficult to take possession?"

"From what I understand from Fred, he made it difficult for God to take the property away."

"What happened that God had a hard time handling the situation?"

"You misunderstand me. God handled his job with ease. It was us, his servants that struggled to handle the task at hand."

"Oh, I see. That sounds normal."

"I'm learning that quickly. We still have our human feelings, even though Jesus comes in."

"Yes, we do. Feelings will find a way to get in the way as well."

Bill turned the Benz onto Power Lane. He still anticipated further attacks from Trainer. "You don't have to say that too many times."

"The house still affects you, doesn't it?"

"In a big way. We are giving it to God today. I know how Trainer thinks—well, a little—so I know this is going to stir up the pot and create trouble for everyone involved."

"God is in control, and if you're having this meeting in the house, then he has already taken control of the situation. You can see the past. God looks at the present and future. This is a test for you to allow your faith to grow."

"What is the proof that I passed the test?"

"You'll walk boldly in that house thanking God for the victory he provided the group and confident that what God has begun, he will finish. That is how you will know you passed the test."

"Do you believe I have the faith to do all that?"

"I know you have the faith to do all that and more. I will do all I can to bring out the strength, faith, and patience of God in you no matter how much it hurts."

Bill saw the drive getting full, but knew there was a lot of carpooling going on. "Not many cars for the whole crew to be here. I guess they haven't had the chance to get the stolen cars replaced."

"How many cars were stolen?"

"Six or seven at last count. The thinking is that this is a result of a direct attack of the house or Trainer within it."

"How long ago was that?"

"About four or five weeks ago."

"What about the insurance companies?"

"Same story. Like a broken record. They were all accused of insurance fraud and investigated. It has been an interesting month, to say the least."

"This Trainer thing is really as serious as Saundra said it was."

"Yes. It may be more serious than even she knew. This was left in God's hands the day they disappeared."

Bill caught sight of the house. It looked beautiful—the lawn manicured and the house well taken care of. "This place has changed a lot since Trainer was kicked out."

"What was over there?" Rebeca pointed to a large burned-out area, where nothing grew.

"That was Trainer's barn. Part of taking the house involved burning it to the ground. God had to have burned it after it was lit. Even the old cars and tractors burned to ash like wood stubble."

Bill turned into a secondary drive that led to the side of the house and stopped beside a door that looked like it hadn't been used in many years. "We'll go in the front door. This door goes directly to the basement."

"I'm not sure if Fred has seen this door yet. I'll be around in a second."

Bill shivered at the limited memories of the house, like he anticipated Moloch to jump out and try to kill him. He stepped past looking through the little window for any sign that Moloch waited in there. "Okay."

Bill joined Rebeca, and they walked into the house together and began greeting the members of the prayer squad. Members mingled for a few moments…most broke off to greet the new person with Bill. The food was taken to the table, and a spoon to dip it out was placed in it.

Bill scanned the inside of the house. The only furniture to speak of was the folding chairs used at the prayer squad meetings and the dinner table spread with their food. The threadbare carpet looked as though it once matched the '60s style decor of the house; out of date. A few antiques and it could have been a museum.

They worked their way toward the kitchen where the food was put. Bill followed Rebeca into the dining room, where he filled his plate with a little bit of everything, and then into the living area, where Harry grabbed his attention and waved him over. As Bill led, Rebeca came over, and he noted the several other small groups established around the room and felt a comfort and peace come over him being in the presence of these other believers and warriors. There really was no sign of Trainer in that house at all.

4 THE CHURCH

Fred walked into the living room and saw not three others, as he anticipated, but twelve and all but one he could identify by sight. Praise God for such growth in this little group. May I be faithful to the few?

"Wow, Look around at the blessings God has given us this day."

The conversations in the room broke up as people looked around. Fred was certain they saw the same thing that he saw. The air in the house was filled with the presence of God, and he couldn't imagine anyone mixing up the cause of that.

"Do we need more chairs for the circle?"

"Ladies sit first. Men stand, if necessary. We will need to get another dozen to grow into again."

"That is a problem I can handle." Fred knew he was witness to God's blessings pouring out on them in a way he could no longer comprehend.

The chair reserved for the middle of the circle was slid out to accommodate one more there. As they all gathered around the circle and took their seats, Fred asked Bill about the new face sitting next to him. "It looks like we have a new face in the crowd. Bill, did she come with you?"

"Yes, she did. This is Rebeca." To Rebeca, he said, "You finally get the chance to meet Fred."

"Nice to have you, Rebeca." Fred turned his attention to the rest of the group. "Welcome, all. We have come here to pray, and that is what we are going to do. Remember, first we give thanks, and then we pray for others, and then we will pray committing the property on Power Lane to God's glory and use. Let's start with giving thanks for the victory giving us this property."

The prayers of thanksgiving lifted to heaven for the many blessings and victories. The prayers silenced, and Fred asked, "Does any of you want this group to pray for you in a specific situation in your life?"

The hands went up for many specific situations. One chair was placed in the middle as those seeking prayer sat in the chair and prayed with the group over the matter.

The prayers went around as those who desired began to pray when urged by the Holy Spirit. The prayers continued to flow for an hour more as they ask God to meet specific needs.

As the prayers ended, Fred's face fell somber. "We have a group need to be discussed and prayed about. We all know that God took this house from the demons that resided here. We need to use it in God's way."

He fell silent and lingered in thought, praying for the right words. "The house was emptied of all of the demon's property. Everything that belonged to the demons was placed in the barn and burned to ash. God destroyed every remnant of the demons on the property. It would be easy for me to live in the house thanking God for the blessing and opportunity, but is that really what God wants from this place? I didn't get the money on my own. It came in the mail, God-given for this purchase. What does God want to do with this property?"

No one answered, so Fred continued, "How many of us go to church on Sunday morning?"

Seven of the thirteen hands went up. "This group has grown quickly and with people new to Jesus and his ways. About half of us could call this church. Don't get me wrong. I am proud to be used by God to encourage your growth and teach you the ways of the Lord. There are things that happen in church that do not happen here. Are we going to become what the people need to grow leaving out God's ordinances? This would not be wise on our part. I would encourage each and every one of you to find a church home to help you grow in the Lord as well."

Bill spoke up. "Fred, you are the only pastor I know."

"Yes, you are my pastor. Why do I need another one?" Richard asked.

Tears welled up in his eyes as Fred opened his mouth to speak when someone else said, "I want you to be my pastor. Is this not like church?"

"You are my pastor," someone else said.

"You are more than my friend and counselor in time of need, and you are my pastor too." Came Harry's voice from behind him. "Will you be my pastor?"

Fred's head touched his chest as tears ran down his cheeks. Words could not describe the conflict inside him or the peace in the message. "Go and preach. I have appointed you to lead these children of mine."

When Fred could finally look up, he asked, "You all want me as your pastor?"

The circle nodded and spoke in agreement. "Yes. Will you?"

"We have no church to worship at."

Harry said, "We have an empty parcel of land where a huge barn once stood. Could we build one there? In the meantime, we could hold services here if you would permit us."

"Among those of us working, we could provide the building supplies," Peter said with an air of excitement.

"We could provide the labor. That would reduce the cost," Richard replied.

Bill said, "I can start working on floor plans and permits. I'll try to get through the red tape quickly."

Still in shock, Fred replied, "You all have shown me your seriousness. I will be your pastor. What time do you want to start services on Sunday?"

After deciding that the services should start at nine thirty the following Sunday, the meeting broke up, and all went home. Fred was left with a formidable task and little time to prepare for a church service that he wasn't sure was really his to prepare for.

Jesus never turned his head as he said, "The church is formed. You will have the next phase of trials to get them through. The enemies are waiting and planning. Satan may have changed tactics, but he will not give up this fight."

Ailith said, "We are ready. We will fight as long as is needed."

John sat in his office, his Bible open to Matthew chapter 5, verse 22. He turned his head to the ceiling. "How can I be anything but angry? You are giving them everything they want. Am I going to be left alone and separate from everyone in the prayer squad? Then what? What do I do when I need someone, and no one is available to come? Who will pray for me?"

"John, you will always be part of the team. There are three other men who always come to your side when you need them. That will never change. Your anger is unjust. I will bless all of those in obedience to me in the fullness of time."

John's spirit was immediately comforted, and he knew who was talking to him. "Why is everyone else getting the blessings but me? What have I done wrong? Why don't I deserve your blessing?"

"Look at my servant Job. He felt the same way and asked the same questions. Look at how I answered him. My blessings come in the fullness of time and never sooner."

Anger swelled inside him. Accusations fell like rain from the sky. His heart hardened to the message of love, choosing instead to live and act in an unforgivable attitude. "I am justly angry. You are not being fair to me, and I hate that I have to wait."

The silence in his heart was all that was left.

The scent of willful disobedience filled Satan's nostrils. Oh, how he lived for that smell. But this particular victory was particularly sweet. John. John was his way into the prayer squad. With the barrier erected between John and God, it wouldn't take much effort for John's anger, resentment, and jealousy to spread through the rest of the group. John would be the henchman that he would use to open the door and plant the right seeds. With that realization came a new scent—the scent of victory.

Gary was at the gym talking to Coach Hogan. He had increased in ability above and beyond what was possible. Coach Hogan accused him of taking steroids. He began to walk out of the gym leaving Gary behind. Staring at the coach's back, Gary called after him, "What can I do to prove to you that I'm not using drugs?"

Coach Hogan stopped and turned around. "Would you take a drug screen at your cost and guarantee that I can screen you anytime I want?"

"I'll do whatever you want me to do. I'll take the test tonight. You can go with me to verify that I have done nothing to alter the test."

Gary knew from the coach's expression that this was more than any athlete had been willing to do in the past, so it should have been proof enough. Gary knew coach had seen too many athletes fall to steroids and had decided early in his career not to coach any athlete on steroids.

"You know my standing on drug use? For me to remain your coach, you have to take that drug test now."

"Then let's do it. I won't even go to the locker room."

They left the gym together for the clinic that drug screened potential employees. An uncomfortable silence engulfed the car on the drive over. How could he do something like this knowing how I would feel?

Gary could see the disappointment written on coach's face. There was no use trying to talk it off. He knew better than that. He would wait for the drug screen results before saying anything else. The accusation hurt, but he understood where it came from. For the coach, there could only be one explanation for the vast improvement in all areas of his physical activity. "Moloch, how can I explain this improvement to Coach after I pass the drug screen?"

Moloch didn't answer for a while. "Whatever you say, you cannot bring up my name or my presence. No one but you can know about me. Go against me on this, and pain will follow."

"How do I explain you without talking about you?"

"I never tell how. What I promise is that I am listening to your conversation. I can control your increase so it will no longer look like you are on steroids."

"That is a start. You have to work with me, or this will end badly."

"I will work with you, and you will work with me. I can offer leniency so you can come up with any spiritual reason you want as long as my name doesn't come up."

This is going to be difficult to make Coach understand. I hope he still takes me on.

A nurse emerged from the back of the clinic. "Gary?" He rose and followed the nurse into the testing area. The test took about five minutes to complete. The hardest part was waiting for the results. He spent the time mulling over a thousand explanations for his improvement, but he didn't like any of them. *How am I going to explain this?*

5 War Preparation

Four days had passed, and Fred was determined to have a sermon ready. He had dedicated his life to these believers and knew that it would end the way God wanted it to. He knew God touched him and gave him a message to speak. The time was quickly coming for them to be pulling in. He sat in his office reading over his notes one more time while continuously saying little popcorn prayers.

He picked up his Bible, notes, and guitar and headed out to set up the living room for the service. Harry and John had delivered twelve more chairs and a podium. He picked up some chairs and arranged them six across and four deep with an aisle down the middle. The podium stood near the east wall, as did a chair for him to sit on. On the long table at the back of the room stood a one-gallon pickle jar marked, "Help build the church." The room is ready for the congregation. Are you?

"I'm as ready as I'll ever be," he said to himself in response to the thought. Five minutes before the service was to start, the twelve from the Wednesday night's prayer meeting arrived. The conversation struck between them made it sound and look like a church. Everyone seemed taken with the Spirit, all except John, who was off in a corner by himself.

He bowed his head, and a voice told Fred he was struggling.

He walked up to him. "What's wrong, John? Are you feeling well?"

"I'm fine. I just wanted to pray."

"John, why is Peter not here praying with you?"

"Peter is busy with Patty. I don't want to ask him to part from her to pray."

"John, are you going to face the spiritual battles alone? What happened to the strength of two?"

"Patty." His angered flashed with the name. He wanted to take it back as soon as the name escaped from his lips.

"John, are you letting something get between you and Peter?"

"Do you have room to speak? Your family lives, while mine have died."

"Have you let your words be tested for accuracy by Jesus's blood? Learn God's truth before you judge others."

Fred left him alone to pray.

Rebeca walked out of the changing room and into the gym wearing a white GI. The heavy material snapped when her hands and feet moved quickly enough. She'd learned ten years ago to snap the uniform with her leg. She'd been training in the martial arts since the age of twelve and had reached a level where she competed in amateur tournaments. Now her instructor wanted to take her to tournaments that tested her skills against others. The instructor had been a professional fighter, having retired a few years before to teach. He was tall and muscular with speed that Rebcca was learning to defend against. She started stretching with the rest of the class, focusing her mind on her goals for that session.

Every class was different but included one major lesson: Life throws surprises at you; be ready for anything to happen. Some classes were aimed at that one lesson. The instructor bowed onto the workout floor and said, "Let's get started."

The class got up and took their places on the floor. They stood an arm's length apart, the uniform fabric snapped as they went through the warm-up exercises. She was relaxed and ready. It wasn't until the main lesson came that she realized the object of this class.

She could hear the instructor say, "I am trying to surprise you and catch you unaware. Remember that this drill is no contact. Not only are you to be aware but also in control."

Rebeca stood in the center of the floor with two other students. The remainder of the students walked around them. They could only move if they were being attacked by another student. She stood still, ready for anything. *Which one of the students is going to try me?*

A tall, skinny, fast young man placed his flat hand on his belly as he walked behind her. She moved her head just before his hand smacked the back of it. Her foot was up, stopped just short of his gut, and put back before he could do anything else. She set her arms for the block and her mind for the takedown. It was his move. She was in a defensive posture; he in offensive.

When his hand shot out, she caught his wrist, twisted it around his back, and dropped him to his knees. A quick grunt escaped his lips. "You're not trying to pick on me, are you?"

"No."

A second student came from the rear. He reached out and grunted as her free hand grabbed it and flexed it to a position of pain in his wrist. He fell to his knees. She looked intently at a third student. "Are you interested in seeing what I do next?"

The other student just backed away. She released and pushed both students away and fired both feet straight back. They landed beside the head of a fourth student. "You're out of this now."

He backed away to the wall as she landed upright with the other three students facing her. She held out one hand and signaled with two fingers for them to make their move, but no one moved.

"Positions," called the instructor. The five students took their positions and bowed to each other. They took their seats with the students sitting on the floor.

"What did Rebeca do that helped her keep the other students from surprising her?"

A few answered, and after a thorough discussion and a few more demonstrations, the class ended. They all bowed off the floor. The instructor caught Rebeca's arm before she reached the door.

"Take a twenty-minute break, and then we can work on your tournament."

"I'll just get a drink. Do you have some new victims for me?"

"Yes, and one of them will be me to make sure your skills stay sharp."

~

Gary still hadn't made up his mind on an explanation when Coach Hogan asked, "How did you do it? You didn't use steroids. What are you taking?"

"Coach, I started taking the protein powder and multivitamin you recommended and started doing push-ups before going to bed. Just a few on upper body days and doubled on lower body days."

"That doesn't sound like anything that would cause the change I saw. You're sure you're not taking anything other than what I recommended?"

"I know you, Coach. I want your help. My father monitors everything I take to make sure I comply with your recommendations."

"All right, I know you're not cheating. I'll continue to work with you.

I'll see you at the gym tomorrow."

"I'll be there ready to go. Same time as today?"

"Yes. Take only what I recommend and stick to the schedule. You will be a champion one day."

"I'll see you tomorrow."

Nine-thirty—it's time to begin the service; pain, concern, and frayed nerves mixed and flowed through Fred's body. He didn't understand how this was going to do anything for God's work. He would just have to trust God to work and go on with the service.

"Good morning."

"Good morning," the crowd answered with cheer.

"Welcome to the service this morning. It's good to be looking at all your friendly faces. I wanted this to be as much like a church service as possible, so we will praise the Lord with song, prayer, and message. It is as important that you show you are willing to help your local body financially to cover standard expenses to operate. I put a pickle jar in the back for our financial expenses. All money will go to church expenses. May the Lord lead you in your giving. All I ask is that you remain obedient to God in the matter of your finances."

He picked up his guitar. "Let's open with a song of praise to the Lord."The music flowed from the guitar easily, floating from one chord to another as the song took form before the words flowed from their mouths. They sang several songs without a break. Fred swore he saw the words flowing to the heavens with the fragrance of the sweetest rose.

Everyone joined in giving God glory and praise. As the music continued, the words turned to prayer. Fred knew the Holy Spirit was there flowing through him to the congregation in front of him. When the time was right, the guitar fell silent, and the prayers drifted into silence. The Spirit held everyone's hearts as he opened up his Bible and spoke.

"God's Word is clear to me on the importance of obedience. What is it to be obedient? Obedience means to follow instructions, to do what you are told to do. How God applied this to my life in the last few days was to look at this day and ask, 'Are you going to follow through with the commitment no matter what the cost?'"

"God hit me where it was most challenging. I didn't know what the cost would be and even now can't say that I know the full extent of the cost of the decision to be your preacher. That is a challenge I am taking seriously. I had to ask the question again to myself. The easy answer is yes, but is it really? Is it easy to be obedient in everything no matter what the cost?"

"Second Corinthians two nine says, 'The reason I wrote you was to see if you would stand the test and be obedient in everything.'"

He paused to try to read the expressions on the faces in the crowd, but he could not be sure as to what the Spirit was saying to them.

"How easy is it to be disobedient when you think you are going to get away from the consequences? Just to let you know, the consequences are always worse later than if you go ahead and face them now."

He paused to let the words sink in into their minds and hearts. "Was Jesus as obedient as I am talking about? Philippians two eight says, 'And being found in the appearance of a man, he humbled himself and became obedient to death—even the death of the cross!' Is there a better example of total obedience? Jesus obeyed to the point that he went to the cruelest death man could fathom at the time to bring you back to him. As an example, there is no measure that you can simply say, "Did Jesus disobey on this," and honestly answer yes. To be able to do this, Jesus had to pray every morning. Scripture says that Jesus went away to pray over and over again. If Jesus had to go away and pray, how much more important is it that we go away and pray?"

Fred shook at the realization that he himself struggled with that type of obedience. "There was another point God brought out to me. Who are we to be obedient to? Yes, we are to obey the government authorities. Yes, we are to obey civil laws. Did you know there was a place and time that the Apostle Peter didn't obey the civil authorities, and it was still blessed by God? Let's look what the scripture says again. Acts five twenty-nine says, 'Peter and the other apostles replied: "We must obey God rather than men."' When the apostles were commanded not to teach the good news of Jesus by the civil authorities, they did it anyway, knowing that obeying God always comes first in all matters."

The Spirit's words flowed through Fred, and the challenge hit every heart including his own. When he ended the message, he gave anyone who wanted to a chance to pray. He set a chair at the front, offering it to anyone who wanted the group to pray for them. The chair filled over again. The tears flowed as prayers were offered for two hours. Fred could see the work wasn't done, but those that were in need were unwilling to open their hearts.

Fred closed the service with one prayerful request that God would burn conviction in the hearts of those that would not open it to Him today. "It is two o'clock. I'm sure that we're all hungry. You can decide what you're going to do and enjoy dinner. Follow God in obedience today."

With that, he walked into the crowd to greet those who had come.

John's heart burned. He knew that fire was from God. For the second time, he chose to run and not obey God, his anger pulling him away from God even further. How many people had seen his resistance? Did he really want to continue with this? He knew God had said to obey and be blessed. He knew God's words were true and knew what he had to do. How long had it been since He heard a message from God? I need to obey if I am ever going to hear from God again.

6 The Mission

Trainer and cadet met together in the secure area of Samuel. Even at Samuel's age of three months, Cadet could learn information through the child that Samuel was not to understand. With quick access available to the horde's location, the hunt for their backup support began. He knew the signature of the horde too well and had seen it on the radar screen before. The only thing he could see was Samuel's room.

He had done this a hundred times with human eyes and often spotted something or someone beyond what the human host could see. "I can't even start this meeting without the horde's location. I will be back in a minute. I want to find out what is going on with the horde."

Trainer struggled through the baby's bloodstream. He had forgotten the routing of the bloodstream. He first traveled down to the leg. At least, he could tell where he was in the body. It was just a matter of finding the vessel he needed to get him to the shoulder. Twenty minutes later, he floated by the door of the secure area. He went around again, this time the tip of the tail showed like a needle tip into the bloodstream. He kept floating and found the entrance of the scorpion and entered back into the center where immediately he took on wings and his sword.

The weight of the wings and sword reminded him of the comfort of anger and confusion. Now to the tricks he had not forgotten. He spread his wings wide. With a quick flurry of the wings, he was out of Samuel and into the air. He grew to his full size and flew, a breeze rolling by with the forward motion of his body. He saw far beyond what he had ever thought possible. Then he noticed the house. It couldn't be…it just couldn't be! The horde…where is the horde? The barn…what has happened? Where the barn had been was a pile of ruin and ash. There was nothing left. Who could have done this? Why did the horde leave the house unprotected? Where was Nassor?

There was an indelible image on the roof. Where was the scorpion? What was going on? There was no way it could happen. It was impossible to take the property from his control.

The closer he got to the house, the clearer his answer became.

The indelible image on the roof became clear. It was a cross, and not just any cross but a cross with a sign on top. The sign clearly said, "King of the Jews"

Jesus had taken the house. It wasn't clear what his motivation was, but it clearly bore his mark now. There wasn't even a lick of evidence that the horde had existed at all.

He continued flying, searching, and hunting for one of the hordes at work. No one existed within sight of the house. Now fear spurred inside him. His mind filled with rattling, unclear, and vague ideas that didn't make any sense. Panic followed closely behind. You are alone. You can't complete the mission anymore. Run! Run where you can to never be seen again by the master. Instead of giving in to the fear and panic, he focused on the mission at hand. The first step was to get back to Samuel, take permanent control, and put a deep desire to have sons in him. Control of Samuel was more important than support. But there was just one more piece of important information, the log of his, Trainer's, activities that Bill had kept. They might have destroyed everything else, but that was the link that would make it happen. This time, he will bear three sons, and the spread will take. He would establish his dominion again. Trainer turned around and flew for young Samuel. What? Where did the guardian angel come from? The sword shone bright and arced across the path.

Moloch withdrew his sword, sending his fiery arc across the sky. Trainer flew directly at the angel, sword tip pointed to plunge through his heart. There was complete stillness from the angel. Patience and timing, they work best. The angel's sword deflected Trainer's to one side. As Trainer's body swung with his sword, he quickly shrank and dove headfirst into the center of the scorpion on Samuel's shoulder.

The angel turned quickly and saw nothing. It was as if Trainer had vanished into thin air. Looking all around for any sign, the angel knew Trainer had found his way back into Samuel.

Trainer started his meeting with Cadet. "We have lost our support. It is up to us to accomplish the mission at hand. The magic number is three—three boys to carry Trainer to the rest of the world. Samuel's first house will become our house. Once he gets a car, it becomes ours. The work starts all over as if he were the first person we ever possessed."

Cadet saw one thing he knew—the presence of a group of people that created a feeling of confusion and war. It didn't appear to bother Trainer at all. Trainer continued on, "I have been here before and won, and it will be as before. I know exactly how to get this started. I know what to do to make this work. With the two of us together, we can make this happen."

Cadet replied, "Make it happen," and hissed with a cheer.

Ailith looked to Alexander and Boris. "It looks like the fight just got started."

Boris shook his head. "Here we go. This guy won't ever give up."

Alexander had dropped his head. "It won't start hard for a few years. We need to rest now so we can be ready when it comes again to its peak.

One week after the house had been taken, Fred's cell phone rang.

The short call left an astonished look on Fred's face. "The insurance company just called. They canceled the investigation into fraud and are paying the claim for the stolen car. I should have my check in a few days."

They praised God for the victory in Fred's case, and hope bloomed for the others. Could it be possible that with the fall of the house the attacks on the prayer squad would end? As they got to their answering machines, they all heard that investigations were being canceled and the claims were being paid. Within a week of the house being claimed by God, their lives had returned to where they were before the attack had begun.

The prayer squad sat together around Samuel as he played contently on the floor. Bill's mind reeled at the thought of the scorpion on Samuel's shoulder. What could he do now? His heart ached with the thousand regrets running around his mind. Couldn't he have hid Samuel somewhere?

Fred easily read the distress on his face. "Bill, there is a reason this has happened. God has a plan and knows what must happen to make his plan work. Look at all that has gone on with us in the last three months. With all the bad circumstances going on, God settled everything to his glory. God is working with you in many ways. Learn what you need to learn from this and teach Samuel everything you can about Jesus. Allow him to take your life example to bring your son around to him."

With tears still trickling down his cheek, Bill replied, "You don't know how hard it is to overcome the monster that Trainer can create."

"You do. You will teach him with the help of the Holy Spirit. You will have the whole prayer squad praying for you and Samuel. Trust God to guide you and teach you. He knows exactly what you need. He is ultimately in control of all the circumstances anyway."

Bill couldn't take his eyes off the tattoo. He knew he was left with one choice—pray hard and pray now. "God, show me how I can deal with Trainer and how I can teach Samuel to deal with him."

The prayer squad knelt around him and joined him in that prayer. For the next hour, they sought God for wisdom and direction. Each member had to hug Bill before departing, promising to hold him up in prayer. Joy hung deep in spite of the circumstances going on throughout the group.

7 The Insight

Sakata had joined the heavenly forces, feeling the discouragement around the guardian angels. He felt the loss of the battle and knew the pain of having to surrender to loss because of the choice made by the person in whom you are guarding. It hadn't come to that yet, but it was now left to Adley and Aaron until the time that Samuel actually chooses Christ. He knew the battle was no longer fought with swords but with conviction and choices.

"Welcome back, Sakata." Jesus faced the three leader angels; behind them was the angelic line that had protected the prayer squad during the seven-day march. Sakata now joined the three leaders in front. "You did a great job. The house belongs to me and is now in the custody of the one who will use it and the land around it for my namesake. As you know, that was only half the battle. Just as with Bill, he had to choose to follow me, and he did. Now his son must make the same choice to completely eliminate Trainer from coming back. Adley and Aaron are currently doing the work they need to do. Sakata, I have a special job for you. Protect Bill, guide him, and show him how to train Samuel in the ways of the Lord."

Jesus looked at the angels. "Your job is far from done. There is more to do and more to keep safe. This is the war that we have fought so many times. Winning is based on their choice. Samuel's choice will be the determining factor whether we win or not."

Ailith shot a quick question to Jesus. "Lord, with all due honor, the enemy horde has been dissipated. Who is the enemy?"

"Trainer and Cadet are possessing Samuel. The fight will not be with swords. The fight will be with choices."

"Yes, Lord," the angelic team replied in unison.

8 OBEDIENCE HONORED

Bill looked deeply at Samuel, wishing he had an idea of what to look for so he could recognize Trainer and kill him. The milk in the bottle kept Samuel quiet and content, the warmth and love from Bill's touch kept him secure, and the words from Bill's mouth taught him.

Samuel ate while Bill sang. The song sung was simple enough. "Jesus loves me, for this I know." Sakata saw what he was trying to do from the start. The approval was easy. Sakata could see the strategy Bill was using, daily implanting Jesus's love any way he could. Bill could only hope that it was starting to sink in.

Bill's daily prayers rose often; as he thought about the battle he had to go through, he remembered the battle that almost killed him. The prayers would continue to go up; Jesus had to do the work. Bill held on with everything he had in him.

Aaron was taking every word Bill sang and permanently implanting it in Samuel's mind. He could see the seeds of God's truth sinking deep in the soil of Samuel's heart. The words continued to come like seeds floating in the air for him to grab onto and plant in just the right place for Samuel to recall later. Aaron continued his work smoothly and fluidly. With each of God's words spoken into Samuel's life, he made them exactly what was needed for the growth of the seeds. Aaron had already witnessed the fruit of his labor in those assigned to him; now he just had to plant, water, watch, and rest. The work will be made profitable through the hands of Jesus alone.

Fred's little car had turned into a check that allowed him to buy another little cheap car that worked. His job had gone away and with it the security of a paycheck. He knew this; he was thankful for the gift of God and prayed that he would be able to afford to keep it on the road. He would have to fully rely on God for this to happen since there was no money for repairs.

John's truck was replaced with another. Thanks to his work situation, he was able to help others who struggled financially. God had opened a new door for him that he could not comprehend. He knew what he was to do, but seemingly the opportunities did not come. With the patience of Job, John waited for God to make the next move.

Harry had been blessed, and keeping his job had been hard. Between the walking and praying with the house and everything else going on, he was still able to keep his job. Harry's Mustang had been replaced easily with the classic model that he had been looking at for years as well as an older model to drive on a regular basis.

Peter had not lost sight of the goal to be the best that God wanted him to be. He made it a habit to study to know more about God and how to be closer to living his way. God daily dealt with things in his life, and one of those things was how he handled his possessions. As he obeyed in all matters, God blessed him more and more every day. Peter's escort had been traded up for a better car that worked better than the escort did mechanically.

Sunday morning was tense for Fred. It was the first Sunday the prayer squad would meet in the new house. There was a buzz of excitement all around. He had gotten there early to make sure it was open and ready to go. The room lit up in a way he hadn't seen it. Taking a deep breath, he could almost smell the sweet essence of Abba Father God as if He had already filled the room.

Fred could already see God working and positioning his servants where they needed to be. Whatever God was doing, he suspected every need would be met above and beyond anything he could imagine.

9 Trainer's Meeting

Gary was resting after the workout. The stress of almost losing his coach and the physical strain of the workout itself had taken it out of him. Beside him on the table was the berry protein shake half-empty. He allowed his mind to empty of thoughts. Every time it seemed it was empty and he could close his eyes, something big came into his mind that took five or ten minutes of devoted time to think through.

Suddenly, in his mind, he picked up Moloch speaking to him. He chose to ignore him the first time. It was Moloch who ignored him when he needed his help. So he would talk after a nap. His body was winding down anyway. The muffled ache in his legs was nothing unusual after a hard workout on those muscles. A sharp pain drilled into his muscles in his right leg, sending him sitting up. "Are you ready to listen to me?"

"All right, I'm ready to listen."

"You know Bill Collins?"

"Yes, I do."

"You have to arrange a meeting."

"Why do I need to meet my cousin?"

"You need to make contact with his son often."

"And if he doesn't agree?"

"He must be made to agree. If you can get to where you are raising him, he would be taught that following us is the right thing to do."

"How do you think I am going to get him to give me custody of his son?"

"You have to think. Whatever you can do to make contact is enough. Babysit for a while, visit him, and hold the baby. There are many ways to get in contact with him without that drastic a measure."

"I'll make arrangements to meet with him after the nap."

"I don't think you understand what I am saying. You need to make the arrangements now. I need to get information to Trainer. That requires you make contact with Samuel."

"What difference does it make if I see him today or tomorrow?"

"Remember your leg sitting you up to get you to listen to me?"

"Yes, I don't think I will forget that anytime soon."

"I can put a bruise on your leg that will make it impossible for you to walk on it."

"I believe you. Let me make a phone call."

"Better."

He picked up the phone, dialed the number by memory, and waited for Bill to answer. He was almost hoping he forgot his phone or just didn't answer for any specific reason. He wanted to avoid this contact until tomorrow, but if it had to happen today, he would deal with it.

After four rings, Bill answered, "Hello."

"Hello, Bill, this is Gary. How are you doing?"

"I'm fine, how are you?"

"Doing well. Do you have some available time where I can come visit you and Samuel?"

"Today would be a bad day. I don't see any problem with you coming over on Saturday for a visit."

"Do you have a particular time in mind?"

"Samuel wakes up early and is sleeping again by ten to eleven o'clock. The best morning hours are eight to nine o'clock. Can you be here about that time?"

"Sure, that sounds good."

Rebeca knew that to get stronger, she would have to make her muscles work harder than they are used to. If this happens, they will be forced to grow stronger. Weights are the best way to push the muscles. There are two gyms in the yellow pages. She was going to Judd's Powerhouse to check it out for a few special features that aren't available at the other gym.

The gym was open with lots of equipment and free weights, side rooms, and an open floor section for no weight workouts. The personal trainer option most impressed her. The freedom allowed by her work schedule made this even better. It took her no time at all to make the decision to join.

The aerobic workout for the first day was exhilarating. As she got off the treadmill, she could feel the eyes of someone trying to size her up. The man looked big and thought it best to avoid him but keep an eye open for anyway. She walked to the ladies' shower room away from the workout floor. She showered, changed, and walked out, ready to leave.

Exiting the dressing room, she looked for the man and quickly spotted him. He was not working out and had no sweat on him. She hurried to the front door waving and smiling at the workers on her way. She knew the man followed her out the door. She kept a good pace going to the retail area of town just a block away from the gym.

At the corner, she felt a strong hand rest on her shoulder. She quickly spun, knocking his hand off her shoulder. She ducked the fist that plunged over her head and threw her own fist into his groin. He held his stance, slamming his elbow down. With a quick roll back and away, she got back to her feet and ran across the street to the retail district. He followed fast and caught her before she could enter any store.

She spun around, kicking at the ACL and swatting at his wrist bone on her shoulder. She heard the bone snap and a thud as his body dropped before her eyes. She got up and ran as fast as she could into the closest store, yelling frantically for someone to call the police.

She saw the man get up and run off even with the injuries she knew he had. The police showed up in seconds. It took two hours to make the report. The investigator promised to be in contact if he found anything. Her only real desire was to talk to Bill and get into the comfort of his arms.

Bill answered his phone on the second ring. "Hello."

"Bill, I'm scared. I walked to Judd's Powerhouse to check out the gym. I was followed out by a man. He got aggressive, and I had to flee into a retail store to get help."

"Where are you now?"

"I'm in the shoe store. I need a ride to get back home."

"I'll be there in a few minutes. I know where that is."

Twelve minutes later, Bill walked into the shoe store and directly to her.

"Your ride is here. Are you ready to go?"

"Yes, thank you."

Thursday night, prayer meeting was prepared for as usual until the phone at Fred's hip rang. "Hello."

"Fred?"

"Yes, what's up, Bill?"

"What does anointing with oil have to do with healing? I read about how Jesus fasted and prayed and found out what fasting was from Harry. I have fasted now for three days. I read about anointing with oil today in Acts and felt that I should have Samuel anointed with oil."

"Bill, there are a number of reasons for anointing with oil. One is a special announcement confirming that an appointment is from God. In the New Testament, God tells us to call on the elders of the church to anoint the sick with oil for healing. Another is used in dedicating babies with their parents promising to raise them in the Lord."

"Thank you. That confirmed a lot for me. Could we anoint Samuel with oil tonight?"

"You bet we can. The entire group can gather around you holding Samuel. While they pray, I will pray and anoint you and Samuel with oil."

"Thank you, Fred. I appreciate it. You have been good to me."

"You are receiving no different treatment than any other person in the prayer squad…church."

The click on the other end of the line brought with it the obvious silence and the first load of leadership of a church. He hadn't thought of himself as the elder of a church. The very thought brought him to his knees to pray.

The time with God was needed. As he drew closer to his Heavenly Father, he realized exactly what God wanted to do with Samuel and Bill. The level of faith Bill was going to need was a lifetime of learning. He would gain it by study of God's Word, encouragement, and prayer.

Fred's heart leaped with joy at the opportunity given him, but at the same time felt the potential consequences of not fulfilling the tasks he needed to do. He continued to draw closer to Jesus and draw strength from him. With tears in his eyes, he let his feelings of insecurity and weakness pour out to the throne of God, seeking strength.

Fred had not stopped praying since the phone call two hours ago. He felt at peace and sat in the lead chair in the living room. Alone, he didn't want to control his tears, feelings, and heart. Internally, he knew it was all because of the closeness and relationship he was experiencing with God.

The door first opened as he gathered the chairs into a circle. He put the center chair in place and looked up toward the ceiling. "This meeting is yours. Have your way with it."

Trainer's ears and eyes were open. He saw the circle form, heard the chatter, but could not distinguish the details. Trainer knew he would not be able to until Samuel could. Right now, sounds were enough. They became distinct, but not to Bill or Samuel. For the first time, he knew it was prayer. He went immediately to the safe chamber to pick up anything he could. Then a light pierced the chamber. Shadows and hidden corners vanished. The light cut through everything. It revealed the glory of where it came from. The voice he heard was clear. "Samuel, you were chosen to serve me."

"Samuel will serve me!" Trainer said more out of desperation than strength.

"Samuel will choose who he serves. I will honor that choice, and so will you, Trainer."

Trainer was left trembling, fear coursing everywhere within him.

The voice was gone, and so was any reason to believe it would come back soon.

Bill saw the clock on the wall. Samuel woke him up earlier than usual, but that was a good thing really. He needed the extra time to pray and think. Rebeca had proven she knew well how to take care of herself, but now there was a new threat. He tested his memory of some of the moves he used when he was a child. They weren't as fast, but they were still there. After Samuel's eleven-o' clock feeding, he and Rebeca were going to see if he could get them back up to speed. For now, it was time to wait to see Gary.

Samuel was dressed and playing quietly while he readied himself for the visit. "Okay, bud, let's go down and see your uncle." Bill baby talked to Samuel.

Samuel just looked and cooed back as Bill's baby chatter continued. He saw Samuel jump when he was halfway down the stairs. He knew the feeling when Trainer got close to

Moloch at the house. This was the same kind of jump. Was Gary now possessed by Moloch? What was he to do now?

Bill watched the road in front of his house for a minute and saw the car pull in the drive. Though he didn't have proof, he suspected that Gary was possessed by Moloch based on what he saw from Samuel. Gary was taller than he expected, walked with a little limp, and his right wrist was in a makeshift cast. When he walked closer to the house, Bill saw the left leg was being favored. "Were you the one with the run-in with Rebeca? I'll go around the bush and see what he says."

He waited at the door, out of sight, until Gary knocked. He shook his head, clearing his thoughts for now, and opened the door. "Hello, it has been a long time since I've seen you. How are you doing?"

Bill stepped back and invited him in with a gesture of his hand. As Gary entered, he said, "Good. Other than the surprise in my class, I am doing well." He pointed to his broken wrist as he moved toward the baby. "This must be Samuel. I am hearing so much about him through the grapevine."

"All good, I hope." Bill noticed the first sign that Moloch was in the house. Gary started sweating small beads of water on his forehead only. He could see Gary shaking and knew beyond the shadow of a doubt that Moloch was at the root of this visit. Gary was not controlling the force within him, and it would cause him many problems in the long run.

Bill delayed Gary's actual contact with Samuel knowingly, adding pressure to Moloch. Much later than was comfortable, Samuel went to Gary's arms and settled in with the final proof as to what was really going on. In a tone that made Bill even more uncomfortable than everything else, Gary asked, "Do you really want to keep this one?"

Accepting the remark as a joke, Bill replied, "Yes, I do. I think he's a keeper."

The buzzer on the stove went off. Bill said, "I'll take Samuel to the kitchen, and we can go have a good lunch. Samuel will want his lunch soon anyway."

Gary didn't seem to notice that anything was said except for the slight increase in which he held Samuel. Bill forcibly reached in and said, "Give Samuel to me so I can feed him, please."

Gary released Samuel too slowly for Bill's sake, and they walked into the dining room. Samuel played on the kitchen floor in Bill's sight, while Gary waited for the plates to come out. With ease, Bill carried the food and Samuel to the table—two hot roast beef subs with melted cheese and two small jars of puréed something for Samuel.

They talked about family, child care, and custody agreements through lunch. Bill wasn't fooled at all and was glad to see him go. There was no other free time in the near future, but Bill promised to call if something came open.

Bill and Samuel watched as Gary drove off and Rebeca drove in the drive. Her car stopped, the engine died, but Rebeca just looked at Bill through the windshield in astonishment. Bill could see her saying, "He was the man that attacked me?"

Bill and Rebeca met at the door. They carefully hugged each other and went in to the couch to talk. The conversation quickly turned to Gary and what was going to happen. Although no specific answers came of that conversation, the conclusion was that Gary was to no longer have direct contact.

10 THE SOUL WAR

Trainer felt the war going on, even though he could not see it. He struggled with fear and confusion daily. The Spirit and light that kicked him out of Bill was there around Samuel all the time. The few moments he got with Moloch gave him minimal training and less instruction on how to deal with this Spirit. The instruction that was received was who it was, and no one had defeated him when the human called on him.

Trainer heard the words of Moloch again. "Don't let any instruction of Jesus or his love penetrate into the heart of the boy. If he never chooses Jesus, then he will work for us. If not, we lose."

Somehow, even Moloch's words were censored by the Spirit outside Samuel. The light was not aggressive in attacking, but it had altered everything since then. He must find the way to break this power. If he knew what it was that made it so difficult to deal with, he would simply find a greater power and send it packing. As it was, Samuel couldn't be hurt, and his mind couldn't be shut down ever since that night.

Cadet had done nothing but sit in a corner in fear. Nothing he had tried had done anything. He couldn't even make Samuel hungry. His anger brought no external results. Who was Jesus, and what could be done to break his power?

No answers came to him. Moloch wasn't answering calls for help. Now for the second time, he was facing an unknown enemy with no way to fight. *I can't lose this round. Samuel belongs to me. No surrender, no defeat. I will win this fight.*

Trainer turned to Cadet. "Come here, my son. Listen to me."

Cadet came over to him and listened. Trainer saw the fear and wasn't going to let this go. "I have a fight to finish. I don't know how I'm going to complete the task, but for your sake, I will."

11 The Army Is Prepared

Jesus gathered the archangels and the colonels together.

"It is easy to see the battle escalating with Samuel. This battle is for his soul. I have my warriors in place to deal with Trainer. They are frustrating Trainer to no end, and their power was strengthened by the prayer with oil. There is a bigger problem. Satan is going to attack the prayer squad. These attacks may be easily taken care of by the guardian angels. Some are going to be fierce. Moloch is going to be another battle completely. Moloch and Trainer are not talking to each other yet, but that will soon change. When it does, the prayer squad will need every advantage to separate Trainer and Moloch. It is remembered what happened when a guardian angel was struck by the scorpion. That will be four times stronger on my servants. The enemy's swords and that scorpion cannot, in any way, reach my servants. Alexander,

Boris, you are to pick one of the prayer squad and send a colonel to each of the members."

The silence and attentiveness were broken by, "Yes, Lord."

"Ailith, you and your forces are to perform the task previously assigned to the colonels. There will be a little swordplay, but when there is, it will come from the very pits of hell. Don't be surprised if Satan occupies his time with this group personally. One more thing, I am holding you personally responsible for Samuel. The prayers have come up for Samuel constantly. You know what you have to do."

Ailith bowed his head and said, "Yes, Lord, your will be done."

"Prepare the heavens for the call. You will all be on earth for a while."

All together, they said, "Yes, Lord." The new heavenly leaders were appointed, and they flew to their missions on earth with swords and battle arcs drawn in the sky.

12 Gary's Girl

Moloch battled for patience. Gary wasn't doing anything to get a girlfriend or a wife. He was likely not going to have much direct contact with Samuel. Moloch searched the gym. Was there anyone that may be remotely interested in Gary? This had got to change. Moloch saw a young woman running laps around the track. He got enough of a look to know she was a possibility. Moloch needed to communicate with this woman. The communication would tell the whole story.

She was of average height with long dark hair bouncing with her strides. She was wearing running shorts and a T-shirt that read, "I survived breast cancer marathon." Moloch prodded Gary to work on endurance training by running on the track. Gary followed the prodding easily enough. The easy jogging pace was enough to catch the young woman. "Hello."

The soft voice replied with heavy breathing, "Hello."

"Have you been on the track for a while?"

"I put in ten miles a day." Her exasperated breathing said that she was nearing the end of this run. "I'm on mile nine now."

Moloch could only do so much without detriment to his host body.

"How long have you been coming to the gym?"

"I just started last week. I'm training to be a professional fighter. I have a little holdup right now. I can't do many of the exercises I was supposed to. I need to let my body heal from the injuries."

"Who or what did you get into a fight with to cause them?"

"I fought some metal stairs and lost." He laughed.

"You cover the rest of the bruises, or is that an old injury that you're moving your way through?"

Moloch couldn't let Gary admit to anything that would make him look weak. "The injury occurred a week ago. The broken bone will take a little more time to heal. The ACL tendon is what I'm most worried about. I need it in good shape."

"Yes, you do. Did you already tear it? My father can't do many things he wants to do because of it. The pain on the outside of his knee can be unbearable."

Moloch just watched the conversation and did no more until he might be needed.

"That explains the slow speed. How far are you pushing it in areas other than cardio?"

"Not near enough. My muscles are used to a lot more. By the way, my name is Gary."

She spun around, running around the track backward. "My name is Melissa. You'll be my eyes, won't you? This challenges the quads and calves. You just keep jogging forward. Your right hand is my cue. Where it goes, I'll go."

For a mile on the track, they talked, and she moved around easily, following every cue of his hand. The end of the last mile, they jogged off the track and stretched their sore and tired muscles.

Before Gary left, he asked, "Are you busy for dinner?"

"When?"

"When do you have available? I've got tonight and tomorrow night free."

Moloch could see the smile on her face and heard her say, "I could be ready in two hours."

"I'll be showered and out in twenty minutes. Meet me at the front desk, and I'll get your address, okay?"

"Sure, that will work for me."

They parted for the locker rooms.

Melissa was not in the habit of falling for any guy who jogged up to her at the gym, but something about this guy was different. She could sense he was tough, but his nervousness gave away the insecurities in him. She liked that he wasn't perfect and found him curious enough to, at least, go out with him once. She heard him say that money wasn't an object. She tried him hard on that. He agreed to take her to the most expensive restaurant she could think of. As far as she knew, he had everything she wanted in a man. This would be her chance to find out more about this guy than one mile could offer. She searched her closet for just the right dress to make an impression but not to come off as eager. She settled on a knee-length baby blue dress that many people said looked very good on her. She didn't know what made her think the dress was going to make the date, but somehow it was that important.

All the thinking about her clothes let time slip by. Now the knock echoing through the house confirmed that she was late getting ready, leaving him with her roommate. This wasn't a good idea, and she was dressed in two minutes. She was not given time for any makeup but could not ask him to wait. She slipped into her shoes and headed down to rescue Gary.

"SU…" She started to say but was cut off by the stare Gary gave her. Gary was dressed in a suit and tie that mesmerized her as much as she had him. They froze where they stood. "Melissa? Wow. You are gorgeous."

"Thank you. You are more handsome then expected yourself."

Melissa saw her roommate's sign language coming from behind Gary. "You rocked his world. Now go and steal his heart. He is all yours."

She saw her turn around and walk out into another room.

"I need to go get my purse. Could you wait here for one more second?"

"Make it quick. I don't want to be apart from you long."

She blushed as she turned back to her bedroom. With her purse in her hand, she checked the mirror and tried to find what completely mesmerized Gary but failed to see it. The one thing she knew—Gary really was hers for the taking. She wouldn't leave him to wait long. She wanted to get to the restaurant to learn something more about him.

13 The Prayer Squad Grows

The weekend had come, and with it came chores and prep work for the young church. The normal weekend yard work doubled with two houses to take care of. His original house was a simple ten-minute cut in the front and fifteen-minute cut in the back. The new house, on the other hand, was a different story. Four hours later, Harry and Fred were done.

That would have been eight to ten hours with just the push mower. "Come in for something to drink?"

"You should say hi to your company before going in." He gestured to the car pulling in the drive.

"Hello, how are you?"

The stranger looked at the two mowers. "Hello, I'm fine. And yourself?"

"I'm doing better now that the mowing is done."

"That's kind of why I'm here. I saw you last Sunday morning with a crowd here. What was that all about?"

"I'm Fred, and this is Harry," he said, gesturing toward Harry. Harry waved.

"We started a church here last Sunday."

"A church? With all the demonic activity that went on over here. What type of church?"

"We started as a band of men praying together. Now we are a group of believers of Jesus Christ meeting together to worship and pray. You are welcome to join us if you like."

"I may just do that. Do you want someone to mow this yard for you?"

"We have no money to pay anyone. For now, we will have to take care of it ourselves."

"Fred, I'm Doug. I would be honored to mow this yard without charge. I have much bigger equipment to handle the job."

"We are just going in to get something to drink. Would you join us so we can talk about it?"

On their way into the house, Doug responded, "Just for a minute. I have a nineteen-year-old daughter that I need to get back to. She is teaching me sign language so I can speak to her better. She is ninety-five percent deaf. She doesn't get a lot out of hearing pastors speak, but she goes anyway. I think she prays for the pastor and reads the Bible verses along with the pastor. She has grown tremendously since she started doing that."

"I'm glad to hear that. One of our members was born mute and learned sign language to be able to speak. Since then, he developed his voice but still uses sign language to anyone that knows it. He stutters badly. I think your daughter would feel comfortable here. You are both welcome."

They sat down at the table, and Fred retrieved the iced tea from the refrigerator. "It's all I have right now. It is refreshing though."

"Yes, iced tea is. I have no problem with that."

"On the subject of the mowing, when you mow, please come see me. I'll see what funds have come in to help with the gas."

"Don't bother. The gas is on me. Let's call it my service to Jesus's church. I want to know more about the man who can sign. My daughter has tried to read lips, but the pastors turn their heads away from her, and she misses a lot of the sermon."

"John is one of the original four prayer squad members. He is a good man with a strong heart for the Lord. I'll call him to let him know he may be needed to sign. Most of us are single, but we have one family here that joins us. You are welcome to talk to Harry. He can answer most of your questions." Fred shot a look to Harry to counter the one he knew was already boring into him.

"It was nice meeting you." He held out his hand and took Doug's hand when he offered it.

Doug said as they shook hands, "It is past time for my lesson anyway. I'll bring my family over when the cars start to pull up. I am just next door, two city blocks on the hill. I can see everything you do like a miniature."

"I'll be careful then," he laughingly said as he walked up the stairs to the office. His office was small, but it worked. He shuttered the first time he walked in the room but couldn't find anything that could explain it. He didn't know that all the decisions by the demon leaders had been made in this exact room.

John was the first one to the service. He felt robbed of anything good that was in him. It had been two weeks since he heard anything but conviction from the Spirit. He wanted a reason to leave early before he heard a word of the message. Now he was asked to sign for a deaf girl.

He sat in the front row and sulked. He agreed but was not going to stay behind and "fellowship" with the others that didn't care about him anyway.

The room began to fill with people. He saw Fred go up to a family he hadn't seen before and point his way. He put on his church mask that he used for so many years. He stood and prepared to shake hands with the family. The young lady came up, signing to her father. "You didn't tell me he was handsome too."

He could see her father sign back. "Pay attention to God first, and he will provide the man he has chosen for you."

"Yes, Father. I taught you too much already." The familiar signs spoke more to him than words ever did.

"I love you." The father signed as his daughter turned and walked toward John.

"Hello, I am Samantha. Are you John?"

He stopped. Samantha was beautiful. She was just shorter than himself. Her petite frame was naturally attractive. John felt the infatuation rising from his toes. It would slam hard into his hard heart one day, and there was no way to avoid it.

"Hello, yes, I am John." He was thankful he was signing. "I will be signing for you today."

"I look forward to it. Can he understand what we are saying?"

"Fred, no he doesn't know sign language."

"Is Fred the pastor?"

"By a unanimous vote."

"I hope he is good. He will be the first pastor I can hear."

"I hope he is way off if I have to listen to him."

"I hope he is too. He has some real good sermons."

The people began to take their seats. John saw the familiar faces, including Peter's and Patty's. His heart pained at the anger he fostered inside. He knew better but made room for it anyway. This was not a good sign. Deep down, he knew Fred would be ready. God, I need your forgiveness and healing. Show me how.

He looked to Fred to see when he was planning on starting. He saw the five-minute sign. He turned to Samantha. They worked out a sign for when Fred picked up his guitar. They continued talking as her family came and sat beside her. He signed. "May I sit here?"

Samantha chuckled and signed back. “This is my father, Douglas, and my mother, Glenda. This is my brother, Chad.” She turned to the family. “This is John.”

Chad quickly signed. “Welcome to the family.” Where John could see but might go unnoticed by the others.

Samantha signed to him, “Shush,” and then turned to John and gave the sign for the guitar low for John. John sat up and prepared to start the service. The worship songs went along easily enough. He took a deep breath and focused on the sermon. He knew he would get it twice. The sermon topic was receiving healing from hurts. John focused and signed through to the end.

Peter saw John leave the deaf group and come to him. “Hello, Peter. We need to deal with something. You might not know what it is, but I need to talk to you about it.”

His eyes told John this was not going to be hard. He was already waiting for this moment. He heard him out and listened to him pray. He ended the prayer himself. With that settled, he said to John, “Do you want to bring the young lady with you and join us for lunch?”

“I’ll have to see if she would come, but I think she will.”

John went back to the family and signed something. The signing continued for a minute, and she took John’s arm as he escorted her to them. “Let’s go. You drive. I can’t talk to her with my hands on the steering wheel.”

Peter said, “Deal,” and walked with them to the car.

Jesus gathered the angels that remained in heaven to him. "The war is on. What they don't know is that though everything is moving smoothly now, Satan is now watching this himself. He will not allow this to continue any longer. The attacks will come from all angles, and he'll use many methods. As the new church grows, your job will be more difficult and require more attention. You will not go down in large numbers for open war. Satan is not bringing forces against us on the heavenly front again. What he will do is attack every weakness and hurt they have. Don't ever let them forget that sermon. It will serve them for a long time to come."

"Yes, Lord," all the multiple voices said together.

Jesus pointed to two angels. "Get ready. In the next few days, the tough times will come for this church."

14 The Ministry Established

Fred contacted Harry, Peter, and John for an emergency meeting. They were all there, and the burden he bore was thick in the air. All were silent with a drink in front of them. The glasses remained full, and everyone's eyes remained locked on him. He picked up his glass, took a sip to wet his throat, and decided to go forward with what had to be done.

"No one in here is ignorant of what a church takes to run. I am not prepared to take on all that responsibility alone. I want to know what you think about becoming a committee to help me with some of the decisions."

The others were silent as they sat there and listened. "Not all decisions and discussions need to go before the entire church." Fred shook his head. "It's still a little weird to call this group a church. It seems strange to see more than four people in the room. That is the real reason why I want the support and help in making decisions. One of us may have a viewpoint that helps make the wise decision. Guys, I really need your help."

Heads were shaking yes, and it was obvious they were thinking. Harry broke the silence. "You are right. You should not have to make all the decisions without help. I say that we four would make a good board for the church."

Peter shook his head in agreement, and John said, "I agree. Most boards are odd numbers in members because you cannot have a fifty-fifty split with an odd number. Is there someone else that would be willing to meet with us to make a fifth person?"

Fred said with pleasure, "I think Bill would be good. He is wise beyond his years spiritually because of his experience with Trainer."

Harry said, "Is everyone in agreement with him?"

John and Peter both said, "Yeah."

Fred smiled as he responded, "I will call him and see if he is willing to join us. As well, we will need to take the idea to the church and see if they agree with it. If they do, they agree with the people that have been chosen. I would like to give them time to think about it and then, in a week or two, take a vote to get their opinion."

Peter responded, "That is the only fair way to do it. Give them a chance to nominate a fifth person."

Harry immediately responded, "They need to make sure that whoever they nominate is willing to take the position."

"We are in agreement with what has been decided?"

"Yes." This mutually came from the other three.

Fred sighed, thought for a second, and finally said, "Then after we get the fifth man, we can start meeting and making some decisions about the future of this church."

Bill sat at the entrance of Judd's Powerhouse. The bench placed in the sun was warm and comforting. Samuel lay silently in his arms, sleeping. Gary was easily recognized in the gym. The distance between the nursery and Bill was farther than he wanted. How could he get Samuel to the nursery without getting Gary's attention? Plans formed in his mind and were rejected one after another.

Bill continuously scanned the parking lot for Rebeca's car. The best plan included her to help hide the baby from view. After today, they would definitely have to change the time they went to the gym. Bill got up from the bench and walked out to the car as she was parking. He opened her door before she had a chance to turn off the car and unbuckle. "Wow, I am so glad you're here. We may have one problem to deal with."

The surprise on Rebeca's face appeared as the door opened. "What is going on?"

"Gary is in the gym right now."

Surprise turned to concern as her eyes turned to Samuel.

"What are you thinking?"

"I'm thinking he will not do anything in the gym. It will be in the parking lot that we will have the problem...on the way out. I have an escort coming out because of his last attack. Maybe that will help keep trouble down."

"Are you ready to go in then?"

"I have everything I need to get in right here." She held up her key ring membership card, waiting to be scanned into the computer at the front desk.

"Okay, mine is on my key ring. You keep Samuel. I'll take a position to block the view. Maybe we can get to the nursery without being noticed."

"That's my plan. We will need to work in a different area of the gym. We can use the empty room since he is on the weights right now."

Rebeca rose from the car. "Let's get in there quickly."

We're off." They walked into the gym together, not knowing what to expect from Gary. Walking directly to the nursery, they dropped Samuel into the care of the worker before Gary spotted them and began walking toward them. They walked toward the open room in a way to cut Gary off from Samuel. "Hello, Gary."

Gary responded, "I didn't know you worked out here. How are you, cuz?"

"I'm fine. Just going to start working out. You look almost finished."

"I'll be leaving shortly. Can I see Samuel before I leave?"

"I don't think you're allowed since he is already in the nursery. I only have an hour to work out anyway. Maybe you can call me, and we can work out a time when we're home together."

"You know me, Bill, we're family. I'm sure with your permission they will let me visit him in the nursery."

"Gary, it would be best if you waited until we can visit each other in my home. Please."

Bill could see the frustration coming out in the sweat from his cousin's forehead. One look at Rebeca and he knew she was ready too. "You understand what I am saying. It'll be more comfortable for everyone. Surely you can understand that."

The voice coming from Gary filled with anger. "Oh, I understand, all right." His voice rose as he pointed his finger at Bill. "You'd better watch out, though, because I will see Samuel again if I have to take him by force!"

"Sir." The voice broke in. "Is there a problem?"

Bill looked to see the manager of the gym standing behind Gary. "I believe we have an understanding," Bill said, never taking his eyes off Gary.

Gary scolded Bill with his eyes. "Yes, we do." They all watched as he stomped toward the changing rooms.

The manager said to Bill, "I'll be in the nursery until he leaves. You are not the first customers he's made nervous."

"Thank you." They both turned to the open room and entered ready to continue with the real reason for being there. To find out how much Bill really knew.

Rebeca pulled out the kicking bags and pads. "First, we stretch."

Bill's muscles groaned and complained but slowly loosened a little. "A little work and I will be ready to do the splits."

"Huh, a little? I think you will be doing the splits when you are eighty. Let's just settle for slow increases."

Stretching ended soon enough. It came time to find out what he really knew. Rebeca demonstrated in slow motion a kick as Bill watched.

He did the same kick in slow motion with shocking precision. "That is a mind implant. The more I understand about how it worked, the more I know that I turned it on with my anger. Now I have proof of that."

"What are you angry about now?"

"I just carried the emotion from talking to Gary in here, and that was the result."

She put a pad on her hand. "Show it to me without holding back. Here is your target."

Bill focused, took a fighting stance, and repeated with speed and fury the kick again, nailing the target. Her hand took the momentum of the kick and swung around. "That is not as fast as it was in my younger years."

With each new kick and punch, Bill demonstrated surprising skill and accuracy, surprising even himself. "I wonder, could it be controlled in a sparring match?"

Rebeca threw out a full set of sparring gear at him. "Put it on, let's see. That is…if you think you can take me on."

Bill put on the sparring gear. "I must warn you, I don't lose."

"Prove it. Fighting stance."

They sparred for five minutes straight. To Rebeca's surprise, he blocked and countered with speed and control. "Are you sure that Trainer is out of your system? You fight like you're possessed."

"You don't know what that felt like. There was a power that was not of God. I know you still keep your fleshly desires. That is a power I don't want to have to call on. Is it wrong?"

"I don't know the spiritual answer to that. Maybe your prayer needs to be that you be saturated with the power of Christ. "I know that I need to talk to the church too. I held back because you are not an enemy. I could see me killing a man without even thinking about it. That is a trait I remember from the possession."

"We can pray about this together here and now. I want to follow Jesus too. I know God doesn't want us to fight. Still, I felt it was right to defend myself against Gary when he attacked me."

"Let's pray about it, and later we'll talk to Fred about it." They knelt together and prayed.

"Nassor, Come here." Satan's anger shot fire with the words.

"Yes, Master."

"Break that church! It is getting legs under it. Cut them down! Get the leadership, pastor first. Do what you need to do."

"Yes, Master. He will crumble under our feet."

"Go make it happen! No more house experiences!"

With a nod of his head, Nassor went to the demonic armies to gather forces.

Nassor chose twenty warriors like him and twenty attacking horde. They flew off, swords holstered, silently searching for their targets.

Nassor saw not just Fred but also Peter, Harry, and John standing in front of the burned ground where the barn stood. He stopped the group and lined up the ranks. The frontline was the fighting horde; the second line the larger warriors. Still unseen by the guardian angels, they prepared to draw their swords and fly.

Randolph, Boris, Seth, Elliot, William, Cenewig, Einar, and Justin monitored the four as they talked about what needed to be done. It was not until Cenewig turned to scan the sky that he noticed the demons in the sky waiting. Cenewig yelled, "Attack!"

All of the guardian angels turned and drew their swords. The light was matched by the fire from the first line of attacking demons. The angels flew at the attacking line.

Ailith saw immediately what was happening, and she pointed to ten archangels and said, "Go."

The two lines of angels met in the sky, and sparks were flying. The fighting horde all but vanished as expected. The second wave of demons hit by surprise; they pierced two of the fighting angels. All the angels flew down, defending their post. The demons quickly followed, not allowing the volleying to stop.

An arc from above struck the demons, alerting them to the attacking archangels coming from the rear. The attacking demons split and attacked both ways. The archangels cut the demons off headstrong without any resistance. The guardians held their own against the remaining demons.

When the angels heard, "Retreat!" they recognized the voice and saw the demons fly off to a defensive posture, waiting.

Elliot and Seth flew down with Randolph to look at the extent of the injury. Seth took a strike to his left shoulder that made his arm motionless. Elliot took a deep stab wound to the gut. Randolph knew they would need rest. A voice from above him said, "Join the fight. I will keep them."

He didn't recognize the voice but knew an archangel at sight. He took his spot in the defensive line.

15 CHURCH LEADERSHIP SHAPED

Nassor quickly recognized the scorpion was near. The call thundered. "Scorpion, attack the angelic host!"

As quickly as the host could turn, the winged scorpion was flying a direct course of attack. Boris caught the first wave, flaring it off course.

The scorpion bounced from one angel to another, finally clamping on Cenewig. It swung around, arced its tail, and suddenly and surprisingly flew away from his victim. Another archangel struck and cut the claw in half and threw it off. The archangel said, "Down, rest."

Cenewig flew beyond the protection and healing of the archangel on the ground. The demons flew in attack as they called, "Scorpion, fight."

The lines collided, and sparks flew on the collision. The scorpion flew back at the archangel, tail poised to strike, but the light from the archangel drove all the demons and the scorpion away. The demons fled the fight as the scorpion fled, returning to Samuel.

Ailith flew down, gathered the angels together, and said, "Good job. These will be few and far between but will be deadly with many tricks." He looked at the three wounded angels. "Stand." They stood.

Ailith brought a sword to Seth's shoulder, and it was immediately healed. The sword went to Elliot's gut, and it too was immediately healed. The sword went to Cenewig. Immediately, he was healed. Ailith said to them, "Stand strong. You are warriors of the Almighty God."

"Yes, sir." This came from the three as one unanimous voice.

The archangels flew back to the heavens.

Harry felt a sick feeling standing with the others. His expression fell as the sickness deepened in his stomach. He could see the others' expressions of concern focused on him. The words formed in his mind. "Be true to me, and I will be true to you. When you walk away from me, I can't be the guardian you need. By staying close to me, you stay under my protection and blessing. As my servants remain in my house, you must also remain."

The feeling faded as quickly as it came. Harry said, "God is warning us. The fight for Trainer's property is not over, and we will need the protection of our Lord."

Fred responded, "Then let's remember the words of our Lord and heed them carefully."

Together all said, "Amen."

The service ended Sunday morning, and Fred called the church to order for a business meeting. "God doesn't want one man to be solely responsible for everything in a church. I have spoken with the other three from the original prayer squad. They have agreed to be on a board for this fellowship. They also recommended that a fifth man be chosen to serve on this board. We have spoken with Bill, and he is willing, but the decision is ultimately yours to make. If there is someone you want to nominate to go before a church vote to serve on the board, then stand and nominate him. He will then be asked if he is willing to serve in this capacity."

There was silence for a short time. No one else was nominated, so Fred called the men up. "Would the five that have been nominated and expressed their willingness to serve in this capacity please come to the front?"

They came one at a time to the front. Fred looked to the remainder of the group. "If you agree with having these men act as this fellowship's leadership, say, 'Aye.'"

The ayes rang from across the crowd. "I have to ask," Fred continued. "Are there any nays?"

The room was silent again. Fred turned to the front and faced the men standing there. "Do you accept this service as voted on by the fellowship this day?"

The four men and Fred unanimously said, "I do."

"It is decided. Men, we need to meet at five o'clock this afternoon to make some decisions." Fred turned to the full congregation. "Go with God obediently in his service."

16 THE BOARD TESTED

The guardian angels were already aware of the necessity of temptation and testing. The demonic swords and scorpion had to be stopped. Temptation and testing; they could only provide the way to the escape in Jesus Christ. No matter how much they liked it or didn't, they had to allow it through.

Fred sat and was waiting for the hour to tick away when his mind reeled in a thought that he had fought for so many years. He couldn't fathom where it came from and tried to focus on the subject at hand, prioritizing the topics needed to be discussed in this meeting.

The more he read the list the more the thought persisted. It became a vision that played like a movie through his mind, rewinding immediately at the end. The thought began to echo in the background of the vision. *Just act on the vision, and it will go away. It is that simple.*

Fred knew that acting on the vision would just make it come faster and tried to pray. Quickly, he found himself praying for the vision as it played in his mind. His frustration showed in the words of his prayer. The vision didn't go away; instead, it became more dominant, taking up more of his thoughts. He saw a door appearing in the middle of the screen that held the vision. Standing in the doorway, an angel invited him to come and follow. Moving toward the screen intensified the vision. He could no longer pray. The angel just motioned, inviting, doing nothing to make the images go away.

Each step weighed more on his mind, seemingly strapping on a bigger burden. Yet the angel stood and waved him on. *What is on the other side of this door? How can I get away from this?*

Again, he looked at the angel and saw the answer. Follow me. He looked around for any other way out and found none. The weight on his shoulders already hurt; could he really take more? The memory of the attack at the house where he couldn't even walk haunted him. He heard a voice in the background say, "Act on the vision, and it will go away." He saw the angel inviting, standing in the doorway.

"Please, Lord, help."

He struggled harder with every step. Not until he reached the angel did he take him through the door. The weight on his shoulder lifted like a helium balloon. Peace, comfort flooded his entire body. He saw a presence with him that filled him with peace. "Jesus?"

It was then he saw the open arms. The sight of holes in his palms stopped him from running, even though he wanted to sprint into his chest. His sin glared in front of his face. One drop of red liquid started from the top and covered more and more of his sin, spreading out until it covered the whole thing. It vanished from his sight, and all that was left was the inviting arms of Jesus, saying, "Come."

He broke into a sprint, never stopping until he flung himself into the open arms of his Savior. Jesus stood firm and caught him without any struggle. It was then he heard the instruction of the Lord. "Follow me. Lead my sheep. Keep true to my Word."

He was back in his room, praying. The list was already prioritized by his hand, and he didn't know when or how he did it. It was clear to him now; this was truly God's priority.

Bill's mind reeled. *How many times have I walked through the house and absently called Saundra's name? When will I get beyond that?*

"Bill?" Rebeca called out.

"I'm here. My mind still doesn't want to stay with me. Do you know what I mean?"

"I think I do. You still think about Saundra."

"Yes. It's more that I'll be walking to get Samuel, and I'll call Saundra on the way. Just as soon as the silence comes back, I'll realize what I did and continue on. I hoped this sense of loss would be over, but there is so much she did that I know nothing about."

"Bill, you are still dealing with things that she took care of. This is the most difficult time for everyone, but you're doing great, and believe it or not, you will get through this."

"I know what needs to be done and where to go to get it done. I hope there is nothing else to deal with after this. I will finally clear the last of the bills tomorrow, that's one thing out of the way. Rebeca, I have dealt with so much, but you need to know there are times that I'm pretending to be strong. I still put Samuel down for a nap and cry myself to sleep. Next week, I'm going to the spot where I took Saundra for our last anniversary. I'm hoping that I can get closure from this memory that won't stop dancing in my head."

"Are you planning on going alone?"

"No, I know someone else that also needs to have closure. I don't know how to ask that person though."

Her eyes said her mind was working. "Could you tell me who it is?"

Now his mind was working. *I have to sometime.* Maybe she already knows, or would like to see anyway. "It's you. Do you want to go with me?"

Her eyes said, "Yes." Her motionless body said, "What do I do now?"

Bill saw the expression change and was left with only hope and waited for her response.

"I would love to…but proper arrangements will be made if there is any overnight stay."

"Oh! Of course, but there won't be an overnight stay. I'm leaving Friday morning and expect to return Friday night. Then I can sit and rest Saturday. After everything that's happened, I look forward to doing nothing all day."

"Sounds like a lazy weekend. Why are you worried?"

"Not worries, really. I just know that I will be forced to deal with something that's painful."

"Oh. Are you sure you want me to come along?"

"You already know me well enough to know what can't be let out and what can. You'll just have to honor that. Other than that, yes, I'm sure I want you to come."

"Where do you want to meet Friday morning?"

"I'll drive over to your place and put the car in the back garage."

"Excuse me," a voice from behind him said.

Bill turned around and saw the blade first and then the young man holding it. His arm flinched in gut reaction that he forced to stop. "Look, you don't want any trouble. Put away your toy and leave."

"Oh, it's no trouble. Give me all your money, and I'll be off."

The laughter came from behind Rebecca. Bill turned sharply and saw another man standing behind Rebeca and her eyes already in full fighting stance. He turned to face the man again. "I'm not giving you anything. Put away your knife and leave now." The calmness in his voice surprised him.

"Yes, you will, or your girl will die, and then we'll kill you."

He felt the prick of a knife tip and saw the man's eyes go wide like saucers as he looked over Bill's shoulder. Bill heard the thud and then knew that the second man was taken care of; Rebeca had him.

One quick motion during the distraction and the knife was in his hand. The man was in the air heading for the concrete, back first. His anger flared, and the thought, *Kill him.* raced through his mind with menacing laughter. *Time for blood... You want more. Smack!* The man hit the concrete. Bill lunged with the knife flying fast for his throat. All he could see was the wide eyes of fear and the exposed throat waiting to be ripped open. *You can do it, it's self-defense!*

"Bill, stop!"

Something stopped his hand fractions of an inch from driving the blade into his assailant's throat. "I will not fail again."

"Failure is losing control, and you are dangerously close to that. It's better to just walk away leaving them alive to face their own judgment than have to face judgment for your lack of control." She spoke while keeping her man contained and silent.

"You will leave now before I change my mind and rip your throat in half." He got up and turned to Rebeca, who was already standing. Both men were up and running before anything else could be said.

"Bill, are you going to face the man who tried twice to attack Saundra?"

"No, he is in prison, but I must face my failure to protect her to make sure it doesn't happen again. As you saw, the blood thirst can come out quickly. Just as the self-defense moves that are a tag left behind from Trainer, so is this."

"I understand what it is your dealing with. What stopped the knife?"

"An angel's voice yelled from behind. I honestly don't think I could have stopped with just one slash if I had continued."

"I heard your tone of voice. You're a loving man until your love is threatened. That was anger and hate speaking just now."

"I think that was just a glimpse of what I will face Friday. Do you think you can handle it?"

"I will have others praying while we're there."

Besides being head and shoulders above the rest of the prayer squad, Harry was still strong and fast. Though he hadn't kept up with the self-defense training since graduating high school, he could still kick head height with enough proficiency for the average man. He knew that against a man currently in training, he wouldn't stand a chance.

He kept flexible and strong with specific training that the high school coach had set up for his seniors. The program offered a lot of variety for increasing your strength. Now twenty years later, he was still strong and felt good. Until now, he had never had to use his training for self-defense.

Harry walked up to the front desk of Judd's Powerhouse and asked about a membership. During the tour of the gym, Harry froze. The lady giving the tour saw what he was looking at. The path they needed to use was blocked by Gary.

"So you decide to ruin my choice for a workout location too."

After Harry found his voice, he said, "Gary, this is a public place, and the only person that can keep a person out is the manager. We'll just finish the tour, and I'll be out of your way. Okay?"

"You think your training is going help? You won't beat me again? I didn't stop training. I'm now at the professional level. What do you have to say about that?"

"From the looks of the size of this gym, you would need several professional teams to fill this place. Our paths shouldn't have to cross.

"I agree completely, Gary," the manager said. "One more incident like this and you won't be able to come to this gym. Is that clear?"

Gary responded, "Okay." He wiped the sweat from his face and went back to his workout.

Harry looked back to the girl giving the tour. "We'll forget that happened. Shall we continue?"

They finished the tour without any more trouble. Harry was leaving the gym when he heard, "So you think you can get me kicked out of the gym?"

"Gary, why are you insisting on this fight?"

"You don't know. You want to play all innocent now?"

"What are you talking about?"

"You really don't remember humiliating me in high school?"

"High school? You are talking nineteen years ago. What does that have to do with anything now?"

"Harry, Harry, Harry, you forget so quickly. I told you that I'd get you back. I didn't put a time restraint on that. I'm ready now. And, no, don't reach for your cell phone. That will make things worse for you."

"I don't want to fight you. I don't remember anything but me helping a friend. I never went out to humiliate anyone."

"Stop talking and fight. For each bruise you gave me, I'm going to give you two. One other thing, I will have to break both of your arms. You did such a good job on mine then."

Harry knew he wasn't walking away from this with words and most likely wouldn't walk away at all. Time was almost up, and now he would find out just how much he remembered.

Jogging up behind Gary, someone said, "What's up?"

They both turned toward the voice, and Harry said, "Bill, remember when Gary and I got in that fight in school?"

"Sure. What about it?"

Gary replied, "I am here to finish it now."

"Gary, that's old news. Let it go."

Gary's foot shot up and across, just missing Bill's chin. "Shut up and go. I've got a job to do."

"You want to beat up Harry? You will have to contend with me as well."

Harry looked around and didn't see where Rebeca had gone. It wasn't important now; he had to focus. "Gary."

"What?"

"I don't think this fight is going to last very long."

The police sirens could be heard clearly now. The anger in Gary's voice was loud. "You have not heard the last from me."

"Freeze."

Harry and Bill raised their hands in surrender. Gary, half raising his slightly, turned his head and saw that an officer had a gun drawn on him. His hands raised the rest of the way.

All three men were separated and questioned. Rebeca and another officer came up, allowing her to identify who was who.

Bill, Rebeca, and Harry went into the gym, while Gary was handcuffed and seated in the police car. Harry looked back one more time.

The anger on Gary's face shouted the trouble coming their way.

John had always been in familiar places. He couldn't remember a time when he wasn't already familiar with his surroundings. Heading straight into unfamiliar territory, he could feel his nerves fraying. Turning his head all around, searching for anything he knew, he found nothing familiar except the girl walking beside him taking in everything with pleasure as she walked.

He could see her eyes looking at him with a sparkle. He watched them change from joyous to concern to fearful. What was in his eyes that caused such a change in her? She signed for him, but his hands couldn't move. He knew soon his legs would do the same. He tried to look ahead again. It was then he realized his steps shortened. His heart raced, and fear rose from his feet, on the verge of attacking his mind. Not even knowing where he was going, he found himself sitting on a bench with Samantha. The fearful expression on her face went along with her hands signing nonstop. He gingerly picked up one hand and saw her hands stop. He signed slowly. "Where are we?"

"We're walking the park trail. Are you okay?"

"Do you know where we are?"

"Right now, no. It's fun to be walking in God's nature and letting him lead the way. I'll have you back in time for the meeting."

The "no" was more than he could handle. His whole body shivered in fear; muscles that needed to walk wanted to run but failed. "I'm not feeling well. Let's go back, please."

She took his arms and walked fast as she held tight. His feet stumbled more than walked. Communication ceased, and her own fear wanted to get him to the hospital. She could feel his pulse in his wrist and wondered how much more he would take before it stopped. He felt sweat sliding down his face. The more he was sweating, the faster she walked.

Finally, he saw the familiar park, but nothing seemed to slow. He fell to his knees. She let him drop to the ground and ran to the nearest person. She signed and spoke to the best of her ability. "Help."

A couple walking down the sidewalk saw this woman running at them, hands moving fast, trying to vocalize a thought, and followed her to whatever was going on. They saw the man, sweat-soaked, and eyes closed. The man had dropped to his knees and started checking for a pulse and breathing hard. The woman picked up the phone and, within a few seconds, was talking to someone.

The woman watched her sign something, hold her face, and then try to walk. It was easy to see the look of distraught on her face. Her hands didn't stop signing except to cover her face and wipe away her tears.

Samantha kept signing. "It's my fault, and he's dead."

The women tried over and over to console her but couldn't understand what she signed. How could she? She had walked her interpreter to his death. Every time she took her hands away from her face, she hoped he would be sitting up, but she found him unmoving. Her own tears clouded her vision. Her hands could not stop signing the same words over and over.

Her view was blocked, so she couldn't see him. She was expecting to see the police with handcuffs to take her away when she felt the touch on her shoulder. She turned her head and looked into the eyes of John, understanding and forgiving. "Are you ready?"

"John! You're okay? But…I thought you were…"

"I'm sorry, it was a panic attack. I have a fear of the unknown that gets to me when I get somewhere I have never been. But I'm okay now. I'm so sorry I scared you. I really didn't think just walking into the woods would trigger that." He wiped a tear from her cheek. "Hey, I've got a board meeting to go to. What do you say we get going?"

She reached up to him, pulling herself up using his arm as a brace. She saw in her peripheral vision the police, ambulances all leaving. She hugged him.

When they walked to the car, he signed. "I promised I would take you to the police station tomorrow so you could give them your statement."

She signed. "Okay, thank you." They left the park.

As everyone did, Peter faced his demons and laid them aside, never to pick them up again. He looked at Patty wide-eyed and then back to the box sitting in the middle of the room.

The note on top read, "This is yours. You don't want my lifestyle, fine. I don't want your junk."

He couldn't take his eyes off the box, the words fixed and burning in his mind. He couldn't form a thought that made sense. He struggled against the feeling that the color was fading from his face. *What could be in store for me in this box? I have to open it. I have to face it.*

Patty's eyes never left Peter since he put the box on the floor. "What do you have to face?"

"From the looks of the box, me and all I did before Christ."

"Christ forgave you for that already. Why is this happening?"

"I don't know. This I do know—I will never think straight again until I know what this is."

"Will you think straight after you know what it is?"

Peter forcibly pulled his eyes off the box. He looked into Patty's eyes. "If I knew that, I wouldn't have had a hard choice."

Peter saw her eyes plead for something he knew he couldn't give. "I wish I could follow the pleading in your eyes. Maybe it is just my stubbornness, but I have to know."

Her eyes never changed until they closed to blink back the tears. She said, "I'm afraid of what's in that box."

"So am I. My personal fear isn't the issue. The issue is this will not go away by throwing the box out. I have to walk through it and acknowledge it for what it is."

"Can you do that?"

"I already have. God got me through this once. He will take care of it again."

With that, he walked to the box and pulled the tape back, releasing the flaps. He put his hands down, closing both flaps. "Am I ready to do this?" he asked himself more than anyone else.

The answer came as his hands started shaking. "No, you're not. You don't have to put yourself through this now."

He heard and understood the words but knew that the consequence of ignoring this was too high. Wordlessly, he pulled open the flaps. His past ran through his mind like a flash. His heart raced. He was standing two steps away from the box, frozen in time. The image burning in his mind stopped him cold.

"Peter?"

No response.

"Will you look at me?"

His eyes remained frozen on the small round bottles. He stared at the hardest struggle he ever went through. His heart continued to race, and his mind was reeling. Beads of sweat formed on his forehead. One thought stood out above the other jumbled signals of his brain. "Are those bottles loaded?"

Peter said, "Now I know that I'm nowhere near ready for this," more to himself than anyone else.

"Come on"—she grabbed his arm—"let's close it and wait for another day, please. You're really scaring me."

His answer came with one step to the box and then another. He dropped to his knees and put his hands on the red bottle, and it rattled as it lifted. His mind said, *Oh, for the feeling again. It would only take one pill.*

The rattling became consistent as he lifted one bottle after another. The trembling in his hands was unnerving. Now the cravings came on like a fire. The sweating and fever started rising, begging for a dose. They were pleading for a chance to be calmed. His other hand took the blue bottle; was it rattling to? His hands trembled so bad he didn't know for sure, but he believed it to be true. The feeling rushed in his mind, begging for more of the reality the pills brought. Voices penetrated his ears. Nothing he recognized came through. His phone vibrated on his hip, but he made no motion to still it or answer it.

His steps were haggard and slow. His body trembled, his fingers white from the grip on the bottles of pills. His mind demanded to be satisfied. The feelings flowed from desire and greed, unstoppable and unavoidable. Another step, then another, then another; anticipation did its work on his mind. He became hungrier for satisfaction than ever before.

The touch of another person failed to register at all. He took another step. His steady pacing took him to the bathroom sink. One bottle was placed on the sink with trembling hands. It tumbled over and rolled onto the floor. He opened the other bottle in his hand. He raised it to his mouth. It drew closer and closer, the overwhelming anticipation stirring more desire. Just about the time it looked like the bottle was going to dump in his mouth, his wrist turned, and the pills dumped into the drain of the sink. His hands steadied some. Another bottle dumped more easily into the same sink.

Out of the corner of his eye, he could see Patty.

"Now you know what I have the hardest time with. Please understand there is more, but it will go easier from now on."

"How bad was the habit?"

He explained more of his past as they finished throwing away what needed trashed and keeping the one book that he thought he would never see again—his first Bible.

He calmed down completely with the sound of the running water washing down the pills forever. He already knew what else was in that box. The rest of the contents would be taken care of without the drama.

17 THE BOARD APPOINTS ITS DIRECTOR

The five gathered together in the church office. They silently stared at Fred. Fred understood what had to be done. He looked to the paper in his hand for the first order of business. "Let's all five of us pray," he said, and they bowed their heads and prayed.

"All right, the first on my list is for you four to select one person to be director of the board. I'm going to get the iced tea while you decide."

He got up and left for the kitchen.

Harry looked at the other three. "Something is eating at him from the inside out."

Bill replied, "If his afternoon was anything like mine! The other thing is that piece of paper. It seems to get worse when he reads something on that paper."

John asked, "Did anyone besides Bill and me have a difficult time this afternoon?"

All hands went up.

"I can only imagine what he is going through. This I know—he is trying to hold this work together. I'm the only one here with experience dealing with Trainer. It's not something any of us wanted to go through, I'll tell you that!"

Bill commented, "It must be harder on him. He is our leader and example and takes that task to heart."

Harry took Bill by the shoulder. "You are right. The experience you have and insight you've demonstrated qualify you for director. What do you say?"

"Does everyone else agree?"

Harry asked the question for all to answer. "Are we all in agreement?"

"Aye."

"Aye."

"Aye."

"Bill, the ball is back in your court. What do you say?"

"I say you guys are passing the buck, but I'm up for the challenge."

I'll go get Fred so we can continue." Bill left to help Fred.

Bill walked in to the kitchen and stopped. Fred was on his knees, praying that God guide them in selecting the man he wants to lead the board. Bill picked up the tray of drinks and headed out. "Get the notepad, the director's been chosen. We're ready to move on."

Fred got up and followed Bill. After the drinks were dispersed, he asked, "Who did you decide on?"

Bill raised his hand.

"This is yours to continue with." Fred handed him the notepad.

Bill read the agenda. Under point one, it read, "Vote Bill to be director of the board."

It was Bill's turn to stare blankly at Fred. "How did you know?"

"You think I wrote this?"

"Fred, if you didn't, who did?"

"I think you know already."

Bill looked at the other three and saw the confusion on their faces.

He didn't know how to explain this to them and looked to Fred. Fred simply replied, "Go on to point two."

Bill took the lead and continued, "On to the second item. We need a church building. I would like to open the discussion on building a gym that we can use as the church and fellowship hall."

"Can we put on a gym on this property?" Harry asked.

"The property is zoned residential and falls under those rules. Yes, you can put a gym on residential property," Bill answered.

"How big of a gym could we put up?" Peter sat dazed at how exactly the meeting rolled along. "Just using the plot of ground the barn was on, we could put up a three multipurpose court gym with space on both sides for rooms."

"Bill," Harry continued. "How much have you researched this?"

"None, my grandfather did the research before Trainer got his attention. I found the plans drawn up a while back and just three days ago pulled them out."

"Are they up to current standards?" Peter asked.

"No, but it will be cheaper to get them up to date than to have them redrawn completely. This is the tricky part. Trainer is out there, coming to our church services every Sunday. Once Trainer and Moloch get this news, we will think this afternoon is a walk in the park."

Bill saw John shiver at the illustration. "They killed my grandfather because he planned to build on that plot of land. That will not change just because I'm not possessed anymore."

Fred sighed. "God is still in control and wants this built. How much is it going to take to get it done?"

"I will get the contractor here for a quote. He will get the plans approved and all permits taken care of. He'll also come to a service and answer questions for the church members."

"That sounds like a plan. So you have a new assignment," Fred said.

Bill was certain that they had no clue of what was coming in the future.

18 MOLOCH'S ANGER

The next day came, and a quick look at his filling daily agenda reminded him of yesterday's meeting. Right on top in capital letters sat the words: "Quote for the church gym." He picked up the phone and dialed the number for the contractor.

The phone was answered on the second ring. "Hello."

"Hello, this is Bill. I have an old estimate here with your phone number on it for putting a building on some land I have on Power Lane. Are you still interested?"

"You had an estimate done on that property?"

"Not me. My grandfather did sometime back. I have it here if you are interested in looking at it."

"Yes, I would."

"Let's set up a time where we can get together, and I'll show you what we want, and you can see what you can do."

"That sounds good. When's a good time for me to come out?"

"I've got sometime after three this afternoon. The next available time I have is on Thursday."

"Three thirty this afternoon, okay with you? I've got to see that estimate."

"It would be nice if you can do the job for this price."

"I will reserve my judgment until I see it. My grandpa was fair, but the prices may have changed since then. How about I see what I can do?"

"That sounds fair."

"Who am I speaking with?

"Bill Collins."

"What is the address?"

"Five-seven-five-seven Power Lane."

They finished making the arrangements and then hung up.

With one phone call done, he called Fred to inform him of the time the contractor was coming over to give an estimate. He went to the next task on the list—*Great, bills*, he thought.

Gary was driving by the Power Lane house for the hundredth time in just three weeks, looking for a "For Sale" sign so he could purchase the house. He saw three men standing in front of the plot of land where the barn had stood. Though he couldn't hear what they were saying, he knew what was happening. They looked at printed documents, measured the ground, and gave all the signs that they were planning a building project.

"They can't build on that land!"

"What happens if they build on that land?"

"That spot is the original location of the possession. If they take that spot, they can completely crush my ability to build and grow. Without that, you are back to who you were before me."

"What was wrong with that?"

"Let's focus on what has to be stopped. That building cannot be built, even if we have to burn it down before it can be finished."

"Stopping a building from being finished is easy, but I've got to keep from being arrested again. I'm out now temporarily, hoping to show the judge that I will behave so he doesn't have to put me back in."

"We stop it without getting caught. Here's a place to start. Can we talk them out of it?"

He walked up to the men and said, "Excuse me, may I speak to the owner?"

Fred turned to the voice and said, "I am the owner. May I help you?"

He recognized two of them immediately. Fred and Bill were together, and he knew that talking alone may have already been exhausted.

"I want to buy the property."

Fred shook his head no at the same time as Bill. "The property is not for sale."

Bill turned to the contractor. "You know what we want. You can start working on that."

The contractor left with a handshake.

Bill turned to Gary. "You've got some nerve. The property is not for sale."

"Bill, you are not the owner anymore. That decision belongs to someone else."

Fred said, "I'm the owner. Bill is right…it's not for sale. I'd like for you to leave my property now. I really don't want to discuss it any further."

Gary left, angry and feeling the burning inside him and the desire to take it by force. He had to get that property, even if Fred and Bill had to die to make it happen. "I'll see you again." He stopped himself from saying more, but the message got through.

Melissa sat in her car in front of Gary's house. What got into him that he would be so stupid? She understood anger and a desire for revenge, but the total lack of control, she didn't understand. She had to talk to him, and maybe she could square this away in her mind. Yet she sat; nervous or scared or both, she didn't know. The reality was she didn't know how to start.

She decided the best way was to just ask and hope for an honest answer. She got out of the car, dropped the keys in her purse, and headed toward the house. She didn't know what was worse—the feeling of confusion or the feeling that she lost her mind. Did she start falling for a violent man?

The sound of her fist knocking on the door startled her thoughts. *Relax, missy. You're going to go crazy before you even get a chance to talk to him.* Gary's voice came from inside. "Just a minute."

The minute became the welcome break she needed to calm down and, at least, get a starting place. A couple minutes later, the door opened.

She saw the shocked look on Gary's face. "Hello, Gary."

"Hello." His body filled the door.

"May I come in?"

"Sure." He stepped out of the way, closing the door behind her.

"I'm sorry about that. I wasn't expecting you."

"I'm not sure I should be here, but we need to talk."

The inquisitive look on his face asked the question for him, but he spoke it anyway. "What about?"

"Violence."

She saw his face change from curious to knowing. "Oh. I guess you heard about that."

"Yes, I'm the one who paid your bail. I can't keep seeing you if you're going to be getting in trouble like this."

"That was an old high school thing. I took it way too seriously. I've decided to let it go completely. I don't know if they will even talk to me now."

"Would you want to talk to someone that threatened you like you did him?"

"No, I guess not."

"The question is, are you violent like that often or just when you're mad?"

"I don't make a habit of hurting people. My days of bullying are over. So are my days of revenge. I promise no more violence unless I'm in a professional ring in competition."

"That's only fair. Next time, I won't bail you out."

"No problem, there won't be a next time."

"Okay, how about a walk? I need to get some air."

"Sure, let me get the keys and lock up before we leave."

His hand went down to where they normally were and found nothing but an empty table. He dropped to his knees and searched the floor underneath the table; nothing. Sitting on his feet, he shook his head.

"Have you ever had one of those days that you would forget your head if it wasn't attached? Of course not. How silly that I even ask."

He sat without moving, retracing his steps after getting home. No more than thirty seconds later, he jumped up, did a complete flip, landed on both feet, and darted off in a flash to the back of the house. Seconds later, he returned to the room. "Here they are! We can go now." He took her hand and escorted her along the way.

She looked on curiously without speaking. *Who is this guy really? Can anyone be so awkward and smooth at the same time? I just can't figure him out.*

They walked together without talking. She took in everything she saw about him like a sponge. She saw the boy shining with delight, but there was more. She couldn't quite put her finger on it, but it was obvious there was something deeper going on with him. Something that would overshadow everything else before this was over.

The silence gave him time to think. For a long time, she just stared at him. He thought she must have seen something that brought on this silence. They were together, but she seemed guarded, uncomfortable. He allowed her to think without interruption while he gathered his thoughts together. He feared the little boy was trying to get out again, and he didn't know how to stop him this time. She wasn't an opponent in a ring wanting to win a fight. She was beautiful, caring, and more.

Treat her like a delicate flower, or she will wither before your eyes. The words of his father flashed like a neon sign in his head. Knowing what he meant was easy; doing it in these circumstances seemed harder. For now, the little boy was out to play, and no selfish motivation would make him put the boy away.

"Melissa, I'm sorry about the awkwardness back at the house."

She held up a finger to his lips, stopping the words. "What awkwardness? I saw a handsome young man preparing to take his girl for a walk. Isn't that what you were doing?"

"Yes."

"Oh, here's the trail. Take it to the right. It will only take a little while."

They both walked onto the narrow trail, which was wooded on both sides. It curved into the woods and sloped to lower ground. The clearing came into view. He could see the smile reach across her face. "This is my favorite spot. Wait until you see the wild flowers on the other side. They are gorgeous this time of year."

The trees cut away into a big circle. One side was bordered by lush green leaves standing tall. Then the smell of the flowers hit his nostrils. His head followed the scent, and the lush green stems with tiny white flowers gave way to lilies of all colors mixed in with baby's breath. It looked to him like someone planted and tended to this section just to make this look the way it did.

"I told you. It takes my breath away every time I see it."

Gary noticed the opening on the other side of the circle. "Where does that go?"

He could see her thinking. "I'll show you later when you have more time. You have to be getting ready for the gym soon."

The confrontation with coach was today too. He wouldn't be handled so easily. He offered an awkward smile and said, "You're right. We can do this again some other time."

They walked back hand in hand, chatting about what they saw and whispering secrets to each other.

Fred sat in his study looking at the plans for the gym or, at least, a general picture of it. He stood for several hours holding the picture in his hand, trying to imagine what it would be like to be inside the building after it was built. With all surety, he knew he understood a tenth of what it would be in real life. The time in imagination lifted the burden he so carefully placed and adjusted on his back every day.

They were the dreams and desires that only God knew. He carried them by choice, though he knew that God shared the task with him. And now back in his office, he enjoyed the luxury of resting, while his mind walked through the courts, dreamed of big revivals, and patrolled the halls and classrooms for misbehaving kids. He smiled with the dream rolling through his mind. The dream was so far away, and yet the light was shining from the other end of the tunnel.

His mind shifted gears from his dreams to his deep pain—the one thing he carried with him as much for balance as anything else. He allowed the pain to swell inside as the memories slowly rolled through his mind. The boy was a close friend and someone he made plans to be partners with in business.

He made the plans for the third bicycle tour. The previous two, he showed Christ to his friend with little response, but that was changing fast. He was asking questions that encouraged him. The most encouraging question was if he would show him from his Bible how Jesus worked at the campsite. He tried when he asked the question, but he wouldn't listen to anything then.

Three miles into the tour, the cycles were spinning easily into a left turn when the drunk driver raced past Fred, slamming into his friend. He died before he hit the ground. Fred suffered more than the loss of a friend. He suffered the pain of not seizing the opportunity to show Christ to his friend. This pain pushed him to keep spreading the Gospel to everyone he could. The Gospel of Jesus Christ became his life that day. Within three weeks, the prayer squad was formed, and just three years later, the dedication turned into a church.

19 Physical Decimation

Gary sat on the bench looking at the warm-up weights and thinking about the arrest. The total time all of the previous events occurred, his mind froze on his hatred. That was a mistake. Now he would face the consequences in a big way. His coach was going to walk into the gym, lay down the verdict, and make the choice he dreaded.

There were three options—simply to say that he would work through this with him, or there is no excuse for violence outside of the gym, or there is no more professional career. At any rate, he knew it wasn't going to be good.

He saw the manager meet with his coach before he came over. He couldn't hear what was said. He watched as the coach walked up. His struggle showed on his face. He dropped his head and breathed heavily. *Is it over for me because of some stupid decision?* he thought.

"Gary?"

"Yes, Coach."

"I have permission to use the manager's office to have this talk with you. Follow me."

He got up from the bench and followed the coach into the office. He watched the hand indicate a chair. "Sit down."

He sat down and looked at the coach for a sign that this could end well. He didn't see a lot of hope in his face. "I have to know what is going on. Two fights in the gym that the manager broke up and a fight in the parking lot that the police broke up. What do you think the professional circuit is going to do with you?"

Hearing it put so plainly made it even dumber than he thought. He didn't know whether he should break down or not. His heart got heavier than before, and a new pain surfaced in his heart. He had to answer, but the words that tried to form were just plain wrong. "I don't know exactly what is going on with me. It seems that my anger takes over, and I can't stop it."

"Anger—that should be displayed for show only, Gary, never acted on. Do you understand the price you may have to pay for acting on your anger?"

The first tear started to fall from his eye. "No, I don't."

"You won't have a professional career at all if you continue like this. Because the arrest was disturbing the peace, the circuit manager is willing to let you in under one circumstance. Any fighting outside the ring and you will have no professional career period. Do you get it? You can train, spar, and drill all you want, but no more trouble!"

He dropped his head and muttered through his hands, "What about the gym?"

"That is why we are in here." He got up and called the manager in the office. "The manger wanted to talk to you himself on that."

He didn't dare look up now. His shoulders shook with quiet sobs, which told the story anyway. "Son," the manager said. "We have rules that have to be obeyed. There hasn't been actual fighting but too many threats. Your coach has assured me that you will deal with the anger issue. I'm offering one chance for you to stay in this gym."

A ray of hope entered where none had existed. He looked up at the manager for the first time, wiping the tears from his face. "What is your offer?"

"This gym has a professional training area on the back side. You pay the same fee, but you schedule the time for that training area, and you go to an anger management program. Any more problems and you are out for good. I hope you understand."

"I do, thank you. I will do that."

The manager turned to the coach. "If you are wrong on your guess, you will be removed from the gym as well. I will not tolerate anymore."

The coach replied, "There will be no more disturbances."

The manager threw him a piece of paper and walked out.

The coach looked back at Gary. "I am paying the ultimate price for you, staking everything on what you do now. You have to watch everything you do from now on closely. You had better not get me kicked out of this gym, Gary."

His head fell again. "I won't, Coach. I'll do better. What do we do next?"

"First, we get a time blocked out. Second, we come back and work you out so hard that you don't have the energy to get into trouble."

"That sounds like a plan."

"I'll go with you to get the time. Stay away from those guys that have you so riled," he said as they left the office.

Gary struggled with the thoughts and feelings from the past week. His control of every situation was faltering. Thinking back to try to find the time when it happened, he could only come up with the time shortly after Moloch's possession. He needed to find out for sure what Moloch really wanted. "Moloch."

Was Moloch willing to listen anytime, or was he just in this for him? "Yes, Gary."

"Can you tell me why I am losing it lately?"

"Gary, you need to surrender yourself to me, and I will make sure your desires are completely fulfilled. Do you see the value in that?"

"I am to give you my life for what reason?"

"For the accomplishment of the mission. It is time we start working to that end."

"What mission, Moloch? I don't like playing games."

"Your mission is simple. All you have to do is have three boys and raise them to follow me. The rest I will take care of."

"Are you serious, Moloch? Just like that? What do you want me to do? Find three hookers and get them pregnant?"

"Gary, that would accomplish nothing. Calm down. It is best if the mother of all three boys is the same woman. Does that sound like a better plan than yours?"

"Yes, it does. One problem—the violence and revenge you are driving me to do are driving away the potential mother of these three boys. What can we do about that?"

"All right, no more fighting. I need something from you."

"What do you need from me?"

"I need you to take Samuel and raise him as your own."

"And you think that won't result in a fight?" Gary shook his head and laughed.

"Samuel belongs to me. He is part of the mission. Please understand the mission is everything to me."

"Moloch, that much I understand. Do you think Bill is really going to legally sign Samuel over to my care? Why would he do that?"

"How you get him is not important. The fact that you get him is."

"Bill won't let me within half a mile of him without perking up and going into defense mode."

"The only way I'm going to get him is to kill Bill."

"You can't be serious. What are you thinking? Or are you?"

Gary sensed the silence and realized how serious he was. "You know that the result of that would end any chance I had at a professional fighting career and, more importantly, any relationship with Melissa. So there go the three boys."

Gary could hear the silence and finally said, "When you want to make sense, let me know. Maybe then we can come to a mutual agreement."

"Gary, we don't have to come to a mutual agreement. The only agreement we have to come to is this. You will find a way to get Samuel, or your fighting career won't mean anything to anyone."

"Maybe I need to talk to Bill after all."

"Gary."

"Gary."

Gary felt the stab in his leg first. The pain shot up from his leg to his hips before he gave out and fell to the floor. "Are you listening to me, Gary?"

"Yes."

Gary felt the pain subside immediately. "Why did you do that?"

"Because you quit listening. I have ways to get your attention and will use them."

"Who are you, and what is your mission?"

"Never mind about that. You will not—and I mean will not—talk to Bill except for one thing, getting legal control over Samuel. You do understand that now. This mission is everything to you too."

"Okay. I get the point."

"Good."

Patty's mind began racing in ways she didn't understand. Every doubt that she had ever experienced came racing into her mind. Patty didn't know what to believe or what to do. She could feel her body giving out. Pain from everywhere ran through her nerves. She fumbled and stumbled for the phone. As she fell to the floor, the phone dropped with her. God help me.

Patty dialed the number for Peter. On the third ring, Peter answered, "Hello."

"Help…me." Then the phone went dead.

"Patty…Patty…Patty!"

Peter disconnected from the call and dialed the speed number for Fred. He answered in two rings. "Hello."

"Emergency prayer meeting, Patty's place, now."

"On my way."

Fred speed-dialed Harry and John. He knew they were on the way. It became a race to get to Patty's. Fred saw that Peter was already in the drive; Harry was right behind him, and he suspected the car behind Harry was John's.

Peter ran in first without knocking. Immediately, the other three ran in behind. Peter yelled, "Patty!"

A soft groan was all he heard, but it was more than enough. All four ran in the direction of the sound. Peter saw Patty on the floor reaching out; soft whimpers seemed to be all she could get out.

Peter dropped to his knees, placing both hands on her, and began praying. He knew he was joined by the other three. "Father, we come together on behalf of your daughter. You are almighty and all-knowing. Come now and touch her. We pray that you would overcome any attack on her, bringing victory in her life."

Garold drove up to the house, parked by the curb, and ran into the house just behind his wife. He could see the panic running through her. He almost pushed her down from behind when he saw Patty on the floor with the four prayer squad members laying hands on her and praying.

"Honey, get in the circle and pray."

She moved more quickly than he expected. Following the example before them, they laid their hands on the shoulders of the prayer warriors and started praying. Garold could hear the sobs from his wife and knew she was breaking down. He wrapped his arms around her and prayed for her in her ear.

Garold's prayer brought with it peace. He released her when he saw Patty sit up on the floor. He wasn't surprised when he saw Vera grab her daughter. Garold led the way, placing his hands on his wife and continuing to pray. He felt the strength of the others joining in. An hour later, Patty turned to Peter. "What happened?"

Peter looked to Harry. "You want to answer that?"

Harry looked to Vera and Patty. "The assaults we have experienced spiritually are expanding. The person that last received Christ as Savior is going to be tried."

Vera said, "If I'm being tried, why is Patty being attacked?"

"Vera, Satan is using an attack method that almost crushed you before. Hurt one of your children and create doubt and fear in your life. Do you know that God is in complete control and will never leave or forsake you?"

"This is God's provision. He is trying to show me what he has already provided."

"The question is, did he?" Harry asked.

"Yes, you will come whenever we call?"

"Anywhere, anyplace, anytime, all you have to do is call. That is the agreement we have."

Peter's arms wrapped around Patty. He felt her arms around him as they held each other on the brink of tears.

Jelani (Patty's angel) couldn't interfere until help had arrived. She prayed to Jesus to send the help and knew her prayer had been answered when Peter answered the phone. Jelani was getting anxious waiting for the help. It was too long; Patty had not moved for two minutes and could barely get out a sound. She bowed her head in a silent prayer.

She heard Dustin shout, "Jelani, let's go get those imps!"

Their swords whipped out flashing light that penetrated into the soul. Jelani saw Randolph, Cenewig, and Einar with swords drawn and coming in right after. All five of the guardian angels attacked the imps that were attacking Patty's mind and body. The imps withdrew quickly and said, "You can't stop us. We have your Lord's permission."

Jelani said, "You only have permission as long as I'm alone. Do I look alone now?"

"We have help if we need to use them."

"Bring them all on. We are ready."

Twenty of the attacking demons flew at the guardian angels with the imps. Swords clashed and sparked, but the guardian angels didn't break. Jelani saw three more angels coming. Boris, William, and Elliot joined the line. Boris said, "No more, the test is over now. Leave."

The imp responded, "Just because you're here you think that we're going to run. Patty is almost dead. Jelani will be out of a job soon. We're going back in to finish the job. You won't stop us ever."

Boris commanded. "Hold the line. Let no one in."

The guardian angels took a defensive stance around the praying children of God and locked. The lead demon said, "We're leaving for now. This is not over. We'll have our day yet."

They flew away.

20 The Lost Logs

Bill walked into the office carrying Samuel. It seemed to him that he had not been in this room for too many weeks. His briefcase sat on his desk loaded with paperwork that needed to be inputted into the computer and phone numbers that needed called. He gathered himself together, turned on the computer, and mentally prepared himself for the work ahead.

The desk was more cluttered than he liked. He cleared the papers of the stack and scanned them to see what needed to be done. The first sheet needed to be contacted in the afternoon. The note took him to researching specific needs for the customer. The second one needed a follow-up call to make sure that the work was staying on track.

His cell phone sat on the desk beside the pen and pencil holder. He rolled out the chair and sat down. *Okay. Let's see if you and I can make some things happen now.* He tapped a few keys on the computer, and it went to work. He turned to the stack again to find out what was still there. His mind froze in panic. What he recognized immediately as Trainer's logs lay there. The phone chirped seconds after he discovered the logs. He picked it up and said, "Hello."

"Bill?"

"Yes, Jeff? What's going on?"

"We received a call from Bernard's Title Company. Justin McKay is a real estate agent. He is looking to list your property in Van Burean. Are you looking to sell all of Trainer's houses?"

"All of Trainer's houses? There are more?"

"I have a list of addresses in four states. You have almost one million in land value that is completely up-to-date."

"Is there more property I don't know about?"

"I would have to do title searches, but I believe our records have been kept up-to-date. I will look and see what I can find."

"Would you give me the real estate agent's number so I can contact him?"

"Sure, you can call him at 318-555-9134."

"Thank you. I'll contact him, and you can get on that title search. When do you think you'll have anything ready for me?"

"Next week early. We already have most of the information in the office. I'll check for further information though."

"All right. I'll expect a call from you then."

"Good-bye. Talk to you next week."

"Next week."

Bill hung up the phone. What more can come up of Trainer's? He dropped his head and began to pray. "Father, show me what to do with this property that belongs to Trainer. Guide me and show me how to get rid of Trainer."

Bill prepared for the board meeting, never able to get his mind off the logs that weren't destroyed with the rest of them. His knowledge of Trainer told him that they would be sensed and hunted for until they were found.

Bill stopped at the thought. *Trainer and, most likely, Moloch know these logs weren't in the house when everything else was burned. Trainer is currently in Samuel, and Moloch is currently in Gary. Samuel is too young to worry about now, but Gary must not know they are here, or he will be here looking for them.*

Bill realized that the protection he needed came from God. He would be the only one who could protect them from getting into Trainer's hands again. Bill was about to walk out the door when he thought to take the logs with him. They could be hidden in the house that now belonged to God and protected there. The board would have to agree, but there was always a hope.

I'm getting tired of Trainer already. I'm sure the others are going to get tired of him too. "God, give me the words to say. This isn't going to make anything easier."

Trainer jumped inside Samuel. There was something he needed and would have to get help to get. He called out to Moloch as he had so many times before. Trainer felt the response. He sent out a message: "Logs on the way to Power Lane. Bill has them."

He sensed the answer more than heard it. But it was a start. They could now communicate to some extent with each other.

"Gary," Moloch called.

"Moloch." Gary mocked.

"Be careful with the attitude. You are being sent on an important mission."

"I haven't had a chance to arrange a meeting with Samuel."

"This mission is more important than Samuel. The logs we need to gather the information from the past has been found. You are going to retrieve them."

"Who has them?"

"Bill. He is on his way to the house on Power Lane. We have to intercept the logs before they get there."

"Trainer, isn't that where you wanted me to go before?"

"That was until I found out about the circumstances around the house. Please listen. He is on his way now. We have to get going."

"I have things that I have to do as well. Missing practice with coach is a big no-no. He's doing me a favor, and I've no intention of forgetting that."

Use your skill, and you will not have to be late. Just get in the intercept path."

"Ailith, Power Lane intercept. Get the prayer squad and Rebeca doing what they do best. Those logs are to be protected at all cost."

Rebeca jumped up from the chair she was sitting in. Somehow, she knew trouble was coming, and it would be near the house on Power Lane. Without reservation, she got into her car and headed that direction.

Fred sat in his office chair, working on getting the business meeting organized so the information could be covered quickly. The Spirit told him to pray. Somehow, Bill was in trouble. Though he didn't know how or where, he began to pray.

Harry was on Power Lane, heading to the house, so he could be there a little early when the car stalled. He got it over to the side of the road and stopped, but it refused to restart. The voice he recognized to be God's told him not to call anyone and to just wait. He would be needed shortly at that spot.

Peter was driving with John in the passenger seat. John said, "Keep driving. We both need to start praying for Bill. Something is going on." They both began to pray.

Rebeca turned in front of Bill's car and continued toward Power Lane. She felt unrest and peace at the same time. This was different to her, but she knew to keep going. *Was this what Fred talked about when he said obeying God in all circumstance?*

Gary pulled up to the corner and stopped. He was there and just had to wait for Bill's car. He didn't feel Trainer getting closer, so Samuel wouldn't be with him. He decided he could still persuade Bill to give him Samuel. A little force may be necessary, but that was fine with Gary. Coach wouldn't find out if he did this right.

The other car was broken down with hazards flashing. It looked empty and shouldn't pose a problem. In fact, if he played it right, he could put Bill's car into it to stop him. The wait wasn't long until he saw two cars coming down the road. *Time it, Gary. Wait and strike quick and hard.* Gary held one foot on the brake, the other above the accelerator. He recognized the first driver immediately.

Rebeca will make things tougher, but it can be handled easily enough. The second car was Bill. Anticipation built inside him like a roaring steamroller begging to go. He waited and slammed hard on the accelerator while simultaneously releasing the brake. The car shot out just in time to catch the front of Bill's car and slam it into Harry's car, stopping it cold. He jumped out of his car and ran toward Bill's car. He saw Rebeca running at him, holding nothing back.

Gary didn't see Bill in the car, and the passenger door was already open. Before he could get around the car, his arm shot across his body, blocking Rebeca's flying kick. Gary turned to follow her. He saw her land upright in a defensive stance he not only recognized but also used. Before he could say a word, his side gave way. Pain shot from something striking beyond his sight line.

He turned and saw Harry standing in a defensive position. Keeping an eye on both parties, he said, "Two on one, I see. You"—he pointed to Harry—"have kissed the death angel, and better be afraid! You"—pointing to Rebeca—"will bear me a son, and I will enjoy that. I hope you're ready to party."

Bill could see Gary's back and knew where to strike, but he also knew that he would strike back. He couldn't let Harry get killed and would not, under any circumstance, let Rebeca get raped. "Not if I have anything to say about it." He leaped over the hood of the car, his foot already in striking position. He saw Gary turn and fired his foot across his jaw. He watched as Gary spun around by the blow, dropped to his knees, and then landed upright, ready for the next move.

He saw Harry spin Gary into a pin hold with his arm behind his back. Bill felt Rebeca standing beside him. He heard her say, "Be ready, boys. This dance has just begun."

Gary felt the knee lock on his back below his arm. He heard Harry say, "Move one toe and I will crush your back. I may have forgotten some moves, but a few tricks never leave." Sirens could be heard, and as blue lights came into view, Gary gave in.

"Moloch! You have done it again! I will lose the girl, the career, and freedom all for some stupid logs. I hope you like looking at bars. You will be seeing a lot of them."

"No, Gary, I won't, and neither will you. Because when I leave, you will die. The secrets you know about me will never get out."

There was only one hope. Gary took one last chance. He spun under Harry, freed his arm, and ran for the woods across the way.

Harry looked up from the road where he lay. "Didn't expect that."

Rebeca said, "That's okay. He is gone now, and whatever he wanted went with him."

Bill said, "Try again. What he wanted were these logs, and I'm holding them. Rebeca, our cars are a little out of action. Would you mind driving them to Fred's and tell him why we're delayed?"

Harry looked to Bill as Rebeca left with the logs in hand.

Rebeca ran into the church, yelling, "Fred!"

She saw him running down the hall and heard, "What's going on?"

She ran to him. "You have to help me. Where is your office?"

"Follow me."

She watched as Peter and John entered and closed the door. She followed Fred into the office. She said, "Peter, John, I'm glad you're here too. Is there someplace that these can be locked up tight?" She extended out the two Trainer's logs. "Bill said to get them locked up."

She watched as Fred dialed the combination to the safe and opened the door. "In here." She threw them in and closed the door.

Making sure the door would not open, she said, "Bill and Harry are talking to the police. I think those books have something to do with Trainer."

She heard the concern in Fred's voice. "Rebeca, slow down. Everything is locked up and safe. What happened?"

"Gary can get in. He will kill us all for those logs."

John said, "The front door is locked. What is going on?"

"I don't know. Bill is in trouble, and I'm not there to help him. Gary is out there on the run from the police. Fred, he's crazy!"

She jumped at the sound of the phone. Fred answered, "Hello."

"Hello, Fred. Did Rebeca make it there?"

"Yes, she is a wreck. What happened?"

"Can I talk to her first?"

"Yes." Fred extended the phone to Rebeca. "It's Bill for you."

She took the phone quickly. "Bill, are you okay? Do I need to come back? Is Gary there?"

"Rebeca, calm down. Everything is fine here. The police are here and K-9 units are on their way to search for Gary. No one knows where he is right now. There is an officer on the way to sit by the house to make sure he didn't double back that direction. They want to talk to you and get a statement. Can you calm down enough to do that?"

The shaking and trembling in Rebeca slowed and finally stopped. "Am I in trouble for leaving?"

"The officer here assured me that all they want is a statement. They aren't arresting anyone but Gary if they find him. He said we have the right to defend ourselves."

"Okay, I can do that."

"Good, they'll be there soon. I love you."

"Bill, I love you too. See you later." She handed the phone back to Fred. "The police are on their way to talk to me and keep watch on the house in case Gary shows up. He wants those logs, Fred. He'll do anything to get them."

21 5857 Power Lane

Gary's mission was incomplete. The logs still were in the wrong hands. The decision to double back was easy. Get into the house and steal the logs. Harry and Bill were back at the original scene and would not be able to help. Fred wasn't a threat.

By the time he got to the house, the police sat in the driveway with a policeman standing in the front door and one going in the house. He hadn't planned on the police being there so soon. The dogs that had been on his tail would catch up soon if he continued to sit. "Another day, you can go after them another day, Moloch. We know where they are. We can get them anytime now."

"And I know that house like the back of your hand, every square inch of it." Moloch agreed to draw back. "They can't hide anything in there that I can't find." Gary retreated in the woods toward the stream where he lost the dogs in before.

Harry drove Bill to the house for the meeting. As he pulled into the drive, he saw Fred, Peter, and John waiting at the door. The look on their faces expressed concern. Harry got out of the car and walked to the door followed by Bill.

Fred said, "Welcome. Come on up to the office. We have a lot to talk about."

Harry knew little of the books, but he also knew they were now on the agenda. "And new things were happening every day."

Fred replied, "So it seems. What do you say that we get to the office and start this off with prayer?"

"Agreed," Harry said.

After the prayer, Fred started the meeting. "Bill, do you wish to fill us in on the books?"

"They are the only and the most recent logs of Trainer. We all know the trouble that we went through for the house. I'm certain that these logs will lead to more trouble."

Harry asked, "We have another fight like we had for the house?"

"That may be an understatement. These are the only instructions he has left. The fight for these will involve anyone and everyone, newest to the oldest member."

"What are we going to do with them?" Peter asked.

John said, "Use t-t-them to d-d-defeat him."

Harry continued, "There'll be a time that we need them to defeat the power of Satan. The battle before us will be greater than the battle we had for the house."

Fred said, "It's already started."

Harry said, "The previous battle was here. We've already taken their base. I feel that there will be another base close to here. It hasn't been established yet."

Fred saw Bill shiver. "What are we missing, Bill?"

Bill answered, "Trainer has other properties. My lawyer is looking for those locations now. Anything that I own could become a base of operation. When I sell it, it falls out of his hands."

Peter asked, "Why hasn't he taken one for a base of operation yet?"

Harry said, "Bill is God's property now. If any demon tries to take one now, they would lose it quickly. Bill must sell it though. The image I see is of someone putting a wood statue of a god on a shelf. It will eventually become a hindrance to their relationship with Jesus Christ."

Bill said, "God wants me to get everything that was Trainer's out of my life? If I hold on to them, I can stop the home base from developing."

"Bill," Harry said. "You'll also hold back your growth and blessing. The price is too high for you to stop what would look like a victory for them. Sometimes they have to win a battle for God to win the war."

Fred said, "You'll have the church holding you up. What seems to be right to us may not be God's way. Understand that we don't want more battling but are willing to obey God whatever the circumstances may be."

Fred saw Bill drop his head. "I am getting tired of having to fight."

"Bill," Fred said. "You'll have to fight anyway. As long as Samuel is possessed, the fight will continue. Maybe this is God's way of ending the fight once and for all."

Fred saw understanding in Bill's eyes when they locked on his. The unspoken communication read clearly by all in the meeting. Fred said, "Right now the logs are safe, so let's move on to a new subject."

Harry said, "God isn't done with this conversation. The logs need to be hidden elsewhere. There is a hole in the wall in the basement. They need to go back there, this time with a Bible on top of them. The Bible is a representation of God's covering and protection over them."

Bill said, "Is that a good idea? They were hidden there to start with. Wouldn't that be like hiding them in plain sight?"

"I think that is the idea. God defeats the enemy so we don't have to fight."

"The memories are going to be a lot to deal with," Bill said.

Fred saw the shiver and nerves being displayed prominently on Bill. "That's what we're here for. As a team, we'll place everything where God says."

Fred picked up the logs and an old Bible, looked at the others, and said, "Let's get this done." Fred knew everyone followed.

"Ailith, place an angel with those books. They are a big part of my plans."

"Yes, Lord." He went to the angels in his command. "You are going to protect those books."

The selected angel flew to the place where he needed to be.

Bill walked down to the basement with two of the prayer squad in front and two behind him. The memories and fears flooded back all the way down the stairs. Bill saw the eyes of the other four board members before he saw the figure standing where Moloch stood the first time. He heard the figure say, "Fear not, Jesus has placed protection here. The Father has well in store you."

Bill felt better as he pulled out the brick along the floor, reached in, and flipped the switch. The door slid up and opened. He reached out his hand, taking the logs and the Bible. Making sure the Bible was on top, he slid them in the room by the wall. Sliding out, he said, "I guess this means the war is on?"

Fred said, "God will win it yet. Just believe."

"Let's get back to the office and finish up. I'm not real comfortable down here." Bill meant every word of that and started up immediately. In the office, Bill gave the report on the plans for the church. There would be a few weeks of delay as the company finalizes the blueprints. Everything would be ready for starting the building in five months."

Bill listened to the rest of the reports and made the necessary notes. Bill prayed silently as Harry prayed out loud to close the meeting. Then he walked out of the office to find Rebeca waiting in the church area. She walked up to him with a smile that quickly fell to concern. Bill looked at her. "Hello. You didn't have to wait for me."

"I waited so you could protect me. What happened in the meeting?"

He looked to Fred and heard him say, "Tell her the truth. She will hear about it Sunday from me anyway."

Bill looked back to Rebeca and said, "You remember what just happened with Gary?"

"Yes."

"It will happen again. What the board decided to do will outrage Trainer, and I expect that I and anyone associated with me will pay."

"Bill, you know I'm ready to deal with anything Trainer can dish out. I've helped Saundra through eight months of Trainer's stuff. There's nothing that he can dish out that God can't get us through. Saundra described Trainer perfectly to me. Gary is just the start."

"Rebeca, I'm in this so deep. I'm not just going against Trainer. I'm standing against the whole horde this time. I've seen what the horde can do to a person. And now the only thing standing between them and me is Jesus and praying friends. That had better be enough."

Bill saw Rebeca smile. "I know it is and will never let you forget it."

Bill smiled and said, "Let's go somewhere else. This place is too crowded."

Bill heard Fred say, "Good night. Take care of each other."

They left, closing the door behind them. Rebeca asked, "My car is right here. Where do you want to go?"

"Right now home would be great. I'm not ready for more excitement tonight."

Bill closed his eyes in the passenger seat and tried to forget the crazy day.

"Bill," Rebeca said. "You're home. Are you going to be all right?"

"Sure. It looks like Grandma and Grandpa are here. They make everything all right."

He got out of the car and went inside. He watched Rebeca drive off from the door before entering.

22 The Rejection

Rebeca drove home, praying. She couldn't feel anything because of the confusion running rampant through her head. From all she knew of Bill, this was different from anything she had ever heard of. She knew he liked being in control, and she would have sworn she felt a lost feeling and confusion coming from him.

There were a few people who could or would help her with this. She picked up her cell phone, struggling with her emotions; she was next to tears. She dialed Harry's number and waited. He answered on the third ring. "Hello."

"Hello, Harry."

"Rebecca, how are things going?"

"I don't know. I thought good, but Bill…" She could feel her voice break, and there was nothing more than sobs after.

"Listen to me. Bill loves you more than he can express right now. The entire board fears that Trainer is going to come after his soul again as well as trying hard to take Samuel. He doesn't want to hurt you in any way. He doesn't know how to react now. Bill needs you to be there. Please, Rebeca, stay strong and pray for him. He needs all he can get right now."

"He didn't talk at all on the way home. I don't know what that means."

"He is the type of man to think through things before talking about them. With the battle he fought last time, it may take him sometime to talk about it. Be there to help him when he is ready. One of the four other board members is stopping by in the morning to pray with him. I have tomorrow morning. Feel free to meet me there in the morning. Maybe he will open up some."

"He wants me to come?"

"You need to come for your sake. Show him you love him and allow him to reciprocate that love. God put you in his life for a reason. You will be together for a long time. This is a God-planted love that he will never escape."

"Thank you. What time in the morning?"

"He gets to his office about nine a.m. I want to be there fifteen minutes before."

"I will be there. Thank you for talking to me. Good-bye."

"See ya then."

Gary found the stream and ran along the middle heading toward town. He kept looking back for signs he was spotted but found none. He didn't hear the dogs barking until after he turned the corner out of sight. Still in a dead sprint in the stream, he suddenly dropped into the water. He gasped for air just as his head went under. He regained enough control of the fall to kick his way back to the top. He started swimming with the current of what was now a river. Quickly, he found a pace that allowed him to breathe and take advantage of the river current for speed.

He could feel fatigue trying to set in and slow him down, but that wasn't going to happen now. His training kicked in, allowing him to keep going. The dogs were still behind him and lost by the sound of their barking.

The command came from within the river. The police were working the river. He arched his back, driving his whole body under the water, and swam for the shore and the camouflage of the trees on the edge.

His head surfaced behind a big tree. Listening for any sound at all, he slid deeper into the thicket as the voices and barking got louder. *Why did I double back and lose all that time? No time to think about that now.*

He stayed motionless in the thicket as the dogs sniffed about. The barking focused on the thicket. He dipped his head down under the water and held himself under. The sounds from under the water calmed down as he waited until he had no more breath and had to come up.

He listened again knowing that coming up and out too soon would put him back on the run again. The voices and barking became more distant. He remained still until all sound from outside the woods vanished.

He went back under and swam out of the thicket to the shore. He saw nothing but woods. His heart was racing with excitement and nerves shaking more than he could imagine. He cautiously got out of the river. Gary ran southeast back to where the police had already searched and kept listening as he ran. Ten minutes later, he stopped just before a clearing, caught his breath, and listened. All he could hear was traffic. When he peeked out, he saw the main road going into town. He waited for a while until traffic was quiet and slid out of the forest.

How much the police knew, he didn't know. This was for sure: he had to come up with a good reason for this or lose everything. "Just keep walking and let the sun dry you off. You can work out the details on the way."

"Thank you for your vote of confidence, Moloch. I hope you understand what is at stake now."

"Believe me, I do. No girlfriend, no baby boys. No baby boys, no plan fulfillment."

"Is that all you think about, Moloch? What about helping me with my professional career?"

"Your professional career will be great after this plan is going in the right direction. Relax about that."

Gary quit talking and walked on concentrating on what to say. I will have to take her on a walk and hope she doesn't walk away from me forever.

Gary was walking down the road when the car pulled up and stopped.

"Gary."

He looked up. "Coach?"

"Hop in. I'm on my way to the gym. We can stop by and get you some clothes. Maybe we can get some extra time in."

"Okay, what are you doing here?"

"I heard on the radio there was a wanted criminal around the area, something about hit and run, attempted assault, and sexual assault. You wouldn't know anything about that, would you?"

Gary's face drained of color. "How much is on the radio?"

"The police scanner has a full name and description as well as a full APB out on you. Didn't you think I was serious? You can't have a professional career with any fighting organization with APBs and warrants out for your arrest."

"I'm sorry, Coach. I don't know what to say."

"There is nothing for you to say. I have already contacted the gym manager. He gave the police your photograph and vital information the others didn't have. To take you home is to take you to the police."

"You're not going to train me anymore?"

"There's no more training until this is settled. I can't and won't train anyone who can't abide by the law. It is my reputation that is at stake as well. You fail to see that, but I don't."

"Oh, man, I need some real help."

"Yes, you do. Talk to the police and face this. You have to clear your name before anyone will move on with you."

"Thanks, I was going home anyway. If the police are there already, then I'll get that opportunity."

"Don't run, Gary. Go straight to the police. No one can help you if you run."

"Okay."

Gary started the walk to his house. Moloch asked, "Where are you going?"

"I have to face the consequences of my actions. This may be the only way that I will have any help at all."

"You cannot accomplish anything in jail, most importantly, the children."

"I think my last action took care of the children's problem. It's safe to say that Melissa isn't going to be doing much with me anyway."

"Melissa will if you take her to the right place."

"The old house? I want to get a look at it first."

"That is exactly what I want. Let's follow the trail."

Gary knew he was counting on the wrong help, but he liked the way it sounded better than jail. He walked to the trail, his mind wandering to Melissa. His hand instinctively reached out for another that became air at the moment the connection should have been made. He walked on alone with his memories. The open circle came into view. The grass and flowers blackened immediately upon his entrance. He ran through the circle onto the trail on the other side. A new excitement filled him. It pushed the darkness within him to the surface. The first bend just led to trees. The carving on the trees shocked him and then made him smile. "Yes, I know these markings. It is the place I hoped it to be."

He felt the power of Moloch saturate every muscle in his body. It felt good to be one in spirit with the demon. Now one more turn to the opening and then in the back door. The demons didn't call, but that was okay. They will be back soon enough.

The clearing opened up in front of him. The house, seemingly dead in the middle of the clearing, brought memories of wanting and burning desire for the days of old. The welcome sign beckoned a long past host that fled instead of seeking the freedom and power available. Then a different feeling poured into him—comforting, welcome, but not Trainer. It felt like meeting an old friend or a distant cousin for the first time. He walked to the basement, taking in the sight. The wood floor shone brightly of wealth, furnished in the eighteen sixties of money and leisure. He opened the door that he knew led to the basement, even though he had never been in this house before. The steps down were steep but a pleasure to walk down. The same feeling that filled Moloch when he led the house on Power Lane drove him to the northwest corner of the basement. The empty shelf slid out of the way, easily exposing the door.

The doorknob didn't turn. The door refused to budge. "This is Moloch. Open and let me in."

The door opened, and the top three stairs could be seen beyond as it was engulfed in darkness. Smiling, Gary took the stairs down to the lower floor. Though there was no light, he walked directly to where he needed to go. He stopped in the center of the room. His heart beat evenly and calmly as he lifted the log of the spirit and carried it up the stairs to the basement.

The lights shattered the darkness of the basement. The cover of the log was dark brown with the words, "Log of Didi." He pulled the cover open and read the first line: "The plan is in action; two boys already and the third on the way."

How could they accomplish that so quickly? He continued reading. "The mission will be completed in just a few more generations." *Did they complete the mission, and we don't know anything about it?* He wanted to stop reading but instead flipped over the page and saw the brown spot on the bottom of the page. The journal entry dated July 4, 1902. "Completing the mission was now impossible. A stray bullet from a gunfight took both of my son's lives. When my wife fell to their side, crying, she heard someone say, 'No witnesses,' and then the bang from the gun.

"All the witness accounts said it was an accident for the kids, but my wife was a deliberate act. Didi alone won't complete my life. Assume what you want. If you are reading this, you must be my only other son. I love you and want you to read Didi's lessons learned. It will tell your Didi how to complete the mission in three generations. As well, it may hold a clue to break the gender problem and allow girls in the picture."

We need to spend time reading that. Has this been read by the one living son of the writer? He flipped through the rest of the pages. No more writing, no more words. The one book Gary couldn't feel was Didi's lessons learned. That book held a reservation for Didi and the host. There was a book in the barn reserved for Trainer alone. Only Trainer or his host could feel it. The book would be hidden in a place where it had to be felt.

You have time to get acquainted with Didi and earn his trust. With that, he will allow you to feel the book's presence. Gary molded with Moloch as one completely in thought and person. It didn't matter what you called him; he was and is Gary and Moloch at the same time.

23 THE DOOR

Jeff looked at the list of eight houses, twelve cars, and over three hundred acres of land. Everything on the list combined to over one million in value at auction. The properties and cars sat in seven states with individual values ranging from a few thousand to several hundred thousand.

Bill knows nothing of this list. I don't know what he's going to do with this information. I guess it is time to lay out what Bill truly owns to him. He picked up the phone and dialed the number for Bill.

Bill spent the last hour on his knees. Samuel was sleeping, so he continuously listened for him to wake up. A burden came during the prayer that he knew was bigger than could be afforded by the church or him. He knew God wanted the church to have the building. He struggled through the last hour with the burden for him to pay for the building.

His prayer continued in the same direction, though he knew he couldn't afford it. He didn't know how long he had prayed, but he just sat in silence, listening for answers from God. The phone rang once, twice, and then three times before he answered it. "Hello."

"Hello, Bill. This is Jeff from Coleman, Schmitt, and Brand, attorneys-at-law."

"Yes, you have the information I requested?"

"Yes, I do. Do you have a fax, or would you rather I e-mail the file to you?"

"You can e-mail the file to me. Could we take a minute and preview the file for me?"

"You have eight properties, twelve cars, and more acreage of land than you can imagine. I will tell you that you have over one million dollars worth of property."

"All previously owned by family?"

"Yes. By the middle of next week, you will have the legal right to sell or keep what you want. You need to look at all the options before making any decisions."

"Thanks for the information. I will think everything through."

Two more days of prayer didn't change anything. His heart still burned for the church, and now he knew something was really wrong. Bill felt constant concern for Samuel's welfare.

The child stayed by his side or Rebeca's or most preferably both. After the last attack, he decided it was time to take extra precautions for everyone's sake.

No one heard a word from Gary, and the police had all-points bulletins out. Because he was wanted, he would be quick and ruthless with a ready route of escape. Bill wasn't going to let him take Samuel without a fight. That was one of the main concerns. Another concern was the fact that Gary could and would attack at all cost to get the log that was now in the protection of Fred. And last but not the least, the concern of the building cost. For the size and type of structure, it would cost almost one million dollars.

The first two, God gave Bill peace about, but not the answer he wanted. The third concern, God clearly guided Bill to sell Trainer's property and use the money to build the church. He had all the addresses and had the cars already together on one lot. One piece he prayed about longer than he thought he should. The Greyhound bus ran well and offered more comforts than he imagined. He didn't know exactly what it was, but something stopped him from selling it.

That wasn't an issue at the moment. He had an appointment coming up and needed to get his head together. This Jacob seemed to be exactly what his business needed. The work skills and experience fit exactly. It was a matter of getting the interview done and seeing if he fit like the application said he would.

Jacob's job search took him to the Internet three weeks ago. Just last week, a new job opening caught his eye. He was familiar with the location of the job and the type of work he not only loved but also did well. Sending his resume was an automatic. He couldn't have ever imagined it would get a response so quickly.

His interview was set to start in two hours. The drive would be at least one hour. The extra time would give him a chance to look at available housing in the area. The drive up was uneventful until he turned onto Power Lane. Memories began flashing through his mind that he didn't recognize. Images popped up, begging to be understood. Houses that he knew nothing about were jumping out and had no indication they were for sale. The fields of corn and soybeans drew him to stop and admire them. Like he had been there and knew it from the past.

He stopped the car on the side of the road and looked at the house. Nothing out of the ordinary appeared to make it jump out above the rest. It was not a verbal call that he could hear with his ears, but it was a call he could hear with his heart.

The "For Sale" sign jumped out from the yard almost literally. The phone number, 555-3587, was one he had seen before. He checked the numbers in his incoming call list to see if it was there. Four numbers down, around the same time the interview was set up, he found the number. *This house is being sold by the same person who is interviewing me for a job. Does someone want me to buy this house?* He went on noting the odometer reading at the house to where he would be working.

The odometer clicked one mile when he pulled into the parking lot of what looked like another house. There was no sign in the yard, indicating it was anything more than another house. The red Mercedes Benz pulled into the driveway directly beside him. He saw Bill get out, head up to the door, and unlock it. He ran back to the car, slid a box out of the passenger seat, and walked back to the door.

Jacob got out and followed him into the waiting area. He saw the desk with nothing on it, the couch against the north wall, the chairs against the south wall, and a coffee table in the middle. He heard Bill say, "Jacob?"

"Yes."

"I'm sorry…got here a little late because of a call, and you're a little early. Would you wait here while I get the file I need?"

"Sure." He sat on the couch and noticed that you sink into it.

Bill went around the desk and sat down. "Jacob, could you join me over here, please?"

He got up and walked around the other side. The drawers and small file cabinets sat under the top of the long table along the wall. He took the other seat and faced Bill.

Bill started to say, "How was the drive here."

"It was good. This seems to be an open relaxing area to drive in." Bill knew that to be true from past years, but it wasn't to him lately. "Good. I reviewed your resume yesterday and prepared a few questions for you. What do you bring that would be the greatest asset to Collins Enterprises?"

"My father has been training me in business accounting and taxes since I was sixteen years old. My familiarity with tax laws as well as accounting procedures in small business and home financial situations will set me apart from other applicants."

"What type of business was your father in?"

"He was an operations and design engineer specialist. He contracted with companies for special assignments."

"How did he teach you the accounting specialties you talked about?"

"They were his sideline specialties mainly for his personal use. When he got busy, he groomed me to do the sideline work. Ever since then, I have been studying and keeping up with the laws in that area."

Bill took the notes he needed and continued to say, "In the business activities I go through, I deal with customers in all kinds of situations. What do you understand the term customer service to mean? Tell me about a time you demonstrated excellent customer service."

"Customer service is actions you take to bring about customer satisfaction. The time I remember is when my father had to be out and leave me to answer the phones. One particular customer had been a problem from the beginning, and he called with yet another complaint. I did not only resolve the complaint but also convinced him to increase his business with my father while using me for all of his accounting and tax needs."

"How old were you when this happened?"

"I was seventeen at the time. I still serviced his business until last year when his business grew so big that the stockholders required me to get a tax number."

"Why didn't you?"

"I didn't want to get into my own business without the proper financial backing. I could have made it work, but it would have been too stressful at the time. I was still getting my degree."

"I have to listen to my customer's needs and find ways to maximize the benefits while keeping the cost down. Tell me of a specific time where your listening skills helped you communicate better."

"One of my personal clients last year started her own business and needed to set up the facilities and financial situation. I was able to work with my father and do more than she expected for less money and better tax breaks."

"How did that work out?"

"My father showed me how to save money in areas that would increase tax benefit. By using those tips, I saved her money immediately and helped her pay less on taxes. I've learned to use methods like it in other areas that saved money as well."

"What do you expect from me as an employer?"

"I'm looking for work that uses my expertise and skills. I expect to be compensated fairly for the work and respected by my superiors."

"Do you have any questions for me?"

"If this is the office, when is it going to be operational?"

"The goal is to be up and running by Monday. This weekend, I am getting the computers in place. Phone lines will be installed Monday morning, but all the rest should be in and ready before Sunday. Any other questions?"

"How am I paid?"

"You are paid on a commission basis. As your clients grow, so does your pay. From the sound of things, you won't struggle with getting clients."

"No, I won't."

"I'll give you a call when I've made my decision. I thank you for coming in and talking to me."

"You're welcome and thank you for considering me."

They stood and shook hands. Bill watched as Jacob left, paying special attention to the confidence he carried throughout the interview.

Jacob drove back the way he came. When he stopped at 5857 Power Lane, he got out to look at the house, looking for details. The yard was big and green. The house itself still called to him, and this time he listened to the call with ears that recognized the voice that was not his own. "Cousin, come to me."

Something inside him stirred; wanting began to grow. The feeling of a new awakening kindled within his soul. From somewhere inside him came, "Cousin?"

I can't be seeing this right. How can something change in front of your eyes? As the recognition of spirits came, the paint began to peel off the house. The grass in the yard grew tall and turned to weeds. The window glass just fell out of the windows and lay on the ground in pieces.

The light coming through the window glowed green. His interest in the house changed immediately, but his ability to walk away from the house was gone too. Every step he took carried him closer to the front door and closer to the impending heart attack that killed his father. Jacob tried to turn away from the house, and the house seemed to stay in front of him no matter which way he faced.

As seconds ticked by, the house continued to decay and erode away. The four walls still stood, but no paint remained on the house. The windows were holes in the walls and no more. The doors hung open, waiting, calling, and seeming to get closer.

He realized with terror that the house wasn't moving, but instead he was floating to the house beyond his control. He could hear the house calling for help. "All right, I'll buy you and help you if you let me to the car to call the owner."

His feet sat squarely on the ground. He ran to the car and grasped the phone. The number dialed easily. He hoped no one would answer as it rang the second time. The third ring brought a sense of relief that no one was answering until there was a "Hello."

Immediately, he recognized the voice. "This is Jacob. I'm calling about the house you have for sale."

"Well, Jacob, which house are you interested in?"

"You are selling more than one? The house at 5857 Power Lane."

"At 5857 Power Lane. Are you there now?"

"Yes."

"Do you want to look inside?"

"Yes." Was he kidding? "I think that would be good idea."

"I can be there with a key in a few minutes. Or would you rather come back at a later time?"

Bill must know nothing of the spirit inside the house. "I guess now is as good a time as any."

Bill was reading over the notes that he took during the interview. Deep down in his soul, he knew that he interviewed the man God had for him to hire. He wasn't sure if he was the root person to give Trainer an opening back into the battle until he heard the request on the phone. He dialed Fred and waited. It took two rings before Fred answered, "Hello."

"Fred, this is Bill. The guy I interviewed that I know God wants me to hire wants to look at 5857 Power Lane. If he's who I think he is…he's the one that is going to reactivate the war with Trainer. I've got to follow through with this."

"Yes, you do, Bill. It is time for you to obey, and we will start the prayers now. God won the last war with prayer, and this one will be won the same way."

"I'm on my way now."

"I'll make the calls."

"Harry, emergency prayer where you're at. The war is turning up as we speak. I'm making the calls."

All he heard was a click. He knew what Harry was already doing. The next numbers and two rings later, there was a "Hello."

He repeated what he said before with the same response until all of the other prayer squad was contacted, and he took off in his car, praying.

He knocked on the door, praying silently. The door opened, and he said, "Rebeca, may I come in? The prayer is started. Bill and the church are in trouble."

Rebeca said, "Come in. I'm glad you involved me in this."

"You need to be praying too. You are God's assigned helper to him. We all know you will be married. It's time to pray."

"You start…I'm still learning."

He started the prayer for her and her ability to be the helper Bill needed in the future battles. Then it turned to Bill. In the meantime, Rebeca's confidence was rattled at the sound of Fred's words. Her own prayers were mixed with thanks and requesting understanding that apparently everyone else had.

24 The Open Heart

Ailith and the other angels had watched the events alongside Jesus. Ailith looked to Jesus and saw all he needed to see. "We all stay here until we are needed. The guardian angels must be the first defense. Boris, your group is next. Then we will finish off the battles."

Ailith looked throughout the angels, and seeing the understanding on each face, he turned again to Jesus. "They are ready, Lord. Does this have to happen this way?"

Jesus said, "It must happen this way. Your obedience is what I need. This is the way my Father wills it. You understand that my Father has nothing but good in store for Bill and the rest of the prayer squad, right?"

"Yes, my Lord. It is as you say."

Bill prayed as he started the Benz and proceeded to the property. "Father, guide and direct my words and actions so that your will be done in my life as well as Jacob's."

The one mile between the properties went too quickly for Bill. This was the one property he didn't want to sell. He still hoped God would see fit to stop the sell. Bill wouldn't allow himself to be disobedient in this. He couldn't be sure if it was the place God wanted Jacob in, so Jesus could touch his life—or not.

Every bone in his body told him to flee now, but his feet walked toward Jacob, and his hand extended to shake Jacob's again. "Is there any questions before we go in?"

"No, I'd like to go ahead and look inside."

"Follow me." Bill pulled the key out of his pocket as they walked up to the door. The interior room was large, open, and antique-looking. It was clean and looked ready to move in. Bill felt nothing as he was walking through the house. He turned to Jacob and saw the fear written on his face. Jacob's trembling body told him all he needed to know. "What are you seeing, Jacob?"

"I'm seeing a rundown antique house that needs to be torn down. The real problem is what I'm hearing. I don't think anyone would ever understand."

"Are you hearing that if you buy the house it will look immaculate?"

"It doesn't now because you have to be one with the house for that look to come to you."

"Yes, how did you know?"

"Let's just say I've been in your shoes and know more about what you're thinking than you could imagine."

"Why is the house calling me?"

"Is this the first time you're feeling this way?"

"Yes."

"I can't tell you the specifics, but I can help with any questions you may want answered later. Has the voice inside you identified itself yet?"

"No."

"Has it hurt you physically yet?"

"No."

"Has the voice told you anything since I started asking questions?"

"Yes, it wants to know who you are that you can come in here without being involved with Trainer."

"I was deeply involved with Trainer and will be again, I'm sure."

"How is that?"

"The voice is telling me you know too much, and you can't be read. Why is that?"

"There is the first question I will answer. Your voice cannot read me because what the voice sees is a guardian angel of the heavenly host. When Jesus took my life away from Trainer, he gave me an angel to protect me."

Bill could see the curious expression leave his face as anger replaced it.

"No Jesus talk. Just make him buy the house." The voice was mean and rough.

"I won't make him buy anything. What I will do is tell him he should buy the house, though it goes against everything in me."

"Don't make me fight. I know how to make him hurt so bad he can't listen."

"Is this Trainer I'm talking to?"

"No, this is Didi. I am meaner and better than Trainer ever was!"

"I can see that. You are part of the plan as well."

"How do you know so much? Where is Trainer? Isn't this his place?"

"I was a host body to Trainer. I don't know where cast out demons go, but, yes, this was owned by one of his hosts. I now own it, and I'm selling all of the property owned by him, so to speak."

"You can't do that. Trainer will stop you."

"Trainer hasn't influenced my decisions since Jesus Christ came into my soul, though I'm sure he's trying to kill me and take my son now."

"He will succeed, and Jesus will lose the war."

"That's why Trainer had your help with me. I do fear what you are capable of doing, but right now you need me. So why don't you let me talk to Jacob and sell him the house."

Bill just then noticed his body slump and his eyes return to the real world. "What did I do?"

"You just allowed Didi to talk to me. Did you hear what was said?"

"Yes, is Je…" Bill watched Jacob drop to the floor. Bill dropped beside him and prayed for him. He knew the battle was for his soul.

"Jacob, do you have any children?"

"No, but I want to have some."

"That is good. This house is big enough for you to have three children, and each child can have their own room."

"How soon can I move in?"

"You can move in when all of the financial arrangements have been made."

"How much?

"Land and all are worth two hundred twenty thousand. How much do you have to offer?"

"I have one hundred ninety thousand in cash in the car."

Bill opened his briefcase and pulled out the sales contract. "This is all done legally by my attorney." They went through the contract and set the time to finalize it with the attorney. Jacob drove off with the key, and Bill drove off with the money.

Didi felt a burning inside. Jacob had finished unloading the truck, and almost immediately Didi saw the house through his eyes. She saw the green glow coming from within that she recognized from the early days of possession. *Could Trainer be stuck in those days? If Trainer is, I'll soon have him out and getting control immediately.*

Something different yet familiar was calling her, but she couldn't place it. That something possessed great power, which she recognized as her own; but from where? Where did it come from? It seemed so far away but so close. It was new but old. Whatever it was, she had to find it. All the rest could wait, and she needed to respond immediately.

Getting Jacob moving wasn't hard; control was easy on the physical level, but the emotional level took time that she hadn't had yet. She had one chance to make this happen and had to take it.

"Jacob, we need to meet a friend. Someone who can help you understand what is going on. If I gave you directions, would you follow?"

"You know the way to Jesus?"

"This person knows more than Jesus ever did. He will help you in more ways than Jesus will."

"Where do I need to go?"

"Just go in the car, and I will tell you which way to go."

"Okay."

Didi had to get his trust and found that kind words got more trust than anger ever did. She'd used force on occasion but always with gentle guidance to keep the person on track. She struggled to sense the direction the call was coming from. Jacob had already followed everything she wanted him to do and now sat waiting for simple directions. "Go right on this road."

She could listen to the outside world through his ears but she wanted more to listen to the call that came to her alone. The faint call grew louder as they got closer. "Turn left on the next road."

She felt the car getting closer. She felt the strength of the call and realized exactly what was calling and why. Her old house buried in the park. It was occupied and waiting for her and her host. It was time to make two teams one. "The walking trails are one mile from here. There is a four-wheeler path half a mile farther down. I'll guide you to those."

The next three turns brought excitement. Fifteen minutes later, the thrill blew out of her like air exhaling from the lungs. The four-wheeler trails were there but fenced in and locked. "Let's park in the main entrance to the park. You will have to walk in if the trail is still open."

The half-mile drive was uneasy. The call still came, and irritation started to become an uneasy feeling that there was something wrong, really wrong. "Jacob, how about you find someplace to park this car and run down the trail to the open circle? I can feel almost everything from there."

Didi knew the trail was going to the right place. The open circle was as expected. The feeling came in strong. Something was really wrong. "Jacob, run to the house. Run straight into the trail across the way. My house is being messed with."

She could feel him run. The house came in sight, and the iridescent green glow said it all. "Run. Now."

She stormed into the house and watched as Jacob dropped in the doorway. She worked all the magic she could, and eventually he got up.

"Go to the office in the attic."

She focused on the office door as Jacob took the steps two at a time. The office door opened, and no one had been in there for years.

"The desk. It has a power control in it. I need you to hold it into the outlet in the east wall."

She guided Jacob directly to the power supply and the plug. With it in his hands, he attached the supply to the outlet. The red glow flowed throughout the entire house and all the occupants at the same time. The power was enough to knock Jacob and Gary off their feet and onto the floor. Jacob got to his feet and went down the stairs. At the base of the stairs, Jacob stared into the eyes of Gary uncomfortably.

Trainer looked into the eyes of the intruder and recognized the power coming from within him. Trainer could easily see the trancelike state in the intruder and knew that for the first time, Gary was in the same state. Trainer heard the voice that wasn't human and realized he was talking to the spirit within directly. "Who are you? Why are you trying to take over my house?"

"I'm Moloch. I'm working here until I get back into my own place."

"Your own place, who are you associated with?"

"I am the lead Trainer sent to start the development of the army that will take control of the earth from Jesus."

"I'm Didi, and I was sent for the same purpose. We were not to meet unless you or I had an army started. Did you get one started?"

"When did you get on the scene? I've never heard of a demon called Didi. I have control of the person that will start the army for me. How are you doing on the mission?"

"You don't know all of Satan's demons. You have failed in completing the mission. I had the mission completed until the mother and children were killed. I never got off another start. I'm lucky to still have one host and have just now come out to his realization."

"I have one child, but his father has rejected my instruction. I'm in the planning stages of getting possession of the child with my host as the training father."

"Criminal activity won't make getting the army easier. I ran into the same thing. Rather than do that, allow the child to grow up and start over as if that child was the first."

"The child is being trained by the prayer squad. They would have to die before Samuel will fall back into my hands again."

"Do you want that arranged?"

"Yes, they have driven me out of my home. Watching them die would be fun."

"Let's get Nassor to help with that. I think you will like the place we can start from."

"Where is that?"

"My host just bought the place at 5857 Power Lane. It belonged to a demon-possessed man. He was controlled by a demon named Trainer. Where is the prayer squad located?"

"At 5857 Power Lane. It is the direct origin of the power that will take over the earth for Satan."

"This land is in the control of the enemy?"

"Yes, but their deaths will change that."

"Then we will have to arrange that."

25 The War Rages

Jacob walked in the door of the house through the garage with Gary. Jacob said, "Didi has promised to lead me in getting help to take back the house next door."

Gary's excitement could hardly be masked. "Taking Samuel to train as well."

"When all of the adults in Samuel's life are dead, taking and training him will be easy."

"How are we going to kill them?" Gary asked.

"That is the deal. We are not. We are going to call on a demonic force that will kill them without us getting our hands dirty."

"Excellent."

"What we need to do is follow the instruction of the ceremony to bring the demonic powers here. From this house, the demons will attack and kill the power of the prayer squad. Once that is done, the related church will fall. The forces open the door for us to take the house back and bring the demonic forces to take over the earth."

"Okay, what are we going to do in this ceremony?"

Fred sat with the other four church board members. "Something is going wrong. We need to pray." The five of them started to pray together. "Father, I don't know why I feel this way. I sense a struggle I can't identify. Lord, you truly are my Shepherd and my Savior. It is your desire to walk me to still waters, keeping me and all your children protected. This small church and I will have to lean on your staff and rod for protection and guidance through the time of trial I feel coming…"

Ailith watched as the ceremony started. He pointed to a smaller team of angels. Go down and surround the house. Make sure nothing happens to the house. The land the barn was on is God's too. Fight for it."

Satan and Nassor heard the request for help during the ceremony and were more than willing to comply with it. Satan said, "Nassor, it looks like you are getting another chance at this. This time, kill those praying fools. Whatever it takes, make it happen."

Nassor asked, "How many do I have to take with me? You know what will happen if I come with too few demons."

"Take as many as you want. This has to happen. Excuses are not going to cut it again. Bill, Fred, Harry, Peter, John, they all have to die. Samuel is to end up in the custody of Gary and Jacob. Don't mess this up."

"Yes, Master, it will be done."

Nassor chose the demons he wanted to go with him. The demons gained power by the minute due to the prayers of the two servants. Nassor led the charge into the house. He felt the power surge into them and could see the following demons powering up for the war coming their way.

"Horde, listen to me. Our objective is twofold. Take back 5857 Power Lane and get Samuel into the care of Jacob and Gary. The faster we get this done, the faster we enjoy the leisure of rest. There will be no stopping until we have accomplished the task."

The hideous hissing from the horde filled the spirit world. Nassor felt his pride rise with the volume of the noise. "Keegan, do a flyover and find out what is going on with the house and the prayer squad."

"Yes, Master."

Nassor watched Keegan take off through the roof. "Aiden, I need you to work on a way to kill Fred. Something has to happen to crush the spirit of that group."

"Yes, Master."

Nassor looked at the rest of the horde and said, "Those set in charge of training, start. We need to be ready quickly."

Nassor watched as the horde prepared for the ensuing war to be engaged.

Keegan saw the cross on the roof first. Jesus had marked the house. What he noticed next shocked him. He expected maybe eight guardian angels. This day, there were at least twenty angels on the roof all ready to go and looking at him. He looked at the cars parked in the street and driveway and noticed any area available for parking had cars in it. There was no question that the fight was going to be against much more.

"It's time to report to Nassor. He'll want to know what's going on."

Aiden found the guardian angels and knew he alone wasn't getting near him then. He stayed high and watched. The moments lingered by, but the group dispersed, and the angels dispersed with them. Now his angel sat on the roof alone, aware of his presence.

It was time to sneak in unseen, though he was sure Randolph wasn't going to make that easy. He turned from his stance and immediately flew back to Nassor.

Nassor saw the two demons return. *This is either too soon and going to be bad news or good news and their return is welcome.* "What is the report?"

Keegan said, "Master, there are over twenty praying servants in the prayer squad now. Together they are a force that will not be easy to defeat."

Aiden said, "And Fred is currently alone. I need fifteen fighting demons to act as a distraction for Randolph, or I will never slip by him unseen. The other fighting demons hold off Randolph, and I will kill Fred."

Nassor turned to the demons. "And so it begins, the war starts today." He pointed to one of the trainer demons and continued, "You and fourteen of your best demons go with him. Make sure Fred dies tonight."

"Yes, Master."

Aiden led the way in the short distance to 5757 Power Lane. The fifteen demons stopped behind him. He faced his army and said, "The guardian angel you see the back of is already aware of our presence and waiting for us to move. There is more. There can quickly be twenty more active fighting angels on their way. All I'm asking you to do is keep the oncoming angels out of my way so I can deal with Fred alone. We move on three. One, two, three."

Aiden led the way as the demons charged right at the roof of the house. It took seconds for the arc of light to come approaching. The power would rattle every demon in flight. Also, there was the question in Aiden's mind: did that arc call the other guardian angels?

Aiden felt the blow from the angel and kept going through it. The other demons knew enough to go through it too. Aiden backed into the middle of the demons and kept pace. He knew his job would be not to fight here but inside with a mere man. The others did their job, and Randolph was moved out of the way. He quickly dropped through the roof under cover of the demon attack.

Boris waited and watched; it wasn't a question of whether or not the attack would come but of when. He knew what trouble felt like long before he ever saw it. Trouble was on its way. His hand laced around his sword. His fingers opened and closed around the handle. Time made him feel more uncomfortable. He looked around the room, but there was nothing unusual. "Lord?"

"You are ready, Boris, and you have enough prayer support to handle what is coming your way. I will honor my word. The prayer squad is praying my promises. You are prepared. Now follow your instructions."

That still didn't comfort him, but he knew what he had to do. He postured himself in a defensive position and stood ready for the battle. A second later, the form flew into the room directly at Fred. Boris threw both fists directly into the midsection of the flying demon. The demon flew hard into the wall and crumpled on the floor. "Fred is not available for you to attack."

"Who are you?" Aiden said before looking.

"Aiden, you are back, and you think that my team and I will walk away? We are always in the fight. I'm Boris."

"You should be on the roof fighting."

"The team of angels has control of that situation. Randolph has retaken his defensive position waiting for me to say if I need his help. Somehow, I think you are going to leave before I need to call him."

Boris watched as the demon vanished before his eyes.

Randolph saw the demon before he cleared the roof. His sword already in his hand, he cleared the distance between them, instantly inflicting the first blow. He watched as the demon dodged, flipped, and flew away.

"Not much fight left in him. I guess he was surprised by our readiness."

Nassor saw the horde of demons reenter the house. The looks on their faces told too much. "Report."

"Master, they were ready for us. We don't know what hit us or who swung the blow."

"There was one angel…you're telling me that fifteen couldn't take care of one?"

"There was one inside waiting for me. He took the fight out of me before I saw him," Aiden said.

"There were twenty angels out of sight to back up Randolph. By the time we knew what was going on, we had already lost the fight."

"It sounds like the prayer squad is well-guarded. What about the newer members of the church? I wonder if they have any protection. Their faith may still be weak."

The decision was made. It was time to go after the new members of the church.

26 SEEKING WEAKNESS

Fred walked the hall, trying to think. No images flashed in his mind, but fear lingered and then left as quickly as it came.

The thoughts flashed through his mind like lightning. He couldn't stop and meditate on any one thought, the one persistent thought—*the war has begun. Get the church informed.* The series of images would quickly flash through. The memories of the attacks on him, Bill, and John and the times of praying through the attacks popped into his mind.

Then they would stop again, giving way to one clear thought, *The war has begun. Get the church informed.* Immediately, flashes of the attack on Patty and the attacks after the house were taken rolled through his mind; then back to the same phrase, and the track started all over in his mind. The sense of urgency overshadowed all others.

Peter sat with Patty, Bill, and Rebeca at the sandwich shop. They each had their sandwiches in front of them. Recanting the blessings of the service, they spent much of the time laughing and enjoying each other's company. The comments and laughter stopped when the smile drained off Peter's face. "Guys, I think we need to go make sure Fred is okay. Something tells me there may be a problem there."

Bill asked, "What kind of problem?"

"I don't know, but with all that has gone on recently, this isn't something to ignore."

Patty said, "If it was anything like I felt, it really is better to check in than wait. I thought I was going to die."

"I'm going back. Anyone who wants to can join me."

Rebeca said, "Well, I'm going with you. I think we all are."

Everyone else agreed.

Fred felt additional weight being applied on his shoulders. He knew trouble was coming. The thoughts didn't stop. Pressure mounted on his heart and mind. Now the weight crushed down on him like he was wearing a one-hundred-pound backpack. *Not this again. Call someone now.*

He reached for his phone, but it was no longer on his hip. His hand groped for it a few more times but still came up empty. *Jesus, where is the way of escape? I'm ready to take it now.*

No answer seemed to come. The weight continued to bear down relentlessly. *I've got to get help, Lord. Where are you?*

Nassor saw the opening he needed. "Aiden, Fred is open for attack. Go now."

"Yes, Master."

Fred could feel numbness working its way into his legs. "Help." The sound was gargled and not loud enough to be heard by anyone. He kept telling himself to pray, listen for the door, and know that God is in control no matter what happens.

Then the thoughts changed. *Is anyone here to help you now? I promise you that I'm going to make your life miserable, or you can volunteer to end your life now.*

"Father, I need you now!" Fred spoke out loud.

Calling on your dad? Your dad has nothing to help you with. Do you see him here now? He's letting me do whatever I want to you.

"Jesus, the voice inside me is lying to me. I know you are always with me and will never leave me."

Never? What?

Fred knew his voice was giving out and began a steady pulse pounding that he would continue until help came, or he finally died.

Where are your friends now? They don't care about you, and neither does your God.

Fred laid his head down and continued to whisper. "He'll never leave me or forsake me."

William flew in with Jelani, Bellatrix, and Finley. "Ailith, it's nice to see you again. I hope you've been practicing. I came with some new friends who want nothing more than to test their skills against you."

Randolph drew his sword with a flash of light. "Welcome! It's time to show this guy the exit."

William saw Ailith change. "Bring it on. You want to play with all of us."

It was clear; multiple demons drew swords of fire. Ailith said, "How about you find the exit so I can finish what I'm doing?"

William saw Dustin and Boris fly in. Boris said, "No, Ailith, you can leave. You may have many more demons with you, but we together are stronger than a thousand of you."

"You will have to prove that to us. I don't think you have all of us convinced."

William turned to the rest of the angels and saw they were ready.

"Come get Fred if you want him so bad."

The light from all the swords being drawn blinded the demons forcing them to draw back and adjust. Boris said, "Defend only. Hold the line. The prayer squad is to be protected."

Ailith held his sword high. "I hope you're ready. I waited a long time to drive you out and kill the prayer squad."

Boris looked over his angels' line. No movement, no statements, nothing but penetrating stares back. "We're waiting."

Ailith held his position, knowing they would be slaughtered if he tried to fight now. "Retreat." In a flash, they were gone.

Randolph said, "Boris, what happened?"

"They knew their limits, and Fred is alive. The obedience of the saints is and will always prove to be more than the demons can handle."

Peter ran in, hearing a steady pounding and knowing to follow it. "He's in real trouble. Follow any noise you hear until he's found."

All four ran up the stairs toward the beating, turned right and then left and then back right. "There in the hall," Peter said.

They all four ran and began praying immediately. As quickly as they started, they heard Fred join in with one-word mutters, then partial sentences and breathing, and finally with complete sentences sounding strong in the power of the Lord. "Greater is he that is in me than he that is in the world."

They reached Fred and knelt beside him, each one thanking God for the victory.

Later as they were discussing the events, Rebeca asked, "What made the change?"

"Obedience," Fred said. "When the saints obey, God's power becomes great, and no demons can hold on to the attack."

"You never called. How did we know so clearly?"

"Obedience keeps your ears tuned in to God. When he can talk to you, you know exactly where to go when you need to be there. Did you feel it and come?"

"Peter did. How did you know?"

"Sounds like Peter has the gift of words of knowledge. Rebeca, you are a prayer warrior. I felt your prayer first and stronger than all the others. Bill will be grateful for having that prayer strength to help him."

He could see her try to shy away, but there was nowhere to go. She said, "I never thought of that as a gift."

"God has many gifts that you may or may not think of as gifts. God still calls them gifts. We all have different gifts so we can strengthen each other and build up the body of Christ."

Aiden reported back to the house. "Master."

"Report."

"The guardian angels are distracted. Samantha is with John and has been all day."

"Then John is in a place of vulnerability and alone. Your army should be able to kill them both."

"Suicide is the wrong method for those two. I want to use more force."

Nassor felt concern. "What do you have in mind? Our authority is limited."

"The first attack has to be enough to kill. If I can get my hands on her once, she'll roll to the floor and never get up."

"You will have guardian angels on you fast."

"If one is already dead, I can deal with the others."

"Your call, but if you're sent back to hell, you will explain that to the master, not me."

"I agree, Master."

John sat on the couch with Samantha. The movie was playing, but their interest was on each other. They spent more time talking to each other. John signed. "Are you getting hungry?"

"Yes, I am. What do you have in mind?"

"There is that little restaurant in town."

"That sounds good."

They walked to the truck, all the while signing to each other.

Aiden saw the truck going down the road with both people he wanted dead in it. The truck coming the other way looked more interesting. He found the driver alert and awake.

Ailith said, "You two make sure that both of them survive the crash. The obedience of the saints will have to keep them alive."

The other two angels said nothing but flew off to do the job they were assigned to do.

Aiden flew directly into the cab of the truck. *This is going to be more difficult than I thought, but anything can be arranged.*

"Timing is everything. Stop the heart, steer the truck the direction it needs to go, and move on." He waited until the gap closed.

His hand struck the heart of the truck driver. It immediately stopped. The driver's head wavered and flopped as the truck became a ground missile moving on the road. Aiden steered the truck easily. He felt the impact on the truck and flew out and watched the collision bounce around the bodies in both vehicles.

John saw the truck coming as he approached. He turned his head and signed to Samantha. "This is a God thing."

He turned back to the road. His eyes instantly grew as big as saucers, and he slammed on the brakes. The tires squealed and came to a sliding halt. The sound of crushing metal overpowered the sound of squealing tires. The truck spun as the eighteen-wheeler jack-knifed. He felt his body flailing around and saw Samantha was doing the same.

Both bodies stopped. "Samantha? Samantha?"

Her voice silenced, and blood dripped from her head. Peter managed to reach his cell and press 911.

"Where is the emergency?" The operator heard the name of the road before the phone slid to the floor of the truck. "Hello? Sir?"

His head went fuzzy, and then blackness filled the truck.

Within minutes, the lights flashed from the rescue squad, and police cars were coming on the scene of the wreck. The radio chirped. The police officer ran to the truck to assess the driver and passenger. He found them both alive but knocked out. He motioned the EMTs over.

The officer saw the driver of the eighteen-wheeler moving. He called in for another EMS. They were already on their way.

Fred's phone rang as the prayer meeting was ready to break up. "Hello."

"Fred? This is John's mom. John has been in a bad accident. The doctors don't know how much longer he has."

"Which hospital?"

"St. Matthews. Will you come?"

"On our way. See you soon. Good-bye."

He turned to the rest of the group. "John and Samantha have been in a wreck. They are at St. Matthews. Start praying. Let's go."

All ran to their cars and took off.

Fred speed-dialed Harry's number. He heard, "Hello."

"Harry, it's John. There's been an accident. Meet us at St. Matthews Hospital emergency room."

"Gone."

Fred parked just seconds after Peter and his group. They met Harry at the entrance door. Harry said, "Fred, you need to show your ID. You're their pastor. The lady will only give the room number to you."

Fred walked quickly to her and showed her his ID. "I have special instructions for you. You and anyone you wish can go with you. He was just brought into the ICU with the passenger."

"He read the instructions out loud to the group on the way. The elevator was the slowest part of the way up. Those praying were still in prayer as they followed."

When Fred turned into the ICU ward, he was barraged by John's mother. "He won't wake up, and it looks like he never will."

The chair was already sitting up in the waiting room. He heard, "Fred, let's get to work."

Fred looked at John's mother. "I'll be right back."

Nancy watched as the whole group gathered around that empty chair and started talking to Jesus. She heard their prayers and understood what they were doing. John had told her that if anything ever happened to call Fred first. He had put Fred's number into his mother's phone under speed dial 3. She didn't think she would ever use it, but now... Nancy turned to her brother. "Brandon, do you know what they're doing?"

"Sis, I don't know, and I don't really care. Your son is lying on a hospital bed almost dead, and you're looking at some idiots gathered around an empty chair. Who are you more concerned about?"

Nancy's eyes teared up. She looked into Brandon's eyes. "There is only one thing I know that will save John and Samantha. Those 'idiots' are praying to the Great Physician, Jesus Christ, that John talked to you about."

"I know this, sis. You're trusting that the prayers of those people are going to change the circumstances. I'll tell you this. I'll look into it when someone can show me a miracle that only God could have done."

Nancy turned her head toward the beds and saw movement from Samantha. "Look, Samantha is moving."

"Don't play gam..." Brandon lost his words at the sight before him.

The last thing Samantha remembered was the impact. She felt pain from her head hitting something. Then blackness overtook her. In the darkness, a form of a human walked up to her. She couldn't see what she was standing on or where she was, but something flowed from the form. The light that she saw wrapped around her, filling her with peace and comfort. She didn't recognize the face, but she saw the holes in both hands. Then she heard the voice. It was as if her spirit was talking to her. She not only recognized it but also knew it to be the voice of Jesus. "Jesus?"

"Yes, my child." He held out his arms like a mother to her child.

She immediately ran into them and landed firmly in his chest. Why she cried, she didn't know, but she began to weep.

"Shhh, my child, you have no reason to fear. You are safe in my arms."

She stayed there for what seemed to be forever. Just listening to the song of Jesus reverberated in her ear. When she broke her grip on Jesus, she asked, "Am I dead?"

"No, Samantha, you are alive. I'm here to keep you calm and well until you need to wake up."

"Is John dead?"

"John is alive too. I'm with him too. There is more work to be done with him, but I'll worry about that. He'll be just fine."

"Jesus, what is happening to the church?"

"It is being tried to prove that it will stay with me and follow my plan. Fear not, child, I am still and always will be in control."

"Thank you." Then she fell again to his chest and cried.

"Child, the time has come for you to wake up. You have a job to do on earth before I can take you home with me."

She didn't want to see the distance grow between Jesus and herself, but it did. The first thing she felt was pain. Her head ached the worst, but trying hard to catch up was her left leg.

Movement came slowly. Fingers and toes came first and then her arms and painfully her legs, and then her eyes fluttered, taking in light from the outside world. She tried to lift her head, but that was met with outside and inside resistance. The newfound pain from that was more than bearable, and she ceased the activity immediately.

She blinked and opened her eyes to a dimly lit room, metal stands holding bags on both sides of her. She lay flat on a bed with rails on each side. The only noise was steady beeping and mechanical sounds. The footsteps coming toward the bed scared her and increased the pace of the beeping.

"Samantha, Samantha, it's okay. Everything is okay. Relax for me. Can you relax?"

She saw the nurse and let herself calm down. She didn't try to speak and didn't know if it was good or bad that she was awake. As time passed, more and more people were gathered around her.

Realization set in that this was a hospital room, and everyone here wanted her to get better. The mouths moved, but not a word entered her ears. She looked to the glass wall where her father stood watching. She raised both arms and signed. "Get an interpreter, or you won't understand me."

One of the nurses signed back. "Do you feel any pain?"

"My head and leg."

She could see the nurse's mouth moving and understood that she was interpreting for her. Her sign language slowed and came with minimal pain. Other nurses checked on machine readings and waited for instructions. The nurse signed to her what was going on and what had happened. It wasn't until she asked about John that the signing stopped. Then she remembered Jesus saying, "There is more work to do on him." She signed in desperation. "Is John alive? I can't see him."

The nurse replied, "Stay calm. John has suffered more extensive injuries. We are doing all we can for him now. He is alive."

Brandon felt shock and terror fill his body. He heard the doctor not fifteen minutes ago say that neither of them was expected to wake up today. They only hoped for tomorrow. Now, signing to nurses and a flurry of other activity buzzed around Samantha. He heard Nancy ask, "Is that enough to look into Jesus?"

He saw one of the men get up and walk to him. "Hello, my name is Bill. How is everything going in there?"

"We don't know. Samantha just woke up, and the doctors are working on her now."

"That's great news. Anything new on John?"

"Not at this time. What did you do around that chair?"

"We just prayed. God does all the work, but we have to ask him to get involved."

"You always believed in this Jesus?"

"No, I struggled a long time before I believed in him. I'm not any different from any other man. I had and still have the tendency for pride and other things that make me want to look to myself when I need to look to Jesus."

"I would like to talk to you more if that's okay with you."

"Sure, what is your name?"

"My name is Brandon, and you are…Bill?"

"Yes, can we take a seat over here and talk?"

Bill explained about all the conversations he had to learn about Jesus and how he finally came to know Jesus and his power. Brandon absorbed every word and took in every emotion. "Such a hard struggle and all you said was 'Jesus save me'?"

"And he did. You may not understand anything else, but this you must understand. He showed him the passage in Romans that Harry showed him earlier. Brandon had seen all those before, but something about Bill's story penetrated deeper. "After all you went through, would you honestly say that you stood any chance of peace, as you say, without Jesus?"

"I would say that without Jesus, I would most likely be dead already or in extreme misery."

The words worked like arrows making holes for the Word to sink through the wall in his soul.

"Jesus said in his Word that he alone is the way to eternity with him. There really is no questioning that. If there was another way that I didn't try sometime in my life, I don't know about it."

"Help me understand one thing. Jesus loved me so much that he died for me, even though I didn't care at all about him? How is that possible?"

"That is the million-dollar question that no one can answer. Neither you nor anyone else can comprehend it completely. We all accept it as fact without proof. He said it, so it has to be true."

"You can trust him that completely?"

"I do trust him that completely. And the others around that chair do as well. Many of them will tell you of things in their life that only that kind of faith could have ever done."

The words began to soften his heart, and the wall around it started to crack and crumble.

Bill continued, "The best part is no one is forced to say anything, do anything, or walk on water. It was as easy as saying, 'Jesus, save me.' He did the instant I said it."

Brandon's head dropped as the wall around his heart crumbled to the ground. There was no more denying the truth. He prayed the only words he knew to pray. "Jesus, save me…" The rest of the prayer flowed like a mighty river rushing to a fall.

27 The Church Tested

John drifted deep into the blackness. He felt swallowed by the darkness until the light form began walking toward him. John tried to retreat away, but it was as if there was a wall keeping him from going back. "Jesus, help me."

"My son, I'm here. Fear not, you need my touch right now." The voice came from the form walking toward him. "I'm dead?"

"No, my child, you won't die from this. I've got more for you to do. Right now, I'm working on the most severe wounds. You have another day to rest."

"What about Samantha?"

"She is fine. She will be waking up soon. I need her to trust me more. Her job will take her farther than she can go right now."

"Where is the prayer squad?"

"They are in the hallway surrounding an empty chair praying for you and Samantha. Enough of these questions, I have something for you."

What could he have for me? I'll listen to him and go from there. "You have stuttered all of your known days. When you wake up, you won't stutter anymore, and all related symptoms will go with it. Your power in prayer will be the saving power of the church."

The first tear filled John's eye. "You will fall under Fred's leadership in a special way. I need you to become Fred's left hand standing beside him."

The tear trickled down his cheek and toward the pillow. "What I'm about to tell you, you must keep between you and me. Fred must go through severe trials for the church to unify in my power. Satan's plan can't be defeated without my power unified throughout the whole church."

"Fred?"

"Satan believes that crushing the leader will divide the church. You will be the one to hold the church together when he is tried. This will place you in the same threat of attack with Fred. Unify the church and the hedge of protection around you, and Satan will not be able to penetrate it."

"Me?"

"You are already prepared and speak all the languages spoken in the church. There is no more qualified than the one that I qualify."

"Yes."

"Keep this to yourself. I will influence the others to make it happen. I know you want to know more, but you don't need to." Jesus wrapped his arms around John and held him close. The finger of Jesus touched the spot on John's brain causing the stuttering, and it immediately was healed.

John's arms wrapped around Jesus, and they refused to let go.

The RN stood in between the two beds. Merton lay silently on the bed, wires and hoses from all over attached to his body. John was speaking in his sleep one word here and there. She was concentrating on Merton, silencing the alarms when needed and keeping a close eye on the numbers on the digital readouts. Her post wasn't new to her. She had been here before and silently prayed continually while actively performing her duties. The numbers were steadily rising. She watched his hands for any motion and listened for any alarms. She scanned Merton again for movement. Still none.

She turned to John again. She checked the readouts and printouts, and everything was steady and good.

She turned to Merton and saw his eyes open briefly and then quickly close. Little grunts escaped his lips. Fingers and hands moved briefly.

She called immediately for the doctor and waited patiently for him to wake up.

It wasn't long before his eyes stayed opened. They flickered from side to side and then up and down. Sounds penetrated into his ears. "Merton?"

Silence.

"Merton?"

She saw his head turn, acknowledging the sound.

"Merton, can you talk?"

"Ye..."

She heard the scratchiness in his soft voice. "How bad is your pain?"

He tried to lift his arm, but it didn't come up far before collapsing back on the bed. The grunt was the only verbal expression he gave. "Can you tell me from one to ten how bad you hurt?"

"Eigh..."

She looked at the doctor, who just entered in time to hear him. The doctor ordered the painkiller while looking over his chart. She administered the painkiller and watched as he drifted back to sleep. "He, at least, tried to speak. I'll take any positive signs," she said to the doctor.

"Yes, keep me informed if they wake up."

"Yes, Doctor."

The church had left the hospital and returned to the house for an all-night prayer vigil. They took turns around the circle for two hours now. Rebeca felt Peter's hand tighten and not loosen.

"Peter? Peter? Peter?"

Silence.

"Fred, it's Peter."

The prayer squad immediately gathered around him and started praying.

Harry broke into the prayer. "Peter, thank God for all he has done for you already."

Almost immediately, Peter started talking out loud. "Thank you. What is going on?"

Harry said, "Wave two. The demons want the house back. It is not as much the house as it is the land the house sits on."

Patty asked, "What is that bare spot in the yard."

Fred said, "That was where the barn was located before it was burned down."

Patty replied, "I don't like this at all. That is the land the demons want control of. Isn't that where their church is planned to be built?"

Fred said, "Yes, that is exactly where the plans are to put it. Bill, do you know why they want the property?"

"It's in the logs with all the rest of the answers."

"I guess a God-honoring church would be a problem if it is on the land they want to control," Patty said.

Fred replied, "Without a doubt. Bill, what do you think we get those logs out and learn from them?"

"I prefer not to, but it looks like we're going to have to."

"Bill, you realize that we are all going to support you and that God is in control of this situation?"

"Yes, Fred, I just wish it was over already."

"Don't we all. God has more that needs to be done. This hasn't and won't leave our prayers."

"Let's get the logs out and to the office. The sooner we learn the better."

Fred walked to the basement with Bill. Fred could see that Bill was uncomfortable and trembling. "Bill, can you think of another way?"

"No, I have to do this in God's strength. At least, Trainer isn't waiting inside me to punish me with pain for my disobedience."

Ailith spoke to one of God's special messenger angels. "You know what they need to see?"

"Yes, Colonel."

"Make sure they see it."

"Yes, Colonel."

"You two go with him. Make sure he gets there and protect the logs and prayer squad. Nassor will go to the end of the earth to stop this."

"It is done, Colonel."

The three angels flew down with their mission in mind.

Nassor sent ten of the best demons to meet them and ten more to meet the logs in the office. The demons saw the angels flying down. The little messenger dropped back behind his protectors.

"We have been sent to stop you. You are not going to complete your mission."

"You don't know what you are up against. That's okay. We're ready for the fight. How about you?"

"Always. Meet the fire of hell."

The ten demons drew their swords, sending fire at the angels. The angels' swords' light arcs cut and extinguished the fire before it reached them. "Messenger, get ready to go fast to your mission. We will draw your fire."

The ten demons charged in flight. The protector angels said, "Hold to the rear. Ready."

The demons reached them with a loud crash and were through the line in a second. The messenger angel flew with all the speed he had to the office. The protector angels said, "Turn and look behind you. You are going nowhere until the messenger is safely in the office."

"We have demons waiting on the roof for him. He will not get through them."

The guardian angels instantly recognized the demons and flew into battle against them in defense of the house and the church.

The demons felt the swords of the angels before they ever saw them. They leaped off the roof, trying to find what was attacking. By the time they found the new targets, the messenger angel flew by with amazing speed and entered into the office.

~

Bill followed Fred as he led the group to the office. The logs were held tightly by Bill.

Fred said, "Bill, we will all listen as you read."

Bill took his trembling fingers and opened the log of Trainer, expecting empty pages. The words written on the pages seemed to be written in blood. His mind couldn't fathom what was happening. "Give me a second. The first time I looked at these pages, there wasn't a word written on them, and now they are full and seem to use blood as ink."

Bill took a deep breath; he struggled to wrap his mind around the words on the pages. He flipped a few pages without saying a word. He gasped and froze. After finally breaking his gaze from the page, he said, "Here is what we're looking for."

He began to read. "'Trainer, your mission is simple. We need one hundred possessed men. Get three sons from your host, and it will happen in a few short years. When that is accomplished, give them the desire to get to the barn. The oldest will know to tell the men where to dig. Those hundred and the millions of demons waiting below will storm the earth, killing anyone who resists, and Satan will have easy reign over all the earth.'"

Bill looked up and said, "Satan wants to take the earth from God's control."

"The church will stop that from happening." Fred and the rest understood the ramifications of the plan. "That is why he has fought so hard. Satan can be god over all the earth, shutting God and his plans down."

"Listen to this…'Once the millions of humans on earth have been turned into demons, they will follow the others on the final attack on heaven. The Father will lose control of the heavens, and I, Satan, will rule all.'"

Bill shivered as he continued to read. "'One warning, Trainer, you must have one hundred possessed men for this to work.'" Bill shook his head. "Can this really be? Can Satan completely break God in this way?"

Fred said, "Apparently, he thinks he can."

Harry said, "Building this church as we planned may set the millions of demons against us. We may not be able to dig deep enough to get the hole for the foundation of the building. We need to get into intense prayer and fasting on this. As well, let's get these logs back into hiding."

Bill said, "I completely agree, especially about getting these logs back in the basement."

The next Sunday morning, Fred walked around the church setup in the living room, praying as he did every Sunday morning. This morning held a heavier burden that he knew would take the entire church unified to carry. His prayers for the following days strictly held the request that the church would be willing to join as one and break the power of the demons waiting to be set free.

It wasn't worry that he felt. He knew the church would surprise him again as they had every time before. The tension he felt was something different. That house made him nervous and frustrated. He couldn't put his finger on it. The feeling that those logs were going to play a larger role nagged at him.

He knelt in front of the empty chair and prayed. He struggled to get started, and just the simple thing of honoring God for who he is seemed to be too much. Finally, with all he could say being Jesus, he repeated. "Jesus, help me."

The words stopped when the weeping started. Through the tears, he felt a peace wash over him. "Son," Jesus started to say. "I'm here with you. Lean on me, and I will hold you up."

The sound of car doors tore him from his prayers but not from the presence of peace that had filled him. He got up and went to the door and escorted Douglas, Glenda, and Chad into the living room. "I thought you would be at the hospital."

Douglas said, "We felt that we could do more by praying with the group than sitting in the hospital. Samantha has been moved to a regular room, but John and the truck driver are still in real danger. Samantha would only let us come if we promised to bring you and the rest of the prayer squad back with us."

"Doug, I'm sure more than the three will be there. I'm announcing where they are and what I know. I guess you're wondering why I have the room arranged like this. I have no sermon planned for today. This will truly be a day of prayer and praise."

Harry walked through the door to the living room. "This is no surprise. You don't plan on ever changing, do you, Fred?"

Fred said, "Prayer is our number one weapon, and we will use it until the battle is won or Jesus takes John home. I refuse to give up."

"Fred, there is the warrior. This time, there is also the whole church. I can't wait to see what God can do when this group unifies with one common goal."

Doug said, "You've seen this before?"

Harry said, "I was the reason for this response the last time. I got on alcohol, and this man with this attitude fell to his knees with two other men, and none of them got up until I walked into the room, asking for prayer. Trust me when I say they didn't have to say a word. The Holy Spirit, to whom they had spent hours praying, flooded into me, and I have never touched alcohol again."

"You've never been tempted?"

"No temptation can penetrate the memory of that moment. You'll see what I'm talking about, I'm sure."

28 MIRACLES

Nassor took one hundred of his best and flew off to the house. Upon quick survey, he saw seven guardian angels and more coming down the road. Ailith waited high in the sky, sword drawn. From behind him, he heard, "Let's take them now!"

Nassor said, "Don't be a fool! There could easily be ten thousand angels waiting behind Ailith that we can't see. We'll sit and scout for now."

There was no answer from the others, which was exactly what he wanted. He watched as every guardian angel took their place for the fight, swords drawn. Nassor knew he was more than outnumbered; he didn't stand a chance at all if he tried to fight.

A quick count of angels settled at eighteen, not counting five colonels. That group alone would be a challenge. The angels in the sky could join them in a second, and that would end it for their enemy.

"I know what I need to know. Slowly back away and go home."

Nassor wanted no trouble with any group this time. All the demons backed away but one. The lone demon charged at the Guardian Angels throwing fire at them. Nassor ordered. "Let him go. Return home!"

The guardian angels waited. There wasn't a spark of clashing swords. The red haze floated away from the assault of the angels. "Does anyone else really want a piece of that?"

"No, Master." This came unanimously from the remainder of the demons.

"Good. Stay low and away. They are ready."

Samantha lay on the bed. Periodical checks from the nurses were getting father and farther apart. Just moments ago, her family left for the service. They left a Bible in her reach as well as her cell phone. It seemed only seconds after they left that her mind drifted to the ICU and John.

The words of Jesus kept running through her mind. "John will be fine. He just has a little more work to be done." Then she prayed. "Father, give me faith. Help me to believe your words. It is so easy to stop believing when everything seems so hopeless. I feel lost already. Don't let him go."

She heard the door open. She turned her neck and saw the doctor. "Hello, Doc."

"Hello, Samantha. How are you feeling?"

"Fine, I just wish John was in here too."

"I just left John. You will be glad to know that we are seeing signs of improvement. We are hopeful that he will be out of ICU when you are ready to leave."

"Then my time will be spent here as a visitor. I want to be around when he wakes up."

She watched as the doctor examined the chart and checked what he needed to. "I have good news. How would you like to go and visit him?"

"Oh, yes."

"Let me see what I can do."

A new excitement wanted to explode inside her. There was a hope, and that was the best news she could have heard. "Thank you."

John held Jesus when he heard, "John, it is time to wake up. Merton is waking as well. Follow my lead. You will know what to do when you need to."

"Do I have to? I don't want to let you go."

"You don't have to let me go. Your work in the world is not done. You will have to wrap your spiritual arms around me like you have so many times before."

The nurse watched patiently as the monitors beeped and readouts flashed, blinked, and printed. Too suddenly, the monitors beeped and changed on both sides of her. She immediately called to notify the doctor. Merton's eyes opened first, and just seconds after, John's eyes opened.

The room was finally clear of medical staff except for one nurse. John looked across the way and saw Merton looking to him. He saw him sign. "I'm sorry."

John signed back. "You are forgiven."

"You know sign language?"

"It is my first language. My second language is English."

"You were alone in the car?"

"No. My girlfriend was with me."

"I hope she is…"

"She woke up yesterday. She was moved to a regular room shortly after."

"That's good. I have a question for you."

"Go ahead."

"How do you live with a handicap? Did you have it from birth?"

"Yes, I had a speech problem from birth. Having it from birth may make it easier to live with, but you still learn that you aren't normal in many people's eyes. I have found that your attitude about the handicap is really the key. If you accept it and live on to the fullness you can with it, you will enjoy your life in spite of the handicap."

"Would you rather have the ability to speak or your current life?"

"I have the ability to speak. That didn't make me any happier than before. My life didn't change until I found Jesus Christ."

"What did Jesus do to make the difference?"

"Through him, I found peace—a peace that I didn't need the ability to talk to be complete."

The nurse just watched and listened. All the while, she continued to pray silently. She prayed for one she knew was going to walk, run, and do anything else he used to before the accident and the other who was not as fortunate.

She knew the pain in Merton's heart was deep but found out both patients had the same pain at sometime in their life. She hoped Merton heard and took to heart the words she saw John sign.

The prayer meeting lasted for three hours before Fred felt comfortable to stop. God had called him to lead the church, and now they were getting an understanding of how deep his love went for those in the church. He looked up at the others. "We have done all we can do. It is time to go to the hospital and visit John and Samantha."

He heard someone say, "What about lunch on the way?"

"Anyone who wants to grab a bite to eat may. I won't until I know John is going to make it."

Harry said, "Fred, are you sure? I'll get your water bottle."

Fred was the first one out of the house. The van held eight, requiring two more vehicles to be taken. The drive to the hospital was filled with silence. It seemed Fred refused to speak, even when he was spoken to. His head buried deep in his hands.

The others followed Fred as he walked directly to Samantha's room. To everyone's surprise, the second bed was full. Fred saw the smiling face first, and he heard the voice of John say, "Fred, go and eat. God is still working, but I'm out of any danger."

"You knew I had to know. I want to stay and talk for a little bit before I get kicked out."

"You can only stay as long your stomach can hold out."

Harry said, "Are you sure you want to say that? You've seen him hold out for four days straight waiting on God."

"Yes," John said. "But he is not waiting on God anymore. I've never seen him starve himself after he got the answer."

"Point made."

Fred said, "You two want me to eat. I can take the hint. Everyone else can enjoy the visit. I could use something anyway."

They all watched as he walked out to the cafeteria.

June was walking to the cafeteria for lunch when she saw the young man waiting, holding the door for her. "Thank you."

She went through the food line taking some roast beef with mixed vegetable and mashed potatoes on the side. After paying the cashier, she saw one open table to sit at. She waited for the young man to pay and then asked, "I don't normally asked this, but…would you share the table with me?"

"Why, yes, thank you for asking. My name is Fred."

"My name is June. I'm a lab tech here. What do you do?"

"I guess I'm a pastor. It's really quite the story."

"I would like to know more about it."

"It might take all your lunchtime."

"I have nothing better to do."

"It all started when two friends started studying the Bible and praying together once a week. It continued to grow…"

She sat, fascinated by every word. "Do you have family in the hospital?"

"No, there are two of the members of the new church. They are doing really well now."

"That is great. I'm always glad when someone gets good news. I see the long-term critical patients for lab test all the time."

"When they get the good news, then my job is done, and they don't have to see me anymore. Most of the time, I can laugh with the good nature of the patient. There are some that are angry, but I have to do my job."

"June, it sounds like you have a job like any other. It has its good times and its bad times."

"Yes, it does. Overall most of the patients are good to me and understanding. When we can laugh together, it makes the rest of the work easier."

"I'm sure it does. It looks like it's near time for you to get back to the lab work."

"Yes, it is. I would like to see you again. You can call me here."

She handed him a napkin.

"Sure, I'll call you to arrange a time."

Fred reentered the room of John and Samantha. "What did I miss?"

John said, "You haven't missed anything other than being crammed in a room too small for the number of people in it."

"I think that describes the cafeteria too. There was one table open when I went down there to eat."

Rebeca said, "So who did you meet down there?"

"What do you mean, Rebeca?"

"I saw the look on your face as you were coming down the hall. That comes from meeting someone. So give it up. Who?"

"No one in particular. I'm just glad John is improving so much."

"You're having the same problem with your friends too?" The voice came from the door.

Fred shot around. "June?"

"Yes. My coworkers didn't buy the line either. It'll go better if you just tell them what they want to hear. Besides, avoiding the conversation just leads to speculation."

Fred could see the smile on Richard's face and could almost hear his thoughts brewing. "I don't think that will make anything easier." He turned to look at John, glanced over at Samantha and, while turning back to June, asked, "Who are you here for this time?"

"Actually, I'm here to be mean to John for teasing you. Since I need two tubes of blood…"

John said, "I haven't done anything to him. It's Richard that will tease him."

"Too late," Judy replied. "The order is for you. We can do this the easy way, or it will hurt."

"I'll cooperate, but I still say I did nothing."

"That's good. You're supposed to respect your pastor."

Fred smiled at her. "You can be nice to him, but Richard, now he's a different story. He's merciless." He said, glancing over at Richard.

"So can I. He'll watch it or answer to me." June smiled at Fred as she reached for John's arm.

"Now I need to get this blood, or no one is going to be happy."

"I'm ready."

"John, this will go quick. Just two tubes." She quickly drew the blood, capped the two viles, and turned to walk out.

"I'll be expecting your call." Their eyes locked as she walked past Fred.

"I'm looking forward to finishing our conversation."

Fred watched her leave and saw the wink and the twinkle in her eye. He looked to the doorway and saw Rebeca standing there, holding the doorknob. "Anything you want to add?"

"No, I think all the details have been filled in."

Richard chimed in. "You can't get anything past a woman."

Patty responded, "That's why you don't have one." Immediately, she ducked behind Peter and wrapped her arms around him.

Richard laughed. "Maybe I need to go to the cafeteria. That seems to work for some."

"Don't. The way you eat would scare any respectable woman off."

"Peter, I have a video for you to see. We're still getting together Tuesday after the work is done?"

"You wouldn't," Patty said, stunned. "You can't."

"I can do anything I want. He's going to find out soon enough anyway."

Fred looked at Peter. "It looks like you are being thrown between the siblings."

"Patty is safe. There is no way that he has anything worse than the one I keep hidden. I still have family looking for it."

Fred tried to get off this track. "Samantha, how are you feeling?"

After John interpreted, Samantha signed. "Very good and glad to be here with John. You know the feeling?"

"Samantha, you're starting to sound like Richard."

"I learned from the best."

John looked to Fred. "She said that she is doing good, thank you."

"What was the rest of the signing?"

"Richard speaking through Samantha. Do you really want to know?"

"I'll never hear the end of this, will I?"

"I'm afraid not. You should feel blessed. God is at work in all of our lives."

"Yes, he is."

Fred couldn't say that he had experienced real trouble with women but had a feeling it wasn't preferable. The napkin, still tucked neatly in his pocket, kept reminding him every time he went for his wallet that he hadn't made the call yet. By now, his stomach played a few tricks, and the number on the napkin itself turned on the nerves.

He knew if he didn't dial the number soon, he would never be able to. He looked at the number written on the paper and at the face of his phone, checked to make sure they were the same for the thousandth time, and nervously hit the Talk button.

What do I really want? Ring. *What do I say if she answers?* Ring. *Does she want to talk to me?* Ring. *Why don't I just hang up now?*

"Hello."

"June?"

"Yes…Fred?"

"Yes, how are you?"

"Good. How are you?"

"I'm doing well. I'm getting ready for the special service tomorrow night. Are you working?"

"I work days. I would love to hear you preach."

"I may not preach. You'll understand tomorrow. I can pick you up at six if that's a good time."

"That sounds good to me. What are you doing to get ready if you're not preaching?"

"I'm picking up John and Samantha from the hospital, that's the good news. After that, I'm getting with the church board to talk about what is going on."

"More of what I'll understand tomorrow?"

"Yes. I don't know how comfortable I'll feel talking about it, but the church needs to know what's going on. I have to prepare them for what I expect to come our way."

"Is it really that bad?"

"I hope not, but I have to be real. It got worse before, and I know we are in for a long fight."

"What makes you say that? What are you expecting, Fred? It sounds really serious."

"The rest of the church will fill you in on the details. I know you don't understand, but we are in a spiritual war that is tough to understand, even for those in it."

"Is there anything in particular I can pray for?"

"Churchwide obedience and unity. God will take care of the rest."

"Are you at the church now?"

"Yes. It seems I live at the church."

"Where is it? I'd like to get a tour."

Fred thought about that and then said, "At 5757 Power Lane. How long will you be?"

He heard the engine of her car start in the background before he heard her say, "I'm on my way. I'll be there shortly. I would rather talk to you in person anyway. Oh, you don't mind, do you?"

"No, not at all…I could use a little backup." Fred looked at the room being used at the church. It looked nothing like a church. The office appeared to be ransacked with the scattering of papers and books all over the room. The realization came to him that he hadn't had time to clean anything, including the bathroom or kitchen.

He took the steps down two at a time and turned into the kitchen to find it immaculate, like a maid came in and cleaned it. He quickly walked to the downstairs bathroom and found it the same way. *Who has been cleaning in here?*

He didn't think it had been very long before he heard the knock on the door.

29 Blessings

June hung up the phone just as she started down the road. Confusion and concern intermingled within herself. She couldn't remember any church being on Power Lane. She couldn't remember ever living on any other road, but her parents told her she moved in this house at just four months old. When she was six years old, she could remember the excitement of having a baby brother or sister. She remembered the day her mom left for the hospital. It was also the last day she ever saw her mother.

Five-seven-five-seven, this is it. She parked the car and headed for the front door of the house. She was even more unsure of her decision to come over now than when she asked over the phone. She forced herself to walk to the door. Her mind reeled with excuses to just leave. She noticed the lawn had been well cared for. The stone walk from the driveway to the porch also relaxed her. The earthy tones reminded her of the trail she used to walk on with her father. He had a way of making the hurt disappear for a little while during their walks.

She raised her hand and knocked on the door. She checked her clothes for the hundredth time. As she raised her hand to knock again, the door opened. "Welcome to the church and my home."

"You actually live in the church."

"Yes, we are planning to build a church on the land so I can have the house, but for now, my home is the church."

She saw the chairs circled around one chair in the center. She became apprehensive. "What kind of service is this?"

"It's nothing weird, don't worry. Just sit in and watch tonight. It's called the empty chair meeting. We get together and pray for someone who is unable to be there for whatever reason."

"This is about John and Samantha."

"Partly, I also got word that Merton will never drive a truck again because of some brain damage that may cause seizures. I know John well enough to know that he would want Merton in this chair."

"You guys are a weird bunch. Even the staff at the hospital says that. But your methods seem to be effective. Those you pray for recover."

"Only those that God chooses to help. The rest just don't."

"Is your mind always this occupied?"

"No, it's just that recently I haven't had a chance to stop. It seems we just go from one battle to another."

Nassor called the demons into the meeting room. Jacob and Gary sat in there, seeing the shadows they now understood to be the support demons.

Nassor said, "What is the battle they're fighting now?"

"They're fighting for the truck driver, Master." A demon from the back reported.

"Why would they fight for seemingly everybody? Is there a connection?"

"Master, none can be found."

"Then tell me why they're fighting for him. He's nobody. In fact, they should be blaming him for hurting their friends, not praying for him."

"Master, the truck driver belongs to Satan. We can kill him while they're praying for his recovery and make them think God isn't listening to them anymore. A fight involves two sides."

"Get to the hospital and make it happen. Take some others with you for support."

"Yes, Master."

Ailith looked to Jesus. He watched him nod in agreement. "Malik, go to him. Once he accepts Jesus, defend him."

"Yes, Coronel. The victory is the Lord's."

John walked with Samantha in the hall with the doctor's permission. Samantha said, "Isn't that the truck driver that hit us?"

"Yes, it is. Let's go see if he's awake."

They walked into the room to see Merton's eyes open. John signed. "How are you doing?"

Merton signed back. "I need to talk to someone who is a Christian. Everything I knew has been stripped away. What does Jesus have against me?"

I know Jesus has a plan for you. Do you have a relationship with him?"

"No, I always thought that my mother's prayers would be enough."

"The eternal plan of God has always been for each man to have a personal relationship with him and not trying to get to heaven on the family. Merton, Jesus wants to have a personal, one-on-one relationship with you."

"How do I get that?" A tear rolled down his temple.

"Just ask him."

Merton's eyes looked to the ceiling. "Jesus, I want a relationship with you like my family and these two have…" The prayer continued on.

Malik saw the demons coming, but they were still far off. Immediately, he was joined by Seth, Cenewig, and Domina. "They're coming to kill him," Cenewig said.

Malik said, "Let's give them a reason to fight. I like eliminating demons."

Cenewig commanded. "Draw your swords. The fight is on."

The distance closed in, and the surprise on the demons' faces showed. Two demons flew to the front, drew double swords, and prepared for battle.

Ailith pointed to another angel. "Go and help."

The angel flew without a word.

The demons called out together, "Kill them all!"

Their flight intensified, and their swords pointed to all four angels. "Make them pay!"

The demons saw that the angels were unmoving and relentless. Then the light circle from Cenewig's sword seemed to float toward them in slow motion. Their acceleration continued until the light circle slammed into the space they were in. Their strength left from them. The fire from their swords extinguished in seconds. The empty blades slapped against the fierce power of the angels' swords, and all the demons were driven back.

"What is it? What has happened?" The demon slapped his sword with his hand, and there was nothing. No fire bolted from the sword.

"That is the power of the blood of Jesus revealed through mankind. You know this power, even if you haven't experienced it firsthand. This is the power of one drop of blood of Jesus Christ."

"Satan, light our swords."The demons began in prayer. "Show your power through the power of the blood of the earth."

Instantly, the swords lit with flames. "I hope your drop is strong.

One of the demons looked to the others. Get the little demons through.

Merton has to die. Anyone else is a bonus."

They formed a line, anger glaring off their faces like the fire off their swords. "We will not allow you to beat us again. It is time for Satan to rule the entire earth and all of heaven as well. Your Lord will fall, and Satan will reign."

Cenewig said, "Satan himself knows that will never happen. The created will never overpower the Creator. You are fighting for a worthless and impossible goal."

"Every power on earth belongs to Satan and he rules the earth. He will rule the heavens as well."

"Every power Satan has, he has been given. He rules only what he is allowed to rule. Now you can leave and tell Nassor that he will not win this fight either. God already knows how you are fighting and where you are attacking. God prepares the people to be there when and where he is attacking. You can't surprise him in any way."

"Fine, we can't surprise him. We don't have to. All we have to do is beat him. We take his creation, turn it against him, give them power to be gods, and they will kill God."

"No, they are created, and because they are, they cannot kill or destroy their Creator. Many will turn and follow Satan, but there is more power in those that choose to follow God."

"We will see. We will see. Demons, charge!"

"Angels, hold the line."

The demons flew. The fire shot ahead. The angels held their swords in defensive position, awaiting the fire coming like lightning. The demons connected with sparks, blinding light, and heat. One demon flew over the fighting angels trying to break free from the angels. Malik saw the demon and broke free attacking.

The demon drew away and back just before Malik's sword slashed the air. He said, "Merton belongs to Satan. I have permission from your Lord to kill him."

"Correction, Merton used to belong to Satan. Merton changed sides to Jesus's fifteen seconds ago. As of that second, you lost your permission."

The demon flew at him. Malik slid to one side and sliced at the demon with his sword. He instantly felt the sword and knew what it meant. "No way. Not no..." The demon dissipated in a red haze.

Malik watched as the other demons flew off, leaving a trail of red haze along their path.

Fred looked at June. "Let me show you what this does. I want you to grab the back of the chair and agree with me in prayer."

"I can do that."

Fred waited until her hands took the back of the chair. He got on his knees and took the seat in his hands. "Abba Father, John and Samantha are improving and healing. We give you the praise and honor for that. There is the other driver in the accident. He needs your touch in a mighty way. He needs you to protect him and guard him. Make him your servant. Father, reveal yourself in a mighty way..."

He fell silent a few seconds and then heard, "Father God, you know more than I what you intend for Merton. You healed him with your mighty hand. Open Merton's heart to your Word. Open John's mouth in a way that Merton will understand and give his heart to you. Father, we stand together as two claiming your promise that where two or more are gathered together, you are there..."

Fred finished. "We thank you for all you have already provided and will continue to provide. We pray this to your glory..."

They both said together, "Amen."

June said, "We are cut from the same cloth. You are a very special man. I'll be honored to come to your church. Is there anything going on tonight?"

Fred's phone rang. "Hello."

"Fred, this is John. God is blessing us in a mighty way. I can't wait to tell you the story."

"Merton accepted Christ as Savior?"

"It is my job to tell you what is going on before anyone else knows. How did you know?"

"June is here and prayed with me. I think you have a little more competition. Why aren't you stuttering?"

"I guess I can tell you that. Jesus took that from me while I was unconscious."

"Jesus is stacking blessing on top of blessing. What can happen next?"

"Fred, don't ask. You can't handle the answer to that question."

"John, what do you know?"

"Too much big picture without detail. I'm not going to say anything without knowing more. Praise God for the blessings and stay obedient."

"What specifically do we need to pray for tonight?"

"Just thanks. Praise in song and thank God for the many blessings."

All right, I'll pick you and Samantha up tomorrow. You take care of yourself."

Fred got up and said, "Will you wait here for me. There has been a change of plans."

"Sure."

Fred left and returned with his guitar in his hands. "We'll be singing tonight. Tonight we celebrate victory."

30 Nassor's Fire

The door opened, and Peter and Patty walked in. June walked up to them and said, "Welcome, come on in. Fred is just finishing getting ready."

"Weren't you the nurse that took the blood in the hospital?" Peter asked?

"Yes, Fred invited me over. The least I could do is greet people so he could finish what he is doing."

"You can expect people to be surprised."

Patty smiled at June. "It's good to have you, June. How long have you been here?"

"Just long enough to pray for someone. I don't think Fred knows who I was praying for."

Peter asked as he walked in, "He's breaking you in already?"

June retorted, "You shouldn't have to be 'broken in' to obedience to God. What Fred did was obey God."

Patty said, "You should know that by now. I think I'll break you in."

She turned to June and then said, "I'm so glad you've joined us. You're just what this group needs."

June watched Fred walk up, took his hand, and asked, "What did she mean by that?"

Fred said, "You know already, I think. Do you want to continue greeting the people with me? Richard will be here soon."

"Richard is the one they said would be teasing you?"

"Richard is the one that will try to give me a hard time."

June just smiled without saying a word. The door opened. "Good afternoon, Richard. Have you met June?"

"Good afternoon, Fred," he said, glancing over at June. "Has she got you yet?"

With a little half grin, she replied before Fred could. "He knows what's good for him. The question is…do you?"

Vera interrupted Richard. "Good afternoon, June. It's nice to see you here. Richard, you're blocking the doorway. Head on in, please." Vera gave him a gentle push on the back and smiled at June as they moved past.

June watched the family go into the living room. Fred said, "They are one of the newer families to the church. The couple coming up now is the newest family to the church. They are the parents of Samantha."

June waited for them to come to the door. "Welcome. I'm surprised you're here. I thought you would be at the hospital with Samantha."

Douglas said, "Between John and Samantha, we were kicked out and told to meet here. We weren't allowed to come back until this service is over."

"From what Fred has told me, that sounds like John. I don't know Samantha that well."

"She sounds like John in a lot of ways. Besides, they are walking around for some exercise. I think the physical therapist was with them. They're under strict, watching eyes. I don't think the doctor knows what to do with them." She laughed quietly.

June asked in surprise, "They're up and walking?"

"Yes, I think the only way to hold them down would be to tie them down."

"They will if they try to stay up too long. They are still patients."

Fred said, "I will call them and see if they can join in the service via the phone."

Douglas said, "That would be great."

Fred said, "The next one coming up is Harry. He has been my friend and a member since the prayer squad days."

June extended her hand and said, "Good afternoon. It's good meeting you."

"Welcome, June. I'm glad you could join us."

Fred said, "That's most of them. The rest will be here soon, probably during praise and worship." June followed as Fred walked to the front.

He stopped short and pointed to a chair in the center aisle front row that was left empty. "This is your seat."

"When did the seating arrangement change?"

"While we greeted people."

She sat on the chair and let the look of the room fill her mind. The church could easily be seen, and her mind drifted back to a day where the small country church she went to looked just like this living room. She listened for soft notes of the organ and the strong voice of the pastor leading the worship.

The guitar strummed, and Fred's voice boldly brought her back. "Ladies and gentlemen, let's stand and sing praises to our Lord for all he has done, thanking the Lord for the miraculous recovery of John and Samantha as well as the salvation of Merton."

The guitar paused. "We have two more people who can't be here, but what do you say we try to involve them by phone?"

"Amen," said those in attendance.

Fred picked up his phone, dialed two numbers, and pressed Talk.

The phone was answered on the second ring. "Hello."

"John, can you take enough time to join the praise service by phone?"

"I have nothing but time. The nurses have told us that we have to get back to our room. I think they're trying to keep us in so we can rest. I think I can leave the phone on speaker and still hear you. They just don't want us jumping around until we get out of the hospital."

"That's understood. We're going to start now." The guitar picked up the strumming, and the songs of praise started.

Nassor's fury burned in his eyes. The guardian angels and Ailith still stood ready. All attacks on the church had stopped. The need to get them going again started the fire. The need to kill tried to stir the burn to an out-of-control rage.

He looked to the demons in the main room of the house. "It is time to prove that we have the capability to kill again. You two go out and kill somebody. I don't care who it is."

Forras flew out with Kasadya following behind. Fear found its way into his heart. This would normally be a pleasure to fill, but Nassor was more than furious. This group of demons had missed every opportunity to kill that came their way. Coming back without kill would most certainly be fatal.

He searched the ground for someone to kill without a fight. As people came into view, so did the guardian angels. Three cars came into view with angels on top for the ride. Their drawn swords made the point. A black Chevrolet van rolled down the road two miles off in the distance. It looked like three people inside. The driver appeared to be a mid-thirties woman; the front seat passenger was a teenager just below driving age, and there was an infant about three months old in a car seat in the backseat.

Forras searched the whole area thoroughly for any possible sign of hidden angels; none was found. "Kasadya, does that look like a target to you?"

"Definitely, I haven't seen anything around."

"I see the perfect way to make it happen. That big tree should do the trick."

"It will work nicely. What are we going to do to make sure they die?"

"If I have to, I will go in and take the heart out of their chest. We fail, and there will be no more us."

"I agree. We both need to make sure there are no survivors."

They flew to the van. Forras checked for enough speed, while Kasadya made sure everything else was right. Nothing seemed to be getting in the way. Kasadya said, "This is too easy. What is going to go wrong?"

"Nothing, Kasadya. Don't start talking like that. Just get ready to make those back wheels lose traction."

"I'm ready. You better make sure they all die."

"You can count on it. They will."

"Isn't that why we're here? We said that too many times to Nassor and didn't accomplish the task."

"Shut up and do your job."

"Take your own advice."

"The time has come. Get this van spinning."

Kasadya went under the van. With a smack of the tire with his sword, the tire exploded. The van dropped and spun out of control. Forras slammed into the front of the van. The screaming coming from the van told them their mission was on the way to being accomplished. With rapid speed, the van slammed into the tree. Bodies bounced and jerked around inside. Forras watched the teenager's head slam through the window and into the tree and then stop. The blood ran from the split in her head, and then there was no movement.

The mother's chest slammed into the steering wheel jerking her neck. Her body twitched for a second and then stopped, applying pressure on the horn.

The infant screamed in fright, kicking and thrashing his arms.

June was driving Fred to an ice cream shop in a neighboring town after the praise service. The car in front of them was the last thing on their mind. Fred asked, "So what got you interested in working in the medical field?"

"That has always been an interest of mine. It wasn't until I was thirteen when a young lab tech came in to take my blood for tests that started to make that a dream."

"What did she have to do that made it a dream?"

"My parents were out of the room for a second when she came in. she explained to me what she had to do and then told me it was her job to take away the pain. She promised me before she left that it would be all right."

"It sounds like someone showed you compassion when you really needed it."

"Yes, I decided then to work in the same field. I try to do the same thing with all the children that I meet. It helped me, and I'm told by parents that it makes things easier on the kids I help too."

"Sounds like a good reason to get into the medical field."

"What?" June saw the car spin, drive off the road, and slam into something to a stop. She drove up to the scene, threw the car into park, and ran out to see if anyone was hurt. Her mind went into automatic pilot and saw the mother. Her eyes grayed over with no pulse. She looked to the passenger and needed no more to know she was dead.

The screaming baby flailed in the car seat for help. She ran around to the door and lifted the handle. It released and opened easily. She checked for external injuries and yelled, "Fred, call nine-one-one."

"On it already. They are already on their way."

"I'm staying until we know what is going to happen to the baby. I'll contact Child Protective Services."

June walked Fred to Pediatrics where he met Sandy. "Sandy, this is Fred. He is my boyfriend."

She looked at Fred. "Nice to meet you."

"Do you know anything about the baby?"

"June, Crystal is now without a family. Her mother and sister were her last surviving relatives. I took the liberty to prepare the paperwork for a foster home. Do you have the space now?"

"Yes, do you know how she is doing?"

"All I know is there isn't anything external injured. She was scared but fine, as far as we know. The doctors are watching her and running more test to make sure that everything is still fine."

June took the forms and signed where she needed to. "How long before I know if I'm taking her home?"

"You should know before the doctors release her. Everything is in order, but I have to process the paperwork. She will be here anyway, and the doctors have agreed to hold her here until we have care arrangements made."

"Can I hold the baby?"

"I will allow it since I expect this to go through without a hitch. The medical staff will have to authorize it. I'll let them know what I am doing."

"Thank you."

She turned to Fred. "I think I just got a little busier."

"Are you ready for her?"

"I couldn't agree if I wasn't ready. I couldn't leave Crystal without care anyway. That's not me. I care too much."

"That shows. Crystal couldn't be under better care."

"Thank you. You owe me an ice cream. I believe there is an ice cream shop close to here, and we won't hear any more here anyway."

I'll go if you want to. You make the call."

"We go. I'm ready for dessert."

Forras flew into the house with Kasadya close behind. They landed in-between the demons and Nassor on their knees bowing. Forras said, "Master."

"Report."

"Master, two are dead. They died instantly in a car crash."

"That is what I like to hear. Tell me more."

"Master, Kasadya blew out the tire, and I turned the front of the car to a big tree. The driver and passenger died in less than one second."

"That is one effective way to kill. Can anyone think of any other way to kill?"

"Master," someone said from somewhere in the crowd of demons. "My stubby fingers can rip out the heart of a man. Without his heart, he dies, and there's be no chance to recover."

"Good. Any other good ideas?"

Ideas came from the demons one after another until finally Nassor said, "Who can take these ideas and kill the prayer squad?"

The demons bowed in submission and remained silent. "What do I need to do to prove that these guardian angels are beatable? Fine, I'll get Ailith in a battle and beat him. When I do, you will do the same with the lesser angels."

"Ailith, Nassor is no joke. He is angry. If you take him on in battle, you will have to be ready for almost anything, including cheating."

"Boris, there is much I fear about Nassor, but one thing I know is that if Nassor has his way and I give up, then the prayer squad will be under constant attack. I have to win this fight. I'm ready to fight Nassor. It's God's battle, and I'm merely his instrument. He is the Great I AM, the Almighty God. I think you should remember who it is we serve."

"Is there any other way?"

"I understand you're dread, even Jesus prayed for his cup to pass. Yet he submitted to his Father's will. We must do the same. We are his army created to serve him and protect what is his. No, I must fight. I must deal with Nassor. The time is coming for Nassor to be vanquished. Right now we both will live and fight again. This is the first that will start the war that will turn the tide. You must trust me. I know what I'm doing."

"Ailith, I don't understand. What are you talking about?"

"Boris, you are a young leader. You will understand soon enough. This is a lesson I learned when I was a young leader myself."

"Ailith, I will follow you wherever the battle takes me."

"Boris, stay here. You'll be in it soon enough."

31 The Champion

Ailith looked for the angelic host. "Be ready for anything. No one can come help unless Nassor gets help. Then only can you match strength for strength. It is time to go meet Nassor."

Ailith saw the faces of the host down and wanting change. He raised his wings and flew with his sword ready to be drawn. The question wasn't where to meet him but if he could handle a raid from visiting demons if Nassor decided to call them. He knew there would be demons on the ready and close. *Boris, please hold back. I have to have you ready if the horde attacks.*

Ailith reached the area that he wanted Nassor in for the fight and waited with nothing but time to think. He refused to look at the angels no matter how much he wanted to make sure they cooperated with his instructions. He looked around and saw the void of air all around. His sword waited to be drawn. He wanted so badly to rip Nassor limb from limb, never to allow him to return. Jesus had already told him what he needed to do. There would be pain, but it was angelic obedience teamed with personal obedience of the saints that made God's power shine strong.

He could feel the anger but couldn't see the demon. His fingers loosened and tightened on the handle of the sword. His eyes searched intently. Then there was smoke rising from the east at a lower altitude. The time came to call him. He drew his sword flashing the light that revealed his location.

He waited for another minute before he knew for sure Nassor was coming. Nassor, you have what you want if you really want it. As Nassor approached with his army behind, Ailith said, "Nassor, I come alone. Why do you need an army to take on one angel?"

"Oh, Ailith, I'm bringing them to teach them. Your angels are beating them, and I intend to show them the trick that will defeat you."

"You are their teacher. I'm the teacher to the angels. I can teach my angels more from a distance than you can with your students watching close up."

"You mock me, Ailith? I'm not in a mood for vengeance yet? You have forgotten our last encounter so soon."

"I forget no encounter with you. I simply state the truth. Are you mocked by truth?"

"You're trying my patience. If you're thinking this is going to help your cause, you're wrong. I'll have to kill you just for the disrespect."

"What are you thinking? You forgot that I didn't die the last time you said you was going to kill me?"

"That can be rectified. Why are you doing all this verbal battering? Show your strength, draw your sword."

"No one gains by that. Your sword isn't in your possession. You get your sword, and then we will both be armed."

"You think you're smart, don't you? It's time to see how smart you really are." Nassor locked with two other demons and prepared for the attack.

Ailith watched, sword sheathed. "Boris, don't leave heaven. Stay put until it is clearly an attack of multiple demons."

Ailith saw the attack as it launched, the fire from his sword thrown just inches from his face. Ailith stayed still, not moving a muscle. He watched Nassor target his shoulder to take out his sword. Again, he remained still. The arc of fire accelerated toward him. Ailith drew his sword, throwing a light arc at the same time it sliced the fire arc in half, dissipating it into thin air. "Nassor, strength doesn't always have to be brute force."

"Shut up! I don't want to hear your voice. Show me what your sword can really do."

Ailith remained braced in defensive position. He remained unmoved and visibly unchallenged. "Give me a good reason."

"You're daring me? Do you not see what is happening?"

"Yes, I see that you're surrounding me. It is like you to get help if you can't handle a situation. I guess I'm more than you can handle."

"You do remember who won the last battle?"

"Sure, what you can't handle is the prayer strength. Isn't that what you tried to break ever since you started making yourself known in Bill?"

"Shut up! Are you going to fight or yak?"

"That depends. Are you going to give me a reason?"

Ailith watched the fire grow red hot and the sword thrust fire forward at him. His sword snapped in front of him for a shield. The fire hit the sword and shook it. The red haze floated off the sword, and fire was gone. "Now that's more like your style. Why are you giving me all these wimpy attacks?"

"You want to see my power? You think I'm a wimp. Maybe I need to show you what I'm really ready for."

Ailith braced for the next attack. He watched still as Nassor launched at him, thrusting his fire ahead of him. Ailith waited for the second the fire would hit and then shifted sideways. The fire slid past him and into the circle of demons blowing a hole where it hit. The red haze of the demons distracted Nassor's attack. The timing of the swing was off by seconds, but it missed its target.

"Ailith, you remember me well. Why do you not counter my strikes?"

"My position is to defend. How I defend is up to me. I only counter when I need to. You will tire of this game soon enough."

"Demons, attack the heavens!" Immediately, Nassor flew at Ailith.

Their swords met with sparks flying. Ailith spun around, defending a blow and then cross-countering with a strike to the neck. His sword sank into his neck effortlessly. Nassor withdrew and flew back to the house. *Boris, I hope you're ready.*

Boris watched anxiously as the fight persisted. He knew Ailith could easily beat him, but he kept playing. The words, this lesson I also had to learn when I was a young leader, echoed in his head. He almost felt Jesus smile when he realized what he had to do.

The smile was of small comfort; with the recognition came a knowledge that brought deep concern. He understood Ailith's pain that resounded from the teaching time. Boris tried to shake off the feelings gripping his heart with confidence but knew why it wasn't going away. He wanted to ask Jesus but knew the answer already. "Be ready, Boris. You will have to be ready."

The verbal volleying continued with no effort from Ailith to even draw his sword. The first of many tears trickled down his cheek as the volleying continued. He heard Nassor shout the attack command. "Angels, hold the line!" He flew, followed by the angelic host. The line formed quickly.

He heard the swords being drawn. "Sheath your swords!"

Satisfied, they followed his command. He looked at the large horde flying toward them. He searched for the leader but found no one demon clearly in command, and he knew why. The one in command had already retreated, defeated.

Boris was now armed with more than swords. He found the one weapon he would use to break the attack. *Boris, be ready. You learned from the demonstration, now it is time to practice.*

The horde flew in and took the position Boris recognized as an offensive attack position and waited. He knew what they were waiting for and decided to start the battle without any further ado. "Why stop there? Do you not know how to fight?"

The demon he assumed was in command said, "We know how to fight. We also know not to disobey Nassor's orders. When Nassor is done with Ailith, he is coming for you."

"Nassor isn't coming. You think I didn't watch every move made in that battle?"

"Then you know he is already on his way here."

Boris saw the horde line split apart and heard Ailith say to the demon horde. "Nassor has returned to the house." He flew to the back of the angelic line.

"Horde!" the demon shouted out. "I am in charge now. These angels will fall."

Boris gripped his sword but left it in the sheath. "Angels, ready. Ailith, I learned this from you." He didn't need to look at Ailith to see the smile on his face.

The horde gripped their swords and stopped with the leader's hand raised. "That is the way you want to play this game? How about a one-on-one? I win the fight, Satan dominates the heavens. You win, Jesus dominates hell."

"You know I can't give the heavens to anyone, nor can I claim hell for anyone. If you want to get the heavens for Satan, then you will have to take them from Jesus Christ, the owner of the heavens and the earth, yourself after you get through us."

"Arrrgh! You fool! We will take you down and burn the heavens until they are hotter than the hottest part of hell."

"Angels, swords sheathed. You will have to prove that to me. No demon has ever followed through with any threat."

"We are the elite warriors of Satan. We took the same stance in the heavens you take now. Your God has given us a fighting ability above all others."

"No one disagrees with you. You fail to remember that not all of you followed Lucifer that day. There are more who stayed true to God. We will not surrender the heavens to you."

"Then you commit your army to death."

"Not until your army proves itself. You're in the offensive. We'll wait for you."

"That is your mistake. Demons, fire the swords."

Boris saw what was coming and drew his sword and braced for the impact. He heard the angels follow his lead. The fire charged at the line. Motionless, they anticipated the wave. No one took a breath as the wave hit the swords. They rocked but held until the wave dissipated.

Ailith sheathed his sword. "Do you have all year to play like this, or are you on a time restraint?"

"Boris, your day is coming when we will be one-on-one. You will fall to hell a captive of Satan."

Boris didn't respond but watched the demon horde retreat. "Angels, return to the heavens."

He heard a voice say, "You learned your lesson well. I know this is a small comfort, but God does still control things. They have a tough choice ahead. They've been here before and made the right choice. I have faith it will be the same again."

"Ailith, how do I handle this?"

"Like you just did, you're doing very well."

When Boris turned around, Ailith was a distance off, moving back to the heavens.

32 CRYSTAL

June walked to the nursery and looked through the window at Crystal. The pediatric nurse signaled for her to enter. June walked around to the door and entered the nursery. "What's going on?"

"I have word that you are going to be the foster mom to this girl."

"I'm trying. They have to approve it. She is a real cutie. It's not fair that she lost all of her family."

She looked at Crystal. "It's hard to think that someone this cute and young has no one to call mom or dad."

"She will. Go ahead and pick her up. She came through the wreck surprisingly well."

"She may be small, but she's tough. She just needs someone to teach her."

She held Crystal securely in both arms while looking where the nurse stood a minute ago. She realized she was alone for the time being and turned her attention back to Crystal. A few minutes later, she heard the nurse say, "Everything is approved. Crystal has a new mom."

She turned to the nurse. "Sandy got that approved already?"

"She got everything approved this morning before coming in here."

"That was fast."

"She's coming to see you today with some instructions."

"I'll get everything going after work. I have to go eat some lunch and get back to work." She laid Crystal back down and walked out of the nursery, saying, "Thanks for the heads-up."

Sandy walked into pediatrics as June was walking out. "Good to see you, June. Do you have a minute?"

"You'll have to join me for lunch. I have to get back to work in half an hour."

The two ladies walked down the hall as Sandy said, "I got the approval for you to be the foster mom of Crystal. That was the easy part. Do you have what you need to take care of a baby?"

"That won't be a problem. The crib and changing table are waiting in the playroom. I'll get some help and convert it over to a nursery. I still have two more rooms for other children."

"Good, I'm looking for more family now, but many of the family members died in a house fire. We have to look though before we can get adoption paperwork going."

"I understand. What makes you think adoption so quickly?"

"I've been looking for six months already. Crystal's mother was looking for someone to put as custodial parent in event of her death. I was trying to help."

"You'll let me know when I can move forward."

"Yes. You take good care of her."

June walked into maternity, followed closely by Fred.

"You're too good to me, Fred. You didn't have to buy this for Crystal."

"I know you wanted to take her home today if you could. It's the least I could do."

"I think they ran every possible test possible on her. She was buckled in right to receive no injury in the wreck."

"That's why we need to make sure she is buckled in right still. You need the right equipment to do that."

"Thanks to you, she's got all the goodies and new clothes to go home in."

"I try to bless others as I'm blessed. Hopefully you can give the kindness to someone else."

"I know just the person to give it to." She looked directly at Fred with a sparkle in her eye that seemed brighter than before.

June went directly to the nurses' station. "We have everything needed here. Is she authorized to go home?"

They pulled out the paperwork and said, "Waiting for your signature."

She signed as the nurse pointed to the lines and flipped the pages and pointed to another line. "Crystal is in my official care. Will you help me with her?"

"Any way I can. I don't know a whole lot, but I can learn."

"That's what I needed to hear. Let's get her in the car and get home."

It took a few minutes to get everything and everybody packed into the car, but they got on their way soon enough. "June, I haven't been to your home. You will have to guide me."

"It is easy. I want to go to your place first." She smiled from ear to ear and turned to Crystal, who was babbling something he couldn't clearly understand.

What trouble have I gotten myself into?

33 THE CHILDREN

Fred watched Crystal peacefully sleeping in her car seat. No need to disturb her. He had some research to do that was going to be time-consuming. If Crystal followed her usual pattern, in about fifteen minutes, she would need a diaper change and a bottle. That should be enough time to get his mind running and start him off for the day. With no more than Crystal's usual distractions, he would get at least one point researched of the entire sermon.

The last thing June had heard about Crystal's case was heartbreaking. Crystal's family was all dead and buried. She had been conceived in a violent assault. Her mother chose to carry the child, even though council told her abortion was an acceptable option in her case.

Looking at Crystal, he couldn't imagine desiring to kill this child before she had a chance to live. The past week with Crystal totally changed his life. He never thought he would have to learn how to work on a sermon while holding a baby. As far as that goes, he never imagined he would have a baby to care for without a wife.

That brought to mind June. What was she to him? Did he consider her his girlfriend? The answer inside his head and heart differed drastically. They were polar opposites. His mind screamed no! His heart pounded, continuing to say yes. From the reaction of the other church members, they wanted them to be together, but they didn't express their thoughts verbally to him.

The one place that he always turned to in similar situations was the heart God planted in him. It never steered him wrong before, but now God seemed silent, leaving his mixed up emotions to settle the matter.

He glanced down at Crystal and saw her eyes open, looking at him. He bent down to pick her up, blabbering in baby talk. "You don't know either. No, we're both confused."

He took his hand under her and lightly tickled her, causing her to kick. "Is it safe to ask you a question?"

Crystal cooed and laughed. "You think it's funny. What am I supposed to feel about June? What do you think? Am I that crazy?"

Is it that obvious, Fred? You're talking to a baby. What makes you think you are ready for this?

Fred kissed Crystal on the forehead. "Well then, let's see how much work we can do together, shall we? What do you think?"

He rested Crystal on his lap and started typing with his one free hand. The typing went slower, but he could get some done. The time ticked by, and Crystal cried out, letting him know she was hungry. Fred prepared the bottle, talking to her. The bottle in her mouth quieted her, and again she effectively stopped any progress from being made.

The time passed, and June walked in the house. Fred walked out of the kitchen. "Come join us in here. Crystal has a surprise for you."

"Fred, you watch the baby for a w—"

"I prepared dinner with a little helper."

June saw the dining room table set for two and two tall pillar candles in the middle of the table waiting to be lit and also smelled an aroma that she rarely smelled but loved. "What is this?"

Fred heard the car turn into the drive. "That should be your mom. She is watching Crystal while we have dinner. Are you all right with that?"

"Yes, you will tell me what this is all about?"

He walked to the door without answering her question. Crystal was in the car seat, and the diaper bag was already packed. "Thank you for coming. Everything is in the kitchen, waiting. Crystal just ate, so she'll be good to go—for a while anyway."

"I'll take care of Crystal. You take care of June."

Fred saw the look that he thought every mother had. The look warned silently of permanent injury or, worse, if the words are disregarded.

"Yes, ma'am, I will."

Fred carried the baby out to the car and buckled her in. As he turned to go back in, he heard, "Don't keep her up too late."

Fred and June watched the car back out of the drive and go down the road. "June, will you join me in the kitchen?"

"Why did you call my mother?"

"I wanted sometime with you alone. Dinner is in the oven. Shall we start with dinner?"

"Sure, what more of a surprise could there be?"

"I wasn't sure I could surprise you. I hope you like it."

"Apparently, you have it in you to surprise me."

"I hope it is as good as your mom's. Lemon peppered chicken in a bed of mixed vegetables and cream of mushroom soup rice."

"It smells delicious. What am I to expect next, a ring?"

"I didn't think you were ready for a ring yet. Crystal distracted me all day, so I couldn't think clearly."

"Crystal was the distraction? We may not have known each other long, but I know there is more to this than the distractions of a baby."

He scooped the food on the plate and served June. "Your mom said white wine was best, but all I could afford was sparkling cider."

As he poured the cider, she tried the food. Her facial expression melted, followed by her body. "Did you actually cook this?"

"Yes, I followed your mother's recipe. Is it good?"

"It is delicious."

"Good. I have a question for you. Are you ready?"

"Yes."

"I was trying to work on my sermon and found my mind wondering back to how I feel about you." He saw the smile shine on her face. "I came to a conclusion. I want to be your steady boyfriend."

The smile he saw beamed on her face. She offered him her hand. He took it while looking into her eyes. "Fred, I want nothing more, yes."

Fred got up and scooted his plate so he could sit by her side. "My lady, your dinner is getting cold."

He saw the tear drop from her eye. She looked up for one second, and he knew what she was doing. With each bite, her eyes would close in delight.

The dinner plates emptied when Fred said, "Save room for desert. I made this." He went to the refrigerator and pulled out a fresh strawberry shortcake and a tub of whipped cream.

"I'll take the ring now."

Fred looked at her. "Are you sure you don't want to counsel with your pastor first?" He put the desert down on the table. She stood and took him in her arms. "You're too good to me."

He returned the hug and kissed her on the cheek. "I can't be too good to you. You are better to me."

Bill and Rebeca parked the car in the parking lot for the gym. Bill said, "We are early. As long as Samuel is sleeping, what do you say we sit here and talk?"

"What about?"

"I need your advice on protecting Samuel from Gary. I worry every time he is being watched by Saundra's parents."

"I understand that. Has anyone seen Gary recently?"

"No, but Moloch has not given up. Gary is around somewhere. What can I do to keep him safe?"

"Maybe we need to be the supervising protection. If one of us is with him all the time, at least, there will be a fight."

"How do I tell Henry and Mary what is going on?"

"Bill, you will have to sit with them and explain the danger. Certainly they will understand that."

"I hope so. Thank you. We need to get into the gym. Harry will be here soon for practice."

Bill unbelted himself and Samuel and carried him into the gym. He took Samuel to the day care room and went into the locker room to change. A few minutes later, he walked out ready to start. Rebeca walked out of the ladies' locker room shortly after him, saying, "You look good in that."

"You look great in yours. I think I fell in love with you a long time ago and just didn't say it."

"I was hoping so. I fell in love with you too."

Bill took her hands. "I love you."

"I love you too, Bill."

Harry walked up beside them and said, "Is this the place for lovebirds or practice?"

Bill responded, "Both. Right now were practicing saying 'I love you.'"

"You two do that really good."

Rebeca said, "I like the way his eyes twinkle when he says that."

"I'll be over there stretching. When you're ready to teach me something, come join me."

They watched Harry walk off to the benches to stretch. Bill said, "Shall we join him and continue this later?"

"Yes. I don't have anything going tonight after practice. A date?"

"A date."

They walked over and joined Harry. Rebeca said, "Okay, men, it's time to make those muscles do something."

Harry said, "Who started this?"

Bill said, "Gary."

Rebeca said, "The spirit behind him, and we need to be ready for him on a second's notice."

They all stepped in to the open space. They drilled kicks and punches, attacking the air. "Okay, guys, I'm going to stand in the middle and show you how to spar against two. You two will try to score on me. Ready?"

Bill snapped into a fighting stance. Harry snapped into the stance right behind him. Rebeca stood ready. "Anytime you boys are ready."

The sparring practice continued for a few minutes. After that round was over, Rebeca said, "Did you notice that you had to look for the opening and take it quickly?"

"That's what we'll have to do with Gary," Harry said.

Bill was breathing hard. "You do understand, Harry, that if Gary is going to fall, it will be by finding the one weakness he's got and hurting him. It's your life if you don't."

Rebeca said, "He's right. You are doing well. You will be a great asset to the team."

"Hey, Rebeca," a voice from the side of the room said.

"Hey, what are you up too?"

"Finding out that you're getting extra practice. Do you mind if I join you?"

"No, if the guys don't mind."

"Bill, Harry, this is Eva. She is one of the black belts in my class. Harry, she can be your sparring partner. She is used to sparring as a teaching method…and she's good at it."

"I hope. I have a long way to go. Nice to meet you, Eva."

Bill noticed Eva's tall and very attractive figure. Her long blond hair and blue eyes accentuated her beauty. "Yes, Eva, really nice to have you join in."

Rebeca and Eva stood side by side, facing the men. Rebeca said, "Ready? Fight!"

The time came to stop practice. Rebeca said, "Hit the showers. I will see you afterward," and blew Bill a kiss.

Eva said, "Harry, will you wait for me?"

"Sure."

34 SAMUEL

Nassor sat in a chair, looking at the rest of the demons. "What happened in heaven?"

"Master, Boris led the charge but never fought. It was an exact duplicate of the match you had with Ailith."

"Ailith didn't take over for him?"

"Ailith waited at the back, Master."

"Boris is being trained and is doing well from what I hear."

"Master, what do we do?"

"Change the target. We have to get Samuel. The hardest part is getting Gary out there without him being seen. We know where his grandparents are. Samuel is with them during the day. Maybe we need to try to take him from them instead."

"We need to talk to Gary, Master."

"I need to talk to Gary. Send him to the office."

"Yes, Master."

Moments later, Gary entered the upper room that was being used as the office. There was no furniture or pictures on the wall. There stood a figure that looked like a knight in armor with a sword clad to his side. His broad wings spread out to full extension, holding his feet off the ground. "Yes, Master. You summoned."

"We need Samuel. You know where he is during the day. Is there a way you can get to him when he is with Grandma and Grandpa?"

"Master, they live on the edge of town. That means their yard will be bordered by the woods. I can get anywhere as long as I have a way to get to wooded land quickly."

"That sounds good. When can we start going after Samuel?"

"Tomorrow. I look forward to getting back at Bill and the rest of the gang, Master."

"Good, you will have all the demonic support you will ever want."

"Thank you, Master."

Bill sat with Henry and Mary in the living room. "What is it you need to talk about?"

"Henry, you and Mary have done great taking care of Samuel for me while I worked. I want you to know how much I appreciate you both. I have a problem that I'll need your help with."

"Problem?"

"Yes, Gary wants to take Samuel from me. He's made threats, and even the law has become involved. Rebeca and I agree that we need to have people who know Gary and how he thinks to be on guard to protect Samuel. Henry, you know his strength. He's been working out more lately. I'm not sure you would be able to handle him if he showed up here."

"How bad is he that I couldn't handle him?"

"He is qualified for MMA fighting. He doesn't use just his hands. He is young and fast. His hands are like yours twenty years ago. Even if you could stand against him for a while, I don't think Mary could."

"What are you going to do?"

"We are going to split up watching him. Rebeca and Eve are free during the day and know how to handle Gary. When they have to work, Harry and I will take over. When none of us have to work, then all four of us will watch him. You will still be able to see him but with us around. I hope you both understand."

"What I don't understand is why you think we can't protect him. I can get a gun. I've never seen a man survive getting shot in the head."

"I understand, but there is no reason to put you and Mary in danger. When Gary is in jail, we will all be able to rest easier. Gary will stop at nothing to get him. And I do mean nothing."

"You know we still want to see him."

"I fully understand that, and I want you to. I also don't want you killed and Samuel missing when I come to pick him up, so please just go along with me on this, okay?"

"Bill, it's your decision. I pray you don't leave us out of his life."

"Henry, you and Mary are the best part of his life, and I want to make sure it stays that way. I can't do this without your understanding. I'll make sure you always know where he is. You can come and help watch him anytime. I didn't want to do this, but I feel it's absolutely necessary."

Bill hugged Mary. "I love you so much and hope you understand."

"I do. I'll come over every day to give my grandson a big hug and sing a song to him."

"You are welcome anytime."

Bill turned to Henry. "I look forward to seeing you. Your prayers are deeply appreciated."

"Take care of your son. I enjoy spoiling him rotten and bringing him back to you." Henry grinned.

"I will. I will."

Bill handed the slip of paper with the address to Henry and left. He then walked in his house to see Rebeca and Samuel playing on the floor. "Hello, beautiful. How's my boy?"

"Hi, handsome. Your boy is rambunctious and wide awake. I will have to charge you double to babysit."

"Mary will come over to help. Can you handle that?"

"That would be great. I know she loves both of you and just wants to protect you."

"I love you, Rebeca."

"I love you too."

Rebeca got up, leaving Samuel to play with the toys, and wrapped her arms around him. He returned her hug and kissed her. She willingly returned his kiss and never wanted to be apart again.

They held each other as they sat and watched Samuel play with a plastic set of keys. "What are you thinking, Bill?"

"We have a lot of work ahead of us. This is the start of a major challenge."

"I know. I know."

Nassor sat in front of the three demons. He grinned a devilish smile. "Now we win. Moloch, acting through Gary, is going to get Samuel. You have a very important job to do. Make sure he is not seen. We can't afford foul-ups on this. There will be two guardian angels ready for a fight. You have to take them."

The three demons looked at each other. "Master, Samuel will return with Gary unseen by human eyes," the tallest of them all said.

"Baghatur, that is a big commitment. You are expected to live up to it."

"Master, Gary will make it easy. He follows instructions, and I blind the eyes of man. When do we leave?"

"As soon as Gary is ready to go, make the humans pay for their actions."

"Yes, Master," they all said in unison.

Gary walked through the woods hidden from sight, reviewing the plan a thousand times. His training made the steps almost completely silent. He knew Samuel would be coming home with him. The death of Henry and Mary would be unavoidable. Through the woods, it would be easy to be unseen. In the house, he had to be quick. The camouflage would stand out.

He knew the woods well enough to make that where he would hide. Now it was time to go. His pants, shirt, boots, and hat would hide him in the woods. The face paint finished the look well. Not even a hunter would see him. The dogs would smell the deer scent, sending them after every deer in the woods.

He walked out the back door of 6757 Power Lane and vanished into the tree line. *Keep calm. The wrong move too soon and you won't watch the outside of the tree line for police.*

Quietly, he walked along, laying out every detail of the plan in his mind again. He stayed deep enough in the woods that the movement wouldn't be detected from the edge. Keeping focused on the plan, he maneuvered himself to the one place he could be unseen but yet see the neighborhood clearly.

The houses sat quietly, too quietly for his liking. He waited for signs of life, and only one house had any. He didn't feel the tingle of Samuel but knew he had to be there. The lights lit the windows in the back door. His safety sat in the woods, so he stayed and watched.

The old woman looked out the door in his direction but made no indication of seeing him. *The time is now. Make your move while you can.*

Gary walked to the edge of the woods, looked both ways for any other signs of life, and saw none. He sprinted across the open space, slamming hard through the back door. He heard the scream of the old woman and caught it short yanking hard on her neck. It snapped easily, and she fell limp as he laid her body down. One down. One more to kill and then the steal.

"Mary?" His ears perked up. The old man was going to be coming in soon. He picked up the phone in the kitchen, covered the mouthpiece, and waited for him to call. "Mary, what is wrong?"

He heard the footsteps coming his way. The three tones from the phone said it all. As the old man cleared the doorway into the kitchen, Gary jumped out, grabbing his mouth and throwing the phone down across the kitchen floor. He spun him around, caught his chin and shoulder, and twisted. The old man slumped into Gary's arms. He laid him beside his wife.

The baby was probably upstairs, he thought. He ran up the stairs and searched the rooms, but to no avail. He ran back down and found no sign of the baby in the house. He tried to feel the tingle, but it never came. He ran out the back door and into the woods. He quickly climbed a tree and hid, waiting for signs of where the baby was.

An hour later passed by, and no one came for a baby. Crime scene was all over the place, and the police tracked the only sign they had that he existed. He watched the policeman stand under him and had to resist jumping down and killing him. He wasn't far enough in the woods to risk it.

Three hours later, Bill showed up on the scene. He talked to the police and left with tears coming from his eyes. *He is weak. He will fall easily now that his spirit is broken.*

It was another two hours before he could get down and return to the house. *This would not go well at all. What can you say to Nassor that would remotely explain this failure? The only advantage is no one saw me that would talk anyway.*

All the way back, three questions repeated itself through his mind: *If not here, where is Samuel? Who is watching him? How do I get to him?*

Samuel vanished into thin air, and, somehow, finding him was now the number one priority. He didn't know Nassor very well but he knew he would be very angry.

Bill no more than walked in the house with the police officer, and he knew who it was on the floor. He said to know one in particular. "Gary is after Samuel and will kill to get him."

"Gary is the one that is already wanted?"

"One and the same. Samuel is my three-month-old son. I need to call his babysitter and let her know what is going on."

"What makes you think it was Gary?"

"They both died instantly of a broken neck. It was a trained hand that killed them. Gary is definitely trained and has made threats. There is no question that it was him."

Bill saw the shock on the police officer's face. "Gary is qualified for MMA tournament fighting. He was training to get into the circuit. His training equals a special ops soldier in the military."

"Bill, will you come in to fill out a report?"

Bill pulled out his laptop and a flash drive. As the computer poured up, Bill said, "This file will be more than I could tell you. I have done many hours of research on him. If I give you the file, can I go protect my son?"

"Sure."

He pulled his phone from his belt and dialed the number by memory. It rang twice. "Hello."

"Rebeca, Mary and Henry are both dead. I have reason to believe that Gary is after Samuel. Is someone else with you?"

"Yes, Eva came over. Are you sure it was Gary?"

"Both died instantly of a broken neck, and they were laid side by side on the floor. The rest of the house was quickly rifled through. The back door was shattered as if a heavy body slammed through it. Do you have any other questions?"

"Bill, we will take care of Samuel. Do you know where Gary is?"

"Not yet. Mary had the address where you are. If he found it, he will be there soon."

"I will call Harry now. Hurry and get here. We will have to hold our own until you arrive."

"I love you." He hung up the phone and turned to the policeman. "Can you send a police cruiser to this address? This will be his next destination."

He heard the officer radio in the information. The radio chirped several times, and he received confirmation that they would have support and fast.

The officer scanned the information in the file. "Bill, how accurate is this information?"

"I confirmed it all. At the end of the file is the list of web pages and resources where the information came from. I have somewhere to go now. If you need more information, call me." He handed the officer his card and gathered his computer. The flash drive was laid on the table with a copy of the file contained within it.

Nassor sat in front of Gary, Baghatur, and company. "Where is Samuel?"

Gary said, "Master, Bill changed babysitters sometime. We need to find who is taking care of him now."

"Who saw you, Gary?"

"Master, no one that is able to talk."

"What do you mean that is able to talk?"

"Master, I had to kill Mary and Henry. No one else saw me."

"I should be happy, but I'm afraid. Two dead, that may be traced to your hands. You can't go back out until we have confirmed specific information as to the whereabouts of Samuel."

"Master, I can track him."

"You are compromised. You will stay here, and Baghatur will go out and find him. You will go out on specific missions and no more. We need you free."

"Yes, Master."

35 THE HUNT

Baghatur flew around, looking for any sign of Samuel. It was guessed there would be guardian angels around the boy, but there were also more adults watching him closely. Closest link he had was the scorpion. Tracking it seemed to be impossible. *Where is the scorpion? How would they get him out of the area without Bill going with him?*

He decided to change what he looked for guardian angels in groups. Jesus seemed to have special angels set aside for baby. Find them and you have a point to confirm. The search quickly identified Sakata hovering with two more guardian angels close by—another interesting point to note. He saw Randolph and an unknown angel hovering over 5757 Power Lane. He heard a voice behind him, "You better think twice."

He quickly turned to see Boris's sword drawn. "Boris? What are you doing?"

"Stopping you from getting to the servant of the Most High."

"What happened to waiting and using your sword as a shield?"

"That only works in certain situations. I'm in a situation in which I have to be battling defender. No, I didn't forget how to use my sword as an offensive weapon."

"I don't doubt it." He retreated back to Nassor.

Baghatur bowed to Nassor. "Master, I have news."

"Report."

"Master, there are two babies. One is located on a ranch one mile from here on a farm. The other is located on 5757 Power Lane. I went to investigate further and was immediately approached by Boris."

"That is interesting. Did he just want to banter with words?"

"Master, he all but attacked and would have if I got anywhere near the house. This baby is somehow linked to Fred. Randolph was near the baby's guardian angel."

"Even more interesting; what will it take to get to Samuel?"

"An army. There were four guardian angels besides the babies. I didn't approach for further details because I didn't feel confident against five guardian angels with swords drawn."

"Leave Gary tucked tight in our protection. Maybe a few demon attacks will break the shield. We have found a way to track him but not to get to him yet."

"Yes, Master."

Gary raised his fists and slammed them down on the concrete wall. *Where? Where? How? Bill, when I see you, I'll show you what these fists can really do.*

His anger boiled inside. He was marked for two more felonies, and that made him less likely to get out of the house. "Samuel is still missing, and you, Bill, are in the way again."

Gary calmed down a little. He ate the lunch put before him. Still, curiosity wanted to take over and go out and investigate for himself.

What was Nassor really capable of doing to punish a human? He didn't have an answer to that and was sure he didn't want to find out. The thirst for blood was set in stone, and Bill's blood or anyone of the prayer squad would do. He needed it to pour out to Nassor for a sacrifice and a good laugh.

The best he could do was to be ready when the time came and stay low until he was needed. He could live with that. He could be patient. It just made the kill that much more pleasurable. The sweetness when he talked to the person before he pulled out their brains with his bare hands.

Fred sat with June watching Crystal play. "What does the Child Protection Agency have planned for Crystal?"

"They are still searching for possible family, but the paperwork is in. She doubts there is family alive and out of prison."

"In your situation, you know what you want, but is it what God wants? The real question is what does God have planned for Crystal?

Enjoy every minute of your time with her, and I will be here for you if it doesn't work out as you planned."

"Thank you." She snuggled up close and kissed him on the cheek. He didn't know what to think or do. He turned to face her and took her hands in his. He searched her eyes for the stars that glowed bright and found them in abundance. He slowly lowered in and gave her a kiss on the cheek.

For several more minutes, he stared into her eyes. *Do I dare kiss her on the lips?* He took the chance and reached in and kissed her on the lips and felt her return the kiss willingly.

"I love you, June."

"I love you too, Fred."

Nassor called Forras and Kasadya in front of him again. "Did you two kill everyone in the van?"

"Master, to the best of our knowledge, we did."

"Then why am I getting reports about an infant?"

The two looked at each other and then back to Nassor. "Master, what infant?"

"You really know nothing of an infant?"

"No, Master, nothing."

"Then why are you sweating? My next-in-command will inform you of the report to see if that jogs any memories."

The second-in-command started to say, "The van accident happened as reported. The mother and teenage daughter died as reported. The discrepancy comes in about the infant in the backseat. It not only lived, but according to sources in the state's office, it is currently in the care of Fred and June. June is new to the church."

Nassor asked again, "Ring any bells, or do I have to?"

"Master, exactly as you asked. We went out, found someone to kill, and killed them."

"Yes, you did. It is the not informing me of the baby that I disapprove of. I could have gotten someone to finish the baby. Now I'm trying to find a way to keep the baby from becoming my enemy. It's not bad enough to have Samuel to get. We have to get another infant from the enemy. Are you responsible for this?"

"Master, attack Fred and June, and we have freedom to kill the baby."

"Yes, and we have attacked them repeatedly and failed. Rather than fail again, I say you find a weakness in them and make sure you exploit it to get rid of the kid."

"Yes, Master."

Nassor looked to his second-in-command, "Finley, you can start looking for the weakness in Bill, Rebeca, and anyone else to exploit for Samuel."

"Yes, Master."

"Baghatur, find a way to implement the plan to start the takeover of 5757 Power Lane. Let's see if there is a way to get that cross off the roof. Also, find the logs that weren't destroyed. I've felt them for the last two weeks."

"Yes, Master."

Nassor sat on the floor and felt the call. The logs called, Trainer called, and most importantly, Satan was calling for a report. There was little good to report, and he certainly didn't want to report his own failure against Ailith. He couldn't avoid the report for much longer. At least, with this plan, he had something. He flew out toward Satan's chambers. He checked his neck. The wound healed up, mostly. He hoped he didn't have to make any further report beyond the plans.

"Nassor, give me my report."

"Master, I have sent Finley and Baghatur to seek out the weaknesses of everyone connected to the babies, to exploit, so we can accomplish the mission. As well, we are trying to take back 5757 Power Lane and freeze the church from anything and everything."

"The end results sound good. What are the plans beyond exploiting the weaknesses?"

"The teams are out gathering information as we speak, Master."

"You have been there two weeks and have gotten nothing done? Where is Samuel?"

"Master, Samuel has been located, and we're looking for the weakness to take him without much fight."

"Are you going to tell me about June, Crystal, Eva, and all the other new members of the church?"

"Master, June I just heard about myself. The others you mentioned, I have no information on. June is the newest member I know of and is dating Fred."

"Does Fred have a weakness after all? How interesting…"

"Master, the weakness he has is strengthened by June's strength. The information will reveal the crack for us to exploit."

"Crystal is the other baby you were so worried about, the baby in the van. The demons you sent out killed all but the one that will become an enemy like Fred. Do we need another Fred to fight?"

"Master, we are looking for a weakness to destroy her. The death of Fred and June will do it."

"They may be necessary for you to avoid being replaced there and here. You of all demons know my hatred for failure. Ailith is a lot to handle. He is full of tricks, don't you think?"

"Master, no demon wins every fight. I'll get him when he is not ready."

"When is he not ready?"

"He let me go. That was a mistake. Ailith will pay for what he did."

"Nassor, the clock is ticking. Your mission is clear. Make it happen and have something positive in the next report, understood?"

"Yes, Master. Live on high."

Forras led Kasadya to the house and found the three guardian angels sitting on the roof. They held their distance and lowered themselves to the ground. They looked into the house and saw Fred and June kissing each other. The young baby sat on the floor playing with toys sprawled on the floor in front of her.

Fred felt tension. Not from June but from a source outside himself. An urge warned him of an unknown danger. The concern must have shown on his face, as it was quickly reflected on June's. She asked, "What's wrong?"

"I don't know. I just feel something…" Before any more could be said, he smiled at Crystal and placed her on his lap with a toy that had her current interest. "Is there someone I can call?"

"No." He reached down and picked up his phone. Two numbers and the Talk button hit and he heard the phone ring twice. "Hello."

"Harry, something's going on, and I can't place my finger on it. With all that has gone on recently, we need to get praying. I know Satan is not giving up this easy. I can feel danger, and it's close."

"I don't either. I'll start the chain moving. Do you want to meet somewhere?"

"I'm at the house now with June."

"I'm on my way. I'll bring Eva with me. Talk more later."

Harry punched two numbers and then the Talk button on his phone as he said, "I'm going to the church if you want to join me."

He spoke into the phone. "John, emergency prayer meeting at the church. No details."

"Done gone."

"Call Peter, I'll call Bill."

"Okay."

He punched the speed dial number for Bill and waited for an answer. "Hello."

"Bill, Harry. Emergency prayer meeting at the church."

"On my way with Rebeca."

John looked at Samantha and punched the speed dial number for Peter. He answered on the first ring. "Hello."

"Peter, emergency prayer meeting at the church."

"On my way."

Peter looked to Patty. "Emergency prayer meeting at the church. Are you ready to go?"

"You're not leaving me here. I'll drive while you pray."

Fred looked at June. "Half the church is about to break through the door. I hope you don't mind if we pray before they arrive."

"No, I don't. Does it typically happen this fast?"

"Emergency prayer meeting and location is all is said on the phone. Word moves to the rest of the group fast."

She looked again into Fred's eyes. "What do you feel? There is fear in your eyes."

"Fear…you see it because I don't know anything other than I sense danger. Crystal may be involved now in the attacks that have happened to me."

"No! That isn't fair."

The door opened, and Harry and Eva entered the house. "What's going on?"

"I'm afraid for Crystal." As he spoke, he hugged the baby on his lap.

"Let's start praying. The others can join in when they get here." Fred sat and prayed silently as Harry started out loud. The door opened and closed again, and who came in was not known. Whoever it was automatically joined the prayer laying hands on Fred. More wasn't heard, but fifteen minutes later, the group agreed with an amen and opened their eyes.

Harry said, "I do look forward to the baby explanation. The pretty lady with me is Eva, and I'm Harry. Fred, your explanation will be more interesting. I think you should start."

Fred said, "I met June while going to the cafeteria at the hospital. Most of you recall that I was sent there by you guys. It was a week later that we went on our first date. On that date, we drove up on a car wreck where two ladies died, but the baby was in the back in her car seat and lived through the wreck. June is approved as a foster parent, so she is now the foster mom, and I'm dating June exclusively."

Harry said, "I almost have the same story. I went to practice with Bill and Rebeca at the gym. Eva came up and joined us. The last three days have been predictable."

Peter said, "I don't know what is going on here. Why are you the only one to get a baby with the girl?"

"Peter, the baby is fun to have at times. There are many more times when work fails to get done due to this little bundle of joy. Be careful what you ask for. We know how to arrange a baby for you."

Forras and Kasadya watched, looking for the weakness. They saw the fear but soon realized that within a few minutes, the wall of guardian angels grew thick. As a group, their strength grew, leaving no weakness. Forras said, "We are leaving now. We'll do no harm to anyone."

Boris stood firm beside Cenewig. "Remember well what you face when you go against them. This will be typical."

Forras flew away with Kasadya close on his tail. "Did you see any weakness?"

"No, Forras. In fact, all I saw was an army quickly develop before my eyes."

"One that meant business. I didn't feel like testing them today."

"Me neither. Nassor will need to know about this."

Forras and Kasadya fell to their faces in front of Nassor. "Master, we have a report."

"Report."

"Master, when we approached from a distance to find the weakness, the guardian angels watched closely."

"And you expected differently?"

"Master, that we expected. Fred felt the tension of the angels and called over friends. In just a few short minutes, there were fourteen angels between us and them. Crystal was in the middle of the group of adults with Samuel close by."

"Really? Samuel and Crystal together? Did you happen to look for any heavenly support for the guardian angels?"

"The two of us had our hands full with getting out of there with all our parts, and that was without a fight."

"There is good news in this report. What I want to look for without ruffling the feathers of the guardian angels is a way to get in past the angelic line. I think a plan is forming."

"Yes, Master."

36 The Information

Finley flew out and stayed out of sight of the three guardian angels on the roof. His plan was to watch for a day and see where Samuel went and who was watching him. In the first few hours, he spent his time at the church in an emergency prayer meeting protected by fourteen guardian angels and heightened the alert that something was going on.

Even after the prayer ended, they all sat there and talked. The only advantage to that was the knowledge of how much protection they had when together.

The more he watched, the more frustrated he got. The two babies sat in the middle of the adults, playing. Finley watched them with a hunger, but when he looked through the path he had to take, there stood the guardian angels looking back. Any sign he was there and he would have a war on his hands. *What will it take to get to the kids and adults?*

The thought flooded his mind. First, get the guardian angels alone and then hit them with ten to twenty demons to each one guardian angel. Any demon getting through starts working on them, while the others keep the angels fighting. Could they really be strong enough to take on ten, twenty demons?

He knew he stood no chance right now, so he settled on watching. Getting the timing right to start the attack was more important right now. He wanted to be ready with a plan and way to implement the plan when the time came. He didn't have to hear what was said to know it wouldn't be good for him. He watched Samuel and June eating supper before he realized that time on earth didn't wait. It kept ticking by steadily. As well, the group hadn't separated.

Finley looked at Bill's guardian angel. He looked strong and powered by their time of prayer. Bill and Rebeca packed up Samuel and headed to the car. Excitement perked up in him. He felt that he might get a small part of the normal routine. He watched them and kept an eye on the guardian angels to make sure they sensed nothing of his presence.

They got to the road where he should have turned right, but he continued on straight. Now Finley didn't know what they were doing, but he wanted to learn. He watched and followed impatiently, wanting to strike. The car stopped in front of a different house. Rachel got out, leaned into the car, and said something before going on in. He mentally noted the address and followed as Bill drove on alone with Samuel. The heightened alert showed as the guardian angels separated.

Finally, Bill pulled into the driveway of his own house. He took Samuel in, threw the diaper bag on the couch, and, holding him to his chest gently sat down in the recliner, rocked the chair back and forth. When the chair stopped moving, he pulled the handle on the side. The foot rest flipped up, and the back dropped. A minute later, Bill and Samuel were asleep.

Finley looked in from a far distance and watched them sleep. He knew more, and it was time to report the information to Nassor.

Baghatur stayed off in the tree line, watching the angels. The fact that Forras and company sent them all together encouraged him. The plan formulated almost immediately. He looked up to the heavens for confirmation. He confirmed what he needed to confirm.

He saw Ailith flying above with his hand locked on his sword. He would get the point of a sword quick if he pushed anything right now. He wasn't there to push, and without any intention, he knew Ailith would keep himself in clear sight.

What he realized kept him back. *What is making the angels so unbeatable?* He doubted that it was the guardians themselves but the heavenly host support on a call. *Could they take the same pressure without that support? Would that increase our chances?*

He smiled as he watched the angels. He knew they had no idea what was going on, and that was the way he wanted it. It was time to go see Nassor. The takeover of the house was going to happen shortly, and he would see it with his own eyes.

He flew off to Nassor's. "Master"—he fell to his knees—"the plan to take 5757 Power Lane is simple."

"Simple? What is simple about it?"

"Master, we are always fighting the heavenly host, which outnumbers us, and losing."

"Yes?"

"Master, what if God agreed to not send the heavenly host if the angels are attacked? Could the twenty-four to twenty-six total angels hold us off then?"

"Get their help cut off, and they fall."

"Yes, Master. When they fall, we can go in and kill off the prayer squad and do whatever we want with the babies. Imagine Satan using Samuel and Crystal."

"I can imagine them in our total control. We could implement the plan to take the heavens and earth in just one hundred years."

"Master, the church crumbles at your feet. Satan would honor you with his highest honor."

"Yes..." Nassor let his imagination run away with the thought.

"Master, only Satan himself can approach God for this permission. Only you can approach Satan directly in this situation."

"Yes, it is time to change the odds by outnumbering the angels. This plan will work."

"Master, I'll go and gather more details so the proper plan of attack can be made for when you return."

"Get with Finley. Make the plan so that we can get Samuel at the same time."

"Yes, Master."

Boris looked at Ailith. "How do we pull this off without your help?"

"Boris, you will be provided with what you need by the prayers of the church. Anything else you need, you already have in you."

"The guardian angels will give their very lives if they have to."

"That is what Satan will count on. Right now, we can interfere with anything they try, and what I see looks like trouble. Want to join me?"

"Gladly. Let's see what those demons are made of."

Boris led the way to Finley and Baghatur. "Finley, that's close enough."

Boris watched both demons spin around, startled. "What are you going to do? Call the heavenly host down to stop us."

"Angels, battle stance!"

One third of the heavenly host flew out of the heavens, swords drawn. "I can call on another third right now if you want to challenge me. We can attack you where you stand. We haven't because it wasn't a necessity."

Finley said, "No need. We surrender."

"Back away now! Go home and stay home. Know this—the church is defended by the entire heavenly host."

Boris watched as Finley and Baghatur retreated to the house. "Angels, sheath your swords. Return!"

Ailith said, "Those two will think twice before coming back out."

"I will not give them an advantage until told otherwise by God. They will find me a warrior difficult to measure up to."

"With the heavenly host on your side, anyone will find you a difficult target. Are you ready to do the same thing with just the guardian angels?"

"I will give my life proving it. God is Sovereign, just, and in control. His plans will stand no matter who stands in their way."

Ailith heard his confidence and boldness and said, "It will take that from all of you. Lead them the way you led this charge, and you will stand victorious."

"Are you with me in spirit? I know the time will come that you can't come in person, but I'll need all the confidence you can offer now."

"Boris, Jesus told his children he will never leave them. I give you everything you want plus more. Stand strong and bold. Remember you're Lord, and you are more than enough to hold a line against one thousand demons."

"Thank you."

Jesus looked down on the conversation. "Father, the leader is ready, the servants are ready, and the heavenly host will be ready for your call."

"Son, the time has come. Nassor is on his way to talk to Satan. It will be a test for all involved. The war for heaven is still being fought, just on a different front."

Nassor fell to his knees before Satan. "Master, a plan has been formulated. Many of our defeats have come because we are outnumbered by the heavenly host. We need you to get God to hold back the heavenly host support. We will attack on a twenty-to-one ratio. When the angels fall, the prayer squad first, then the children, then the church will crumble at your feet. You will have the heavens in your reign in a short period of earthly time."

"You have confidence in this plan?"

"Master, I have seen it many times. Just before we can break the guardian's line, the heavenly host scatters us. Without the heavenly host, we can break them and get to the mission at hand."

"Nassor, I will talk to God. When I tell you the support is stopped, you will have to hit hard. No matter what I say, God will still control the time. When I control the heavens, then I can crush without prejudice all my enemies."

"Master, that day will be soon. You will possess and control every man alive. Jesus's power from the cross will be crushed."

"That is what I like to hear. Show me the angels' wings so I can cast them into the fires of hell and watch them burn."

"Yes, Master. Your will be done."

"Father, your saints pray. The prayer warriors are ready to act in prayer support again. All they need is the call of the spirit."

"We wait."

Jesus said, "What is your business, Satan?"

"Your prayer squad is mighty strong."

"Yes, they are."

"Every time they get in a pinch, your heavenly host makes them stronger."

"Yes, I promised to be there for them."

"If you take the heavenly host support away, they will fall away from you and die."

"Lucifer, you misjudge them as you did Job."

"Then take away the support. Prove to me they will stand in obedience no matter what happens."

"You are aware that your support for your demons is cut off as well."

"My demons do not need support if you don't give your angels heavenly support."

"Satan, you have your request. I will stop the heavenly support. You will stop the demonic support. With this one limitation, your demons may not take a single life from the church."

"Agreed, Jesus. When will the heavenly support be cut off?"

"Immediately. Go do what you must."

Jesus watched Satan leave. "Ailith, Boris, Cenewig, I need to talk to you."

They entered, saying, "Yes, Lord. What is your bidding?"

"Boris, Cenewig, you are to fly down to lead the guardian angels. Ailith, your heavenly host may not help the guardian angels in any way until I say so."

They all three said, "Yes, Lord."

Ailith turned to Boris. "You know what to do."

Boris remained silent, but his eyes spoke volumes to Ailith.

Satan went directly to 5757 Power Lane. "Nassor, we need to have a meeting."

"Master"—he bowed to his knees—"what can I do for you?"

"The guardian angels have no heavenly support. You can attack at will. Bring down that church hard, fast, and furiously."

"Yes master, the plan is ready to be executed. I will prepare the demons for an immediate attack."

"I look forward to hearing from you when the church has fallen."

"I will deliver the message myself! Victory is yours, Master."

"Go get it."

"Yes, Master."

Boris flew down followed by Cenewig. "Cenewig, you go to John. Einar is already with Harry, and Dustin is with Peter. We have no more support, so be ready to make things happen fast."

"Boris, how are you going to get the word out?"

"The demons will get them together. When that happens, we have to win the first battle. Then I can get the angels up to speed."

"You want that?"

"It is the most effective way. The guardian angels know what to do."

"I'm on my way. God be with you."

"Our God is sovereign. He reigns over all. Stand strong."

Boris watched Cenewig take off and take position. He flew down to Fred with a tear trickling down his cheek. Now waiting was all that remained to do.

Nassor stood in front of the horde at the house. "Listen, the angels have no heavenly host support. We have no support from hell. We outnumber the angels easily twenty to one. That does not include the three hundred imps."

He waited for response, but not a sound was uttered from anyone. "Here is the plan. Two imps go down to Fred and June. Do whatever you can to start the emergency prayer meeting. We want all the church together. Make sure all the people gather together. We will come in high and out of sight. When the last one enters the group, we'll become an attacking army that mutilates everything in our path."

The demons' hissing laughter rang throughout the room. Nassor continued when it quieted. "Is everyone's job clear? We don't have time for second guessing."

A chorus of "Yes, Master!" filled the room.

"Good." Then Nassor pointed to two imps and said, "Go get the ball rolling. Don't let me down."

"Yes, Master."

Jesus said, "Father, we promised no angelic support. Between us, we can sense exactly what the other is thinking."

"Son, the Holy Spirit is within each one of mine. The angels will know trouble at sight and will be able to communicate it with all the other angels in an instant."

Jesus nodded his head and watched as crystal-like dust sprinkled down on the guardian angels.

Ailith watched the plan formulate beside Jesus. "Lord, his heart already aches."

"That will be his drive to fight. He's experiencing a similar pain to what I experienced on the cross, knowing that pain will save the angels and the church. The ache you experienced was a little different. I went through both fears on the cross, but this is a good fear. Boris will be fine and ready when the time comes."

"Lord, could you tell me why they needed testing to this extreme?"

"Satan won't be vanquished from Samuel without this trial. I know you don't understand now, but you will soon enough."

"Yes, Lord. We wait for your command."

Nassor watched the two imps leave. "Horde, fly high, follow me, and don't be seen. Draw when I draw. Be ready, Satan is waiting for the message that we've taken the church. Let's go."

37 The Attack

The two imps looked at each other, the location of the target clearly written on each face. One held up four bony fingers, indicating the guardian angels at the location. The other held up a finger and a thumb close together. They both shook their heads, confirming the plan. The two imps flew in attack as they shrank in size to be no bigger than a bug.

They were through the roof without even alerting the angels. One immediately attacked Fred and the other June.

June sat with Fred on the chairs facing the stand serving as the pulpit. They watched silently as if they enjoyed a worship service. "Fred, what do you hear when you do this?"

"This is my time to have Jesus pastor me. This has been how I learned since the beginning of the prayer squad."

She sat silently, watching as his face turned down. He got up and began gathering the chairs to the center of the room. The formation quickly looked like the empty chair arrangement she saw the first time she walked in to the room. She recognized this setup as trouble too quickly. When it was set up, he held little Crystal on the chair in the center and started praying.

She joined in the prayer just as Fred stiffened up. His hands released Crystal. She immediately grabbed Crystal and then her phone. She dialed the number for Harry. It rang twice before he answered. "Hello."

"Emergency prayer meeting at the church. It's Fred."

"On our way. I'll make the contacts."

She stiffened up, not hearing a word he said.

Harry listened for the confirmation and never received it. He immediately took off for the car, grabbed his cell phone, and dialed Peter's number. After one ring, he answered, "Hello."

"Emergency prayer meeting at the church. Fred and June are under attack!"

"On my way."

The click confirmed the message got across. He immediately dialed Bill's number. He answered after three rings. "Hello."

"Emergency prayer meeting at the church. Fred and June are under attack!"

"I'm on my way."

God, keep them for two minutes.

He dialed Eva's number. She answered after one ring. "Hello."

"Eva, emergency prayer meeting at the church. Will you join us?"

"I'm one minute away. Do you know details?"

"Fred and June are under attack."

He heard her car start before the phone disconnected.

Peter took off, calling John. He answered in two rings. "Hello."

"Emergency prayer meeting at the church. Fred and June."

"On my way."

It took a second to free the line, and he dialed Patty's number. She answered after two rings. "Hello."

"Emergency prayer meeting at the church. Fred and June are in trouble."

"What about Crystal?"

"I don't know."

"On my way. I'm with my family. They'll be there too."

He heard the click of the phone.

God, keep them, please.

Patty yelled out, "Dad, Mom, let's load up! Emergency prayer meeting at the church. Fred, June, and Crystal are in trouble."

"Let's go," Gerald said. The family ran out the door with Patty dialing Richard's number. He answered after one ring. "Hello."

"Emergency prayer meeting at the church. Fred, June, and Crystal."

"On my way."

"Hurry."

"Say no more."

The click told her all she needed to know.

John dialed Samantha's number. After one ring, Douglas answered. "Hello."

"Douglas, emergency prayer meeting at the church. Fred and June are in trouble."

"We're all on our way."

"Come on, guys. Fred and June are in trouble. Let's go," John heard Douglas say. The phone line disconnected.

Who else can I call? God keep them.

Nassor waited high in the sky. The guardian angels seemed to come in mass to the church. Some cars had three or four guardian angels on top; most of the guardian angels already had swords drawn. Nassor watched Boris go through the roof.

Boris immediately saw the two imps and sliced them both in half. He shot back to the roof. "Angels, battle positions."

The angels immediately fell into ranks. As they drove in the driveway, the angels continued to fall into ranks. Boris immediately drew his sword and stepped into an offensive attack position. The other angels followed suit. Five minutes later, two more cars came down the road. Boris knew by the angels above the cars who the occupants were. They flew into their positions. Boris said, "Angels, prepare for the attack. Hold the line at all cost!"

The silence behind him told him what was happening.

Nassor looked with satisfaction. "Are we ready?"

The hiss sounded off. Nassor raised his sword without any fire. All the demons followed as if instructed. Nassor aimed his sword at the angels, lighting it up as he yelled, "Charge!"

All the demons repeated as the lines flew forward. Nassor gave one last command. "Tear apart that line."

Boris saw the attacking lines' flying horde. He knew they outnumbered him greatly. He wanted them to call on the heavenly host but knew they wouldn't and couldn't come. "We stand with God's glory and strength. Hold strong no matter what it looks like."

Still silence behind him.

Ailith saw the desire and drew his sword, searching through Jesus's face for a yes. All he saw was a tear. "Ailith, they stand on their own. Sheath your sword."

His sword slid into the sheath. "Lord?"

"No, Ailith. Boris has all the help he needs. He must use everything he has learned. You taught him well. The church is together and praying. The Father, the Spirit, and I already know the strength he has. Satan isn't ready yet."

"Yet, Lord?"

"There is much you are not to know. Watch and be ready. The time will come for you and your host to help the angels."

"Yes, Lord, your will be done."

Douglas ran into the house without knocking. Glenda, Samantha, and Chad ran in behind him. He first noticed both Fred and June lying perfectly still on the floor.

Glenda ran directly for Crystal. She took her in her arms away from the others. Douglas, Samantha, and Chad knelt beside Fred and June and started praying.

A voice from the hallway shouted, "They're awake!"

They knelt beside those already praying and joined in. The church joined together and sat them in the chairs placed in the center. The prayers continued. Douglas heard June praising the Lord and holding Fred.

Nassor's charging demons hissed in laughter. Nassor shot a fire arc at the angels. He watched as Boris easily defended it and sent back his light arc. "Layer wall. Fire."

The demons and angels alike stacked to make a high wall and shoot the arc from their swords. The fire arcs met the light arcs in an explosion that shook into the soul of the demons.

Nassor drew up but didn't back off. He was shocked by the power of their swords. More importantly, the demons couldn't take an assault of that nature for long.

"Boris, we are many more than you. Surrender, and we'll go easy on you."

"Nassor, do you really think that I'm going to surrender to you?"

"Angels, arcs away." Their light arcs flew to the demons.

Nassor countered. "Horde, shields." Their fire swords instantly took a defensive position. The light arcs smashed into the swords, extinguishing the flames. Nassor screamed, "Horde, attack!"

The horde collided hard into the angelic line. The swords clashed with fire and sparks. The light on the angel's swords diminished slightly, but all the demons drew back and up. "Where is your heavenly host support? How many guardian angels will give their lives today? Who do you leave unwatched for us to kill slowly. I promise you this. Once I find someone unguarded, they will not know anything but pain and suffering."

"The angels looked to Boris. Boris kept focused on Nassor. "When you find someone unguarded, you will have taken me out of the picture. There are four of us that can take the place of any one of these. We will not give up a soul without a bigger fight than you want to take on."

"We'll see who wants the fight." Nassor knew the demons had regrouped and taken the attack stance again. "Horde, attack!"

They hit the angelic wall, and the light blinded all those in the first wave. "Nassor, this battle is ours. Go home and regroup before we just take out all of your fighting forces."

"We *will* meet again. We *will* take you."

Nassor flew off with his horde following behind.

Boris watched with satisfaction and then turned to the angels. "Injury report."

No report was made. "As you saw, we have no heavenly host support. You will have to fight and with your last breath on occasion. God has given us the strength to hold on in this tough time. We will be greatly outnumbered, but God will be victorious. He is sovereign and in control of this situation."

Fred looked up at the rest of the church gathered around him. "Thank you…John, what is going on? Don't you think we need to know?"

"Fred, I told you I don't know any details. God's time hasn't come. The only thing I know now is that our faith will keep us. Not even God's prophets are privy to information not given them by God."

"Where are Crystal and Samuel?"

"Better protected than us. God has a plan for those two that is bigger than we could ever imagine."

"John, how do we take these attacks? They are more frequent and stronger all the time."

"The same way we always have. No man stands alone. Remember, Jesus says in his Word, 'Where two or more are gathered together in my name, there I will be also.'"

Fred saw the tear trickle down John's cheek. "What's the tear for?"

"The war is just beginning. We will have to be teamed up in twos every possible moment. This will end badly."

"Do you have any details? How can we pray?"

"Fred, you don't want to know the answer to the first question. The answer to your second question is pray that God holds his word to its true value."

June said, "What does that mean?"

"That answer is limited to those God reveals it to. Please understand this isn't a place I chose to go. God chose me to do this. We held strong together, and God's victory is ours. We must never forget this lesson. No matter how tough it gets."

Fred sat stumped on the floor. John had never been so vague and tearful before with his prophecy. He saw fright, joy, and confusion in the past. What he saw now was understanding and sorrow.

John signed. "Samantha, would you join me in prayer?"

"Yes, John. What about the others?"

"You'll understand as I pray. No one else is to know."

Fred watched John and Samantha leave the church and thought he saw a visible sob come from him. He looked at Harry.

"Fred, don't look at me. This is one message that God gave John alone. From the looks of it, the message is more of a burden than any other."

"I don't even know how to pray other than that God hold his word to its true value. What does that mean?"

"I don't think anyone has a full understanding of that but John."

38 THE PLANS CHANGE

Nassor gathered the horde together. Some were strong, uninjured, and ready for another charge. The others suffered injuries, battled with weakness, and couldn't take another charge right now. Something had to be done to weaken the angels.

"Horde, divide in half. One half is to be the strong, ready-to-go demons. The other half is those who need to rest and heal. The angels are stronger than I have ever seen them. We will take shifts. Break them down one by one. They will continue to weaken. Their lines will crumble around us, and then the prayer squad is ours."

The hissing laughter wasn't loud but encouraging. The horde still held faith in him. "Who is strong and ready? We go now."

About two hundred attacking demons rose up and roared in unison. Nassor said, "That's enough. Everyone else rest. Follow me. Let's find a target."

John drove into his driveway. He stepped out of the car and went around helping Samantha out. He saw concern on her face. Twisted in love and joy, fear and heartache wound their way around. "Samantha, everything is going to be okay. It will end with God's plan and riches shining forth."

"How can that be bad?"

"Good or bad are just us looking at circumstances. God will turn all circumstances to his good. Let's go inside and pray."

She shook her head in confusion. "Why are you talking in riddles?"

"You'll understand soon enough. Please just trust me on this."

They went inside the house to the prayer room where John knelt on the bench and expressed by hand for her to kneel with him. After she knelt, John began signing a prayer. As he went from one to another in the church, she couldn't help but notice the prayers for Fred always remained the same. "Keep, Fred. Lord, keep him."

Nassor and the demons saw John and Samantha drive away from the church, and three guardian angels flew off with them. *Two hundred to three, those are odds I like.*

"It's time, demons. They're inside, praying. Shall we make our presence known?"

They agreed in silence.

"Demons." He drew his sword with full flame. "Attack!"

The demons followed, drawing their swords. The guardian angels saw them in time to deflect most of them. One of the smaller imps got through the line and through the roof into the prayer room. The imp hit John in the back, and he dropped on the floor, unmoving. As the imp continued pounding on John, Samantha called her translating service. "Hello."

She tapped the number for Peter and waited. Peter's voice came on the phone. "Hello."

She grunted into the phone the best she could. "Samantha, confirm. Emergency, John's."

She grunted again.

"On our way."

"Guys, we're on at John's now."

The church ran out to the cars, and they took off. One after another parked anywhere they could in the yard and ran into the house. Fred said, "Harry, check the office. I'll check the prayer room."

They both ran up the stairs two at a time. Fred yelled out, "Everyone, prayer room!"

The group came in as fast as the doorway would allow them to enter. The men quickly surrounded John and began praying. The women surrounded Samantha, praying and calming her.

The imp surrendered immediately upon the arrival of the rest of the group. He knew the real war was on the roof now. The guardian angels were fighting. The time had come to weaken an angel with little attacks, imp attacks.

The imp went back to the battle, ready for the pain he knew he would endure. He saw Boris, their prized leader. He raised his imp sword and struck Boris's ankle. The strength from Boris sent him back, but he charged again and again, each blow sending him away. The imp knew that it withdrew strength from him as well.

He paused after several blows, looked around, and saw every angel had multiple imps attacking the angels in similar patterns. He watched the swords swish at the imps missing most of the time. Each time an imp was hit, it immediately dissipated.

The imps continued as the warriors fought each other. The red haze visible above led to the call, "Demons, retreat!"

The angels watched the demons fly away. Boris took the lead in the front. "Angels, we are fighting two battles at the same time. The battle with the warriors is not what will kill us. The imps are sapping at our strength continuously. They don't take much at a time, but they hit enough, and we will feel the drain. My own strength is weakening because of these attacks.

Normally, I would go to the heavens and seek assistance, but it would be useless. If there is anything I learned from Ailith, I learned that time can be on our side. If we can slay the warrior demons the imps would kill off easily."

Cenewig asked, "How do we withstand a fighting army twenty times bigger than you?"

"Cenewig, that is my job. I'll need all of you to listen to every word I say and follow my lead. First off, don't use swords until I pull mine. The imps will come, yes. If they're going to weaken us, it needs to be by us hitting them. It will pull our strength, but they will dissipate."

Dustin asked, "You want us to stomp on them?"

"Stomp, kick, slap, or whatever battle technique you know."

"What are you going to do?"

"The same thing, plus, keep the demonic horde from attacking while we fight. Now we recharge on the prayers of the saints."

Ailith clinched his hands into fist. "Jesus, send me. I'll take care of the problems alone."

"Ailith, you are forgetting the lesson. Just listen. Boris did not forget. He knows you can't help him. He is already planning on how to reduce the problem."

"Yes, Lord."

"You need to remember the lesson of Job. How long did I wait? My word is true. I will not leave them or forsake them ever."

"Lord, the prayer squad?"

"They will all live on my word. Ailith, what you know and they must learn are two different things. Their faith will hold them in the midst of war."

Fred said a final amen as John sat down on the floor, his back to the wall. As Samantha went to his side, Fred said, "What is clear now is that these attacks aren't going to stop."

Harry said, "Fred, are the attacks against us, or are we the ploy to get the real enemy to the fight."

"What are you saying? We no longer do the emergency prayer meeting?"

"No. That will just get someone killed. I'm saying we need more prayer than we can give alone. I know many of us left churches or know pastors. I think it is time to involve prayer partners outside the circle."

Fred picked up his cell phone, dialed two numbers, and listened to it ring three times. "Hello."

"Pastor, this is Fred. I know your prayer warriors are praying for us. Our church has an urgent prayer request."

"What is it, Fred?"

"In the last two hours, we have been attacked twice by demonic forces, and I don't say that lightly. We need God's hedge of protection around us all, especially the two babies, Samuel and Crystal."

"God is confirming every word to me now. I'll start the prayer warrior's twenty-four-hour prayer. Count on this,

Fred. When this is started, you will have to call us to end it. These warriors don't quit."

"That is what we need. This is long term. Harry will have your number as well. He will be able to give you progress reports."

"I want you to put your phone on speaker and have everyone possible touch it. Everyone else can touch someone touching the phone.

I want to pray for all of you now."

They all followed the instructions. "We're ready, Pastor."

The pastor hung up the phone. He picked up the receiver and dialed Betty. "Hello."

"Betty, this is Pastor Brandon. The small church we have been praying for has requested extra prayer. They are under a heavy attack. I believe God wants us to start twenty-four-hour prayer. How soon can it get started?"

"As soon as you let me off the phone."

"Good-bye."

Betty immediately dialed Landon. "Hello."

"Landon, this is Betty. The small church has requested extra prayer. Pastor wants to start twenty-four-hour prayer."

"I'll get the men started. You know what to do."

"Sure do. Let's show Satan what happens when prayer warriors get going."

Jesus said, "No heavenly support."

Ailith said, "That didn't include human prayer support."

"It's time to fuel those angels like they didn't know they could be."

"Yes, Lord."

Boris sat in the house with the rest of the angels, ready and resting. The other angels began to look at Boris questioning. He could not answer, but he did feel what they felt. Prayer strength from somewhere outside those they guarded. He just looked up and prayed. "Thank you, Lord."

Nassor gathered with the other fighting demons. "They are getting weaker. I can feel it in their fight. I need an imp count."

The lead imp said, "You have one thousand remaining. They are not dissipating us because you're keeping them busy. We can beat on them without mercy."

"Keep it up. Give me your two hundred strongest. Let's keep this up."

"Yes, Master."

"Who are my next fighting demons to keep them busy?"

Two hundred flew above the crowd. "Demons, let's go get another target."

Fred knew better than to ask any questions. At this point, it was enough to have John alive and be ready for whatever came up next. They gathered together one more time and prayed. "Do we dare separate again?"

"John responded, "Could we all stay together twenty-four hours a day? We have to go through this no matter how hard it may seem."

"This is more of the plan. How bad will it get before it starts to get better?"

John said, "Look to the Bible. How bad did it get for Job or Paul?"

"Are you saying it will get that bad?"

"I don't know how bad it will get. This I know, God protected their lives through the worst Satan could throw. That is what I believe is going to happen."

"The faith that held us through the house incident will be what we need to hold on to and never let go."

"No matter how tired and frustrated we seem o be getting. We know this is not really about the house specifically. The control of the land the barn was on is more important."

"Satan's plan, it all comes back to the big plan, and we've stepped in the way of its fulfillment."

"Fred, you're getting it. God has placed us in the way. The only thing left for us is to obey and hang on tight to God's train going through the middle of the danger zone."

"We need to stay in groups as long as possible. If we have to divide, we go ready to call. We all know how to pass on the emergency prayer meeting."

"The attacks are coming to the smallest group. Being aware of that can and will save your life."

The group broke up, leaving John and Samantha alone again. Harry and Eva got into their car and headed back to their house. Their hearts were heavy. They both knew without asking why. Eva asked, "What is going to happen?"

"I don't know, the sooner we get out of this car, the better I'll feel."

"What more can the demons do?"

"From what I've seen, anything but kill us. Knowing both examples given by John, Job lost everything but his life before God restored him. Paul lay on the ground after being stoned. He was believed to be dead. Neither sounded good to me when I learned of the events. Now to think it could be me in those shoes, it almost scares me."

"I'll do everything I can…"

"To stop Satan. I know. How much karate would be needed against an attacking demon? When the only weapon is prayer, we just have to keep praying, keep alert, and respond quickly to any sign of danger."

"If the attack is physical?"

"Then we use physical forms of defense. Until that time, the attacks are spiritual in nature. We are used to this in many ways, with the exception of the fact that we are in repeated attacks without a break."

"I'm calling my church's prayer leaders. I don't know what the results will be, but it can't hurt."

Eva picked up the phone and called Kayla. The phone rang twice. "Hello."

"Kayla, this is Eva. I have an urgent prayer request. You remember that Bible study, 'When Satan Brings It On?'"

"Yes, that study went real deep."

"I'm watching it go deeper than they talked about. I talked to you about Harry. I need to open the prayer channels for the whole group Harry is associated with. The attacks are vicious and fast right now."

Nassor looked to a demon. "I want you to get Gary ready. The moment one of the prayer squad gets alone, he goes to attack. I want that one dead. I don't care how."

He flew out of the house, looking for the angels. The group at 5757 Power Lane was still too large, so he flew on. John's angels weren't letting the imps through again. His confidence was firm on that. The cars on the road didn't have the right occupants.

Then the car came into view. Miles stood between them, and he knew the time factor would be critical. Something about those two unnerved him, and his target was selected. "Imps, you two go find out what's going on in that car."

The two imps flew off faster to stay ahead. It took too long for them to get there. They heard the words said over the phone too late to stop the phone call. They looked at each other and flew at the car as it turned into the drive.

She tried to continue the conversation and heard, "Eva, Eva, Eva!"

The phone clicked. The noise faded and then vanished.

Harry called Fred. "Hello."

"Fred, Harry, my place. Eva."

"On our way."

To June, he said, "We're off. Eva. Could you call while I drive?"

"Go."

June picked up the phone and called Peter. "Hello."

"Peter, June, emergency prayer meeting. Harry's."

"On our way."

The phone went silent.

She dialed Bill. "Hello."

"Bill, June, emergency prayer meeting. Harry's."

"On our way."

The phone fell silent again. "Who else do you call?"

"Bill and Peter will get the word out. It's time to start praying."

⁂

Bill looked at Rebeca. "Here we go. It's on again."

"When are we going to sleep?"

"We're not until this thing stops. Do you want them sleeping if it is you or I?"

"No. I guess we move all night if necessary."

⁂

Harry picked up Eva's phone. "Start praying now. The battle is on."

He ignored what Kayla said and went immediately to praying. Harry watched her eyes as he prayed. They fluttered open and closed but didn't respond to anything.

⁂

Nassor waited for the angelic team to arrive and watched the imps start their attack on the angels there. The imps began to dissipate quickly with the kicks and slaps of the angels. "Why aren't they using their swords?"

The more angels showed up on the scene, the faster they dissipated. "Imps, retreat!"

They immediately fell back to the line of fighting demons. Nassor shouted, "Boris, what is your game?"

Boris said, "What game?"

"No messing around. Draw your swords!"

"You can attack us without us pulling swords. What are you waiting for?"

"Boris, we outnumber you at least ten to one. You will fall to us. Why do you fight it?"

"And yet you won't attack us. We are weaker now than when you started and had no fear. Now you hold back the attack. There's something about us you don't want to fight?"

"I'll fight you. I'll kill you too. Where do angels go when they die?"

"You should know. You followed Lucifer there."

"I see you have a sense of humor. I hope you still have it when my sword is stuck through you."

"Are you challenging me to a one-on-one?"

"Is that the way you want it?"

Boris stepped into the middle. "Angels, form a half circle." His hand firmly gripped his sword. You and I alone."

Boris watched Nassor step out and heard the command. "Demons, complete the circle!"

Fred said, "Sleep isn't coming tonight. If we won't sleep, then we do one better. We pray."

John added, "All night if necessary."

Harry said, "Agreed. If we are going to be forced to fight, it's time to show the spirit world we can fight."

All the rest said in unison, "Amen!"

"Between you and me, may the better one be prepared win."

"You already know I'll win. Boris, I'll give you a chance to surrender before anyone gets hurt."

"I'm not surrendering to you. It is time for you to get hurt."

Nassor drew his sword throwing flame at Boris. Matching motion for motion, Boris drew his sword and poised it for the attack. The flame slammed into the sword. Instead of dissipating around it, the fire sucked into the sword becoming light. Boris threw the light back at Nassor.

Nassor poised his sword to block. The strike hit the sword, causing it to explode. The light penetrated the darkness within Nassor, blowing him into the demons that were watching.

Boris watched the demons flee, carrying Nassor back with them.

"Thank you, Ailith."

He turned to the rest of the angels. "Thank you. Your help is appreciated."

William asked, "Did Nassor know what you could do with us surrounding you like that?"

"No, though now I'm sure he won't fall for that again."

"Isn't he dead?"

"No, not in the sense we need him to be. He will be back. For now, we all need to rest and get strength. Let them continue to pray. The demons should leave us alone for a while. William, take the first shift and keep your eyes open. We don't need surprises."

"Yes, General."

Jesus said, "The lesson he learned. When this is over, you'll have to welcome him to the general's squad."

"He will be an asset to our team." Ailith released his sword with a renewed confidence in the team defending the church.

Fred and the church huddled and prayed. In the center of the adults, Samuel and Crystal slept calmly in their car seats.

39 THE HORDE

Finley let Nassor rest in the office. He went to the horde gathered in the main room. "What happened?"

A demon stepped forward. "Master, Nassor fought Boris one-on-one. The strike of Nassor was absorbed by Boris and sent back to Nassor. He didn't stand a chance against it."

"Boris is supposed to be a colonel. That is a skill of a general. How many angels were with him?"

"Twenty-nine, Master."

"Okay, I need three hundred demons for a strike. We let them go now, and they'll take every inch of space we give them to hurt us."

Three hundred demons rose above the crowd. Finley said, "Let's get in the air."

Finley and the demons flew through the roof. He started searching immediately and found nothing. "Do any of you know where the last battle was?"

A demon halfway back spoke up. "I can lead you there, Master."

"Good, come beside me and lead the way. Don't forget who is commanding the mission."

"Yes, Master."

The demon flew up to his side. He guided the direction until he saw a single guardian angel on the roof. "Master…"

"That guardian angel is one of the group causing all the problems."

"Yes, Master."

Boris felt the trouble call immediately and went up to check on the situation. "That's not Nassor. Finley is carrying on with the mission."

Boris felt anger rise from within and knew it could do more harm to the angels and people than any good it would do. He forced himself to calm down and wait before commanding. "Angels, defensive positions."

Finley saw the angels multiply and the wall of protection form. He stopped the demons in midair. "Demons, we outnumber them. How strong are they really?"

"Nassor took one hit, Master."

"Then we had better have a plan to weaken them before we assault them with everything. Attack in waves of one hundred. Fifty hit high and fifty hit low. Light blows drain their strength. Remember speed. Their swords can dissipate you quickly."

The demons divided and took battle positions.

Boris said, "Angels, be ready for anything. Swords as shields."

Boris drew his sword into the defensive position followed by the other angels. He watched the first wave come in high and low and held position. Time seemed to stop. Seconds drifted farther and farther apart. The line stood still, not a muscle moving. Just when time stopped completely, the demons slammed into the shields and legs of the angels. The second wave diverted the direct course to avoid the demons flailing back at them. Their altered angle of attacks allowed the angels a sword advantage, and Boris wasn't letting it go. "Angels, sword strike!"

The strikes hit both the low and high wave at the same time, stopping the third wave completely.

Finley shook off the attack in time to see the second wave take out the third wave before ever reaching the angels. Frustration and impatience tried to settle in to his bones. He took two deep breaths to regain his control. Demons, return."

Finley led the demons back to the base house. He walked into the secondary room used as the medical checkpoint for the wounded. He walked through the fighting demons there and knew what he failed to account for put them there and ended the battle way too soon.

Nassor called out, "Finley, report."

Finley came in the office. "Master, how are you?"

"I'm fine. Why is it that we have more wounded? If it was an attack, what was learned from it?"

"Master, if the attacks stop, the angels have a chance to get stronger. I led a wave of demons to keep them busy."

"Who was attacked?"

"Master, the angels."

"Again I ask, who was the target?"

"Master, the angels were already together. We had no available target."

"And you attacked anyway."

"Yes, Master."

"What attack strategy did you use?"

"Master, high low three wave."

"Did it work?"

"No. The first wave could shake it off, the second wave was mostly injured but flying, and the third wave never got to the angels."

"How many more injured fighters?"

"Master, at last count, ninety-five."

"Hold off on further attacks. I'll be up and around soon. Something needs to be figured out."

Fred watched as the church stood up slowly from praying. Samuel was secure in Rebeca's arms and Crystal in June's. The church felt peace for the first time that day. That seemed to go on and on. Fred said, "I don't know about you guys, but this one is tired."

Rebeca said, "I think that is mutual with all of us. We all could fall asleep right now. Are the attacks over tonight?"

"Rebeca, I've fallen asleep in praying many more times than you can fathom. Unless John or Harry has a different message from God, I would rather fall asleep praying at my own home. Are there any objections?"

The room remained silent. Most of the church just closed their eyes. "June, do you need a ride to the church to pick up your car?"

"Yes, I do. I also want to make sure you stay awake while you're driving."

Shortly after Fred and June left, the rest of the church dispersed to their own homes with peace in their hearts.

40 TRAINER'S FRUSTRATION

The night's rest was uneventful and much needed. Fred got out of bed, showered, and dressed. He knew the morning would be full, but twenty minutes remained before it all started. He opened his Bible to where he left off and began reading the first chapter of 1 Timothy. The eighteenth and nineteenth verses struck him in an unusual way.

> Now, Timothy, my son, here is my command to you: Fight well in the Lord's battles, just as the Lord told us through his prophets that you would. Cling tightly to your faith in Christ and always keep your conscience clear, doing what you know is right. For some people have disobeyed their consciences and have deliberately done what they knew was wrong. It isn't surprising that soon they lost their faith in Christ after defying God like that. (1 Timothy 1:18–19)

Beside the text, he found a handwritten note directing him to Ephesians 6:10–18.

> Last of all I want to remind you that your strength must come from the Lord's mighty power within you. Put on all of God's armor so that you will be able to stand safe against all strategies and tricks of Satan. For we are not fighting against people made of flesh and blood, but against persons without bodies—the evil rulers of the unseen world, those mighty satanic beings and great evil princes of darkness who rule this world; and against huge numbers of wicked spirits in the spirit world. So use every piece of God's armor to resist the enemy whenever he attacks, and when it is all over, you will still be standing up. But to do this, you will need the strong belt of truth and the breastplate of God's approval. Wear shoes that are able to speed you on as you preach the Good News of peace with God. In every battle you will need faith as your shield to stop the fiery arrows aimed at you by Satan. And you will need the helmet of salvation and the sword of the Spirit—which is the Word of God. Pray all the time. Ask God for anything in line with the Holy Spirit's wishes. Plead with him, reminding him of your needs, and keep praying earnestly for all Christians everywhere.

God's word pressed into a place that was deeply in need of comfort. Fred dropped his head in his hands. The tears swelled in his eyes. He could see himself falling at the feet of Jesus. The only phrase that he could mutter was "Jesus, help me." He could see Jesus reach out his hands, and he felt the strength lift him off the floor and place him on his lap. Without resistance, he rested in the image frozen in his mind. "Hold true to your word. Please hold true to your word."

The answer came in his spirit, though it was as if he was really in the image, and Jesus whispered in his ear, "I always do. My son, I always do."

He just cried into Christ's shoulder for what seemed hours. When Jesus whispered, "My son, your morning starts. I will be with you always. I'm available to you always. When you need my shoulder, it will be just as strong and comforting. Now go and do my work."

Fred felt himself lifted off his lap, and the image vanished. He knew more had to be done that day and waited in the kitchen with coffee brewing to start the day. June's voice rang out. "Honey, I'm home."

"Fred got up and took Crystal from her. The memory of the image flashed through his mind as he placed her on his lap. "Has she had breakfast?"

"She is fed and changed, but you know as well as I the changing won't last long."

"That's okay. I'm learning quickly. Do you have time for a cup of coffee?"

"As many as you can serve, I have today off. I thought you would want to see Crystal anyway."

"Of course, I would pull your chair out, but my lap is full."

"Using the baby as an excuse? You should be ashamed."

"Maybe tomorrow. Today God has protection on his mind."

"What do you mean?"

"Come sit here beside me. This may be a long story."

The knock on the door interrupted the conversation. "Come on, Crystal. Your boyfriend is at the door."

June said, walking behind him, "No dating until they're sixteen."

Fred opened the door. "Welcome, Bill. Come on in and join us."

June said, "I've got free arms for Samuel."

Bill said, "That's up to him."

June clapped her hands in front of Samuel. Samuel immediately raised his hands to her. She took him out of the car seat. "Samuel likes me. Yes, he does."

Trainer felt agitation and knew the demons had been close more than once. They hadn't taken him or given him any information. This he knew. The house on Power Lane was not his anymore, and he didn't like the new feeling. Didi told him one day how to lash out at the enemy from within without hurting the host. Now this was the time to try.

Trainer rode the bloodstream to the spot where the attack would be most effective. He prepared and waited. He searched for the heart. "You will see how much Trainer likes being protected."

Placement was right, and he was ready. He launched out and immediately backed in.

June no more than got Samuel to her chest than her eyes popped wide open. Bill dropped the car seat and caught Samuel and June and gently placed them on the floor. "Rebeca, call an ambulance." Fred and Bill started praying immediately.

They were there in minutes; someone let them in and led them to June. Bill saw the paramedics working on June. "Fred, come with me. They know what they're doing." The paramedics went into their routine and got her into the ambulance.

"What happened?"

"Trainer happened."

"Why?"

"You know better than to ask. Pray."

Bill heard Rebeca say, "Emergency prayer meeting, St Matthews. Start the calls."

"Bill, you ready to go? I'm driving you. Take care of Fred."

"What are we waiting for?"

They went immediately and loaded the car. Bill knew the thoughts going through Fred's mind. His thoughts went back to the drive to get Saundra to the hospital. "Fred, it's going to be okay. She is going to be fine."

Fred never said a word. Bill started singing one of the praise songs he learned from the church. He remembered it so well because he sang it two million times to get through some days when Saundra's death hurt so much.

Every once in a while, he would add an encouraging word to Fred.

Fred's phone rang twice before he said, "Hello."

John said, "Fred, you need to know that Jesus has not authorized any demon to kill one of his own. June is going to live."

"Why her? I'm the one they're after."

"We've talked about this before. You know what is going on."

"I know. I just want to know why."

"Fred, I need you to trust me on this. It is in God's hands."

"Is the whole church coming?"

"Rebeca started an emergency prayer meeting. Everyone has been contacted. Hold it together for me. Harry will be at the doors waiting for you."

Fred let the phone fall to the floor. The pain, hurt, and doubt swelled up, trying to overshadow the image of that morning. The arms of Jesus in the image reached out toward him. Fred ran through the pain and fell to his lap. He tried to pray, but all he could get out were sobs. Fred could hear, "Rebeca, how quickly can we get there?"

"We're pulling in the driveway now. I'll park the car. Get him in there."

Fred stumbled in the hospital as he was held up by Bill. Fred felt the familiar hands of Harry. "She is allowed one visitor. I'll take him to her room. Fred, she is going to make it. Can you stand up?"

"Yeah, I can stand now. Show me where she is."

"Fred looked in the corner of the ICU and saw her hooked up to monitor wires and IV tubes. He walked to her side to hear the doctor say, "She is comfortable now. We will be putting her in a room soon. She is strong. She will be just fine."

"Thank you. Can I go up with her?"

"Of course, but you'll have to use the visitor elevators. You can stay with her until she leaves. They will tell you what room they are putting her in."

He watched the doctor leave.

Dana, June's mother, sat in the room, praying. Her eyes focused on June lying still on the bed. Her mind kept going back to the words of the doctor. "Her heart has a pint-size hole in it. She will need to stay calm. We are doing all we can to help it heal."

She looked up at the noise of the door to see Fred come in the room. She asked, "Where's Crystal?"

"Rebeca and Bill are in the waiting room, watching her and Samuel. They are good friends."

"What happened?"

"She picked up Samuel and fell right after."

"She has never shown any sign of this. How can it wait so long?"

"I don't know. I'm sure the doctors will do everything they can. Do you mind if I pray for her?"

"I would appreciate it. I've heard of what you can do with prayer."

She watched as he took her hand, allowing the tear to drip down his cheek. She didn't hear any words but let him go on anyway. Then she heard him getting louder. "Jesus, touch her with your hands of healing. We give her to you. Make her whole…"

June didn't know what was going on. There stood a man looking at her. He was neither coming closer nor walking away; he just looked. She looked for any sign to identify him. Then she saw it—the marks on his hands…no, not marks but holes. She knew who it had to be and how the holes got there.

"Jesus? Jesus, what happened?"

"My daughter, you have seen many miracles from me for others. Now it is time for you to see a miracle for you." Jesus took his finger and touched the hole in her heart, and it immediately closed, and all the damage around it restored as if the incident never happened.

"Why can't I wake up?"

"The doctors don't want you to yet. Don't worry, the drugs will wear off. You will wake up to many caring visitors."

"Jesus, is anyone else hurt?"

"No, my child. No one else is hurt. The others realize how much you mean to them."

"Fred can't be left alone, or he'll be attacked. I've got to get better."

"Fear not. Fred has many willing to be beside him in this hour. In fact, he will never be left alone, nor will you."

"Help me understand. What is going on?"

"I have told those that need to know. They know what to do. Follow them, and you will be following me."

"I still don't understand. Please, Lord, help me understand."

"You don't need to understand to follow. You need to walk behind them, even when you don't understand."

She waited for what seemed to be forever before she realized she was standing on a cloud. "I haven't died?"

"No, my child. You are protected, and I'm not going to let you die. Your time has not come. You are seeing something that the others haven't seen."

The clouds rolled back to reveal a glass floor. Below it, she could see thousands of people praying all over the country. Jesus said, "This is for you. They are asking me to heal you, save you, and just about everything else possible."

"How do they know?"

"Oh, child. Some know by phone calls, others by my spirit's message, and yet others just praying in general for the health of the church and all the individual members. Either way you look at it, it's all the same. They're all praying for you."

"What's that?"

"That is the bowl of healing prayer. It will overflow to you, and everyone will know I did a miracle that no one else could have."

"The bowl looks too big to fill. How will they fill it?"

"Child, that is where the miracle comes from, the multitude of prayers. The bowl was already here before you needed it. Trust me on this. I'm more than enough to get the job done in any circumstance."

She stood there and watched as the prayers streamed in the bowl, and it slowly filled. The prayers continued for a long time before she looked down. She saw Fred on his knees. The hurt and pain were visible to her. Her mother and two others from the church tried to comfort him. She couldn't hear what they said but knew what they attempted to do anyway.

"Jesus, he hurts so badly."

"Yes, he does. If you look at the bowl, it fills faster the longer he cries. He cries to me. That is why no one can comfort him."

"He is my miracle. He is filling the bowl."

"He is a big part of your miracle. The others with him are adding to the bowl too. I don't orchestrate accidents. You are with him now for a reason."

"Is this forever?"

"That choice belongs to both you and Fred. You understand that your will still plays a role in the overall picture."

"I try so hard to align my will with yours."

"I know, and you are doing a good job, but you are finding your humanness getting in the way sometimes. The spirit is willing, but the flesh is weak. I am your strength. That's okay. That is what makes the Christian life what it is on earth. The bowl is almost full. It's time for you to go back. You keep up the good work."

Fred stayed on his knees in the room. A tissue in one hand and June's hand fit snuggly in the other. He already told the others he wouldn't stop praying until she woke up. He stopped listening to outside voices, trying to get him to move. The voice that entered his ear stood out. He recognized it. "Honey, I'm home."

Fred raised his head. "June?"

"Thank you. God has answered your prayers."

"You're healed?"

"Yes, Jesus touched me in a way that the doctors won't understand."

Fred stood up and said, "Oh, June, I love you so much."

"I love you too. I'm tired yet. I want to take a nap. I'll wake up soon, I promise."

"I'll be waiting."

"I want to wake up to an army called the church."

"I'll work out what I can."

"You do that." She closed her eyes and fell asleep. Fred turned to Dana. Dana said, "What I've heard is true. God listens to you. We can wait together. I want to be here when she wakes."

"I'll make some calls. See if I can get this room full of the church."

Fred called Harry. The phone rang twice before he answered. "Hello."

"Harry, she woke up and talked to me for a minute and then fell back asleep for a nap. The monitors are showing normal heart rate, blood pressure, and oxygen levels. She told me the prayers worked."

"That sounds like we need to thank God for the miracle."

"I already have. She still has a way to go. The healing can continue. She also asked for the praying army called the church in the room when she woke up. I say we pack the room to the capacity the hospital will allow."

"I've got that covered. Your pastor is on his way up there right now. I knew you wouldn't mind."

"You called him?"

"Yes, now I'm going to call the prayer leaders to update them. They have been praying twenty-four hours. They take shifts, but the prayer never stops."

"That's the way it works around that church. That won't stop until God's victory is accomplished. I was part of one of those sessions that lasted for six months. No one gave up."

"What was the prayer for?"

"A friend of a member of the church had a family member in a life-threatening accident. He's now a member of the church."

"God listens to those people."

"And God answers in a way that produces many miracles."

"It sounds that way. I'm glad I met him."

"I'll talk to you later. The prayer warriors need the update."

"Okay."

Fred put the phone back in his pocket just as the door opened. "Fred, you in here?"

"Yes."

"What is this I hear? You have been having similar problems and didn't get our prayer warriors praying."

"God has always answered our prayers. When God gave us the last big victory, I thought it was over. Apparently, this demon doesn't want to give up."

"From what I hear, it is more than one demon. I'm glad you called me. Don't think you have to get in this deep to call on us. It is our privilege and honor to be on your emergency prayer squad. I worked it out with Harry."

A tear swelled in his eye. "Pastor, how do you handle this pressure?"

"I don't. I'm surrounded by many prayer warriors. God takes so many of the pressures that you couldn't understand until now."

"Thank you for coming."

"You're still a lamb in my fold to me. Call me anytime."

"Pastor, this is Dana. She is June's mother. This is June. She is sleeping now, which is probably best."

After they shook hands, the pastor said to Dana, "Your daughter could do no better than this young man."

Dana replied, "I knew that when he called me, but thank you for the confirmation."

Fred interrupted the conversation. "What all have you heard?"

"More than you want me to tell. Harry and John were very helpful."

"Yes, Harry and John can be helpful, sometimes too helpful."

"Your church is strong. They are taught well. You have no reason to be ashamed of anything. The root that God has started is going well."

"You can see that from talking to them?"

"I can see that because I saw it with another church that one of the warriors stood in my office touching the back of my chair for three hours refusing to give up. Sound familiar?"

"Yes, it worked too. There was more than one."

"There was one leader and instigator."

Fred's phone rang. "Hello."

"Harry here. I've got permission to bring up the two babies, so there will be a large group coming. Is the room ready?"

"The room is ready. She is still sleeping. We may just have to talk to ourselves for a short while."

"No talking, we get together and pray together. There is a lot going on here. Besides, I would like to see your pastor lead a group prayer meeting."

"Okay, I'll let him know."

Fred turned to his pastor. "The church is going to try to fit in this room. They want you to lead a group prayer meeting."

"They want to see the example you had. I'll do what I can to honor your leadership."

"It is always an honor to be around you and be influenced by you."

The door opened, and the line poured in, filling much of the room to standing room only. The door closed behind them all. Pastor said, "How tight can we gather in? Fred and I and anyone else that can touch the bed. I think Fred should start the prayer, and when everything is quiet I'll close it out."

Fred said, "Hello, Sarah. We've got to stop meeting here."

"Yes, we do." She turned to June. "Girl, hang on, we need you in here. The numbers completely stabilized fifteen minutes ago. Everything is normal."

"That's what happens when you invite Jesus into the picture." Fred said with a smile.

"Yes, it is. Remind me to call you if someone in my family is in here. You seem to shorten a person's stay by days."

"Not me, God."

"Hello, Pastor. Nice to see you." Sarah smiled at him and then went about her work.

"It's a small world. My sheep tend to end up together in more ways than one."

"So June says in more ways than one."

Fred said, "The only mystery is, how many people know?"

Sarah said, "Look at the faces in the hall. Even the doctors around here know. Do you really think that June is going to hide that from us? By the way, some of the nurses want to come visit during their lunch, so some of you may have to make room."

"We can do that."

She wrote on the chart and said, "Fred, Dana, here is a menu for something to eat. The nurses want to meet the one who captured June's heart. Many have tried and failed."

Fred watched Sarah turn and leave. I think I'm famous around here."

June's eyes opened, and she said, "Famous to some, envied by some, you get talked about often." She looked around the room at all the familiar faces. "All but one I recognize. Could you introduce me?"

"June, this is my pastor. You ask for an army. Some will have to leave soon. You have some nurses coming in during their lunch hour to see you."

"More to see you." She smiled. "When are you getting lunch?"

"I was told to order in on your tab. I also got a warning about the some nurses wanting to see me."

"I'm sure. Why don't you send Harry down to the cafeteria and get your lunch? You can tell him to get enough for two. I'll share with you."

"What about the doctor's orders?"

"Yes, June, what about my orders?"

"Dr. Lockwood. I was just going to ask him to tell the nurses I'm hungry." She grinned.

The nurse said, "She has fifteen minutes to order from her menu, and they will deliver her anything she wants, but only from her menu."

The nurse gave a warning glance to Fred.

"There you go. The shoes on the other foot now, young lady. Lunch delivered just like any other patient. Now let's look at the miracle child. I've scheduled you for another scope to check on your heart. I need everyone out while I'm doing this."

The room cleared out. "Now, June"—he placed the stethoscope in various places—"take a deep breath."

He took her pulse, looking for more than what the monitors would tell him. "June, from what I can tell, you don't belong in here, but I want to see the scope before I let you go. If all is well there, then I can release you."

In the waiting room, the group gathered around John when he said, "This surprised the demons. The original demons we combated kept silent until today. We need to be ready for any and every attack. Things may get personal fast."

The pastor said, "May get personal? It's going to get worse?"

"Pastor, if I may call you that, I know they will. Don't ask anymore. I just can't say what I know. God is preparing the way now."

"How bad is this going to get?"

"We'll see you again. It gets personal."

John saw the doctor leave the room and turned to Fred. "Fred, you can go back in. The doctor just left."

John watched Fred leave while holding his arm out to block the pastor. "I need to express something to you…alone."

They waited until all had left. John said, "What you don't know is that God has to unify this church under me and Fred. The unification will be tested soon. Get your warriors praying that they withstand the test."

"What test? This sounds serious."

"More serious than I can tell you. Please pray. I can't tell you anymore. If you need to know more, ask God."

"This is minor in comparison to what is coming?"

"Yes, I want to tell you more, but I can't right now. It doesn't feel right."

"Then don't. We are already praying twenty-four hours a day. The warriors will know the urgent need. I will look for more information from the updates."

"That's good."

"John, sometimes God gives you a prayer need, even though it is tough for you to handle."

"Thank you. I'm going to pray in secret again. So far, God has strengthened me through these times. He's not giving me the answer I want."

"Do you expect him to answer you the way you want?"

"No. Like David, I don't want to give up."

"Then go with all willingness to obey no matter what God wants."

"That is part of my prayer."

John went directly to the ICU waiting room. He found an empty chair and put Fred in it mentally. The tear trickled down his cheek. "Jesus, if you can do this any other way… what can I do to allow your plans to change? I praise you for all you've done, but Fred…please spare him, Lord. Please make another way."

"John, it is not the way. It is the lesson that needs to be learned. This is the way I choose to teach it. I understand how you feel. I've been there before. I obeyed to my death. You are where you are today because of that obedience."

"Yes, Lord. You'll have to give me strength to get everyone through this."

"John, you have all you need. When you need more, it is waiting here to be delivered."

John raised his head, stood, and started the walk back to the room.

John walked back into the room and found three visitors and no patient. John asked, "Where's June?"

Bill said, "They took her down for, hopefully, one last test. We're hoping she can go home tomorrow."

"Where are Fred and Dana?"

"Harry and Peter took them for a walk. We got babysitting duty."

John looked around the room with the look that scared them most of the time. "The news is good."

"Then why the look? What is bothering you?"

"Nothing. I'm glad to hear the good news." He put on a smile as best he could. "You are talking to Bill, the one that threw fake smiles and lies on a regular basis to hide bad news. That was the worst fake smile I've seen. Something is eating you alive. No one wants to hear you can't talk about it. Please give us something."

"I'd rather tell you the whole thing, but I can't. You've seen this look on Fred before. He bore a burden that he took alone until something happened. Then he could share all of it. I'm in the same situation, different person."

"Those were not good times. John, how bad is it going to get?"

"That depends on the church. God will tell me all soon. Too soon, I'm afraid."

"This isn't over."

"Bill, this isn't over until Samuel is free from the demon possession. Each step makes the demons angrier. I think you realize that angry demons try to hurt their enemy. We are the enemy they are after."

John looked down and seemed to struggle with every step. He left, followed by Bill and Rebeca, each holding a baby. John walked down the hall into the gift shop. He strolled through the variety of gifts to give the patients. He saw a male figure reaching down to pick up a lost lamb. He fell to his knees, bent over, burying his face, and sobbed. He heard Bill say something about the coffee shop but couldn't respond. He felt Bill and Rebeca lift him and help him to a table. After the sobbing stopped, he said, "Bill, am I really ready for this?"

"I don't know what it is, but I know God will give you the strength to do what he needs you to do."

"That isn't what is concerning me. Can I obey God, even though it is going to hurt?"

"You have heard and lived through more examples of obedience that led to pain than I have. You know how and what it takes. You are ready for that part. You just have to keep on going no matter what is thrown at you."

"It all comes back to that. Keep doing what you know is right."

"Essentially, that is what Fred has taught us all along."

"You're right, Bill. Will you stand with me and help me?"

"You have all the help I can give you."

"I'll need it."

The doctor sat in his office, looking at the results of the test. He searched the picture of June's heart taken just after she got in the hospital and then back to the one just taken. He picked up the phone and dialed the extension for the other cardiologist. "Hello."

"Hey, do you have a minute for a consult on some test?"

"Yeah, sure, you got everything in your office?"

"I'm looking at them now."

"I'll be there in a second."

He faced the pictures and shook his head in disbelief for the hundredth time. He heard two soft taps, and the door opened. "What are you looking at?"

"You tell me."

"The patient may need surgery. Why are you comparing the patient to a healthy heart?"

"This one is the patient when she came in two days ago." He pointed to the picture on the left. He changed his finger and tapped the picture on the right. "This one is the same patient today. It was taken less than an hour ago."

"You know what I say to those patients?"

"No."

"You are ready to go home. There is nothing wrong with you. Then I sit in my office and thank God for doing the hard work for me."

"Do you really believe in God?"

"Do you have a better explanation for this?" He pointed to the two pictures.

"No. That works for me."

The room was full again when June saw Fred walk in. She smiled. "It's good to see you. Are you ready for me to go home?"

"Yes. The doctor is letting you go. The paperwork is coming after breakfast. The test results were so good that I don't need to stay anymore."

"Great, I was hoping for good news. Do you feel up to holding Crystal?"

"Always, I got another day off to rest so I can go to the house with you to help take care of her."

put Crystal down with June. "Only if you feel up to it. If you need to rest, you can go where you want. I can handle Crystal."

"I can rest at the house with you. You need to work anyway, and I can nap with her." Dana said, "I've already given her all the options. She would rather go with you."

"I have the car ready for her. I promise to take good care of her."

Dana replied, "You know you're not going to get any work done."

"It can't be worse than Crystal alone. Maybe she can catch a messy diaper. I seem to get a few a day from her."

June said, "I'll just be getting out of the hospital. You may have to change those yet today."

"Is there any way for me to win?"

The room filled with laughter, and June said, "No, but that is the way it is supposed to be."

Dana said, "Any more questions?"

Fred said, "No. She'll need to sleep anyway."

The visitors made room for the kitchen staff to deliver her breakfast. She ate her breakfast and started guiding the packing. The men carried down the gifts and other bags as Dana packed up her clothes and any miscellaneous items that remained. By the time men returned, she was ready with Crystal on her lap. June said, "I'm just waiting on the paperwork."

Sarah said, "Then let's get it signed. June, your ride down is here."

She signed form after form and listened to final instructions. She held Crystal in the chair all the way down to the car. Fred helped her in the car after buckling Crystal in the car seat. He sat in the driver's seat and asked, "Are we ready?"

"Yes." June smiled. "Very ready."

41 Gary Meets Fred

Fred was left alone in the office. June was escorted by Bill and Rebeca to a play place for children of any age. He only stayed behind at the request of June and Bill and the insistence that everything is fine. They were coming back in an hour. Fred had his Bible out and open to the text he was preparing.

The demon flew in to the office. "Master, I have great news."

"Continue."

"Master Fred is alone in the office. There would be no better chance to get revenge."

"Well done. Get Gary on the case. Make sure Fred dies."

"Yes, Master.

He first read the notes he already had written. He reread the text again, listening for anything he may have missed. The notes seemed complete and ready to go, so he took his Bible and notes downstairs to the living room. The knock on the door stopped him from starting his practice. He went to the door. “Hello, may I help you?”

“Yes, my name is Gary. I’m wondering if you have time to answer a question for me.”

“If I can. We can go to my office.”

“That would be great.”

Fred walked to the office with nerves fluttering, trying to send a warning. After both entered the office and the door was closed, he asked, “What can I answer for you?”

“Where is Crystal?”

Fred saw the countenance change immediately. “She is not here.”

“That is the wrong answer. Let’s try this again. “Where is crystal?”

“Gary, she is not here. I wouldn’t tell you where she is anyway.”

“You’re being a brave daddy.” His hand reached across the desk, and he slapped him off balance and then grasped his shirt. “Where is she?”

Fred picked up his phone, dialed two numbers without Gary seeing, and placed it on the desk. Gary asked, “Where is she?”

Harry picked up the phone. “Hello.”

"Where is she?"

Harry remained silent. He recognized Fred's strained voice saying, "She is not here. I couldn't tell you where Crystal is anyway. I don't know."

He hung up the phone.

Harry turned to Eva, Bill, Rebeca, and June. "Fred is in trouble."

Gary grew angrier. "Do I sound like I'm joking in any way?"

"No, you don't. I'm not either."

Gary took his fist and slammed it into Fred's nose, breaking the bone with ease. He saw the blood run out. "Where?"

"I don't know?"

He took his arm and thrust Fred into the door frame, bouncing him into the corner of the office. "Are you awake yet?"

Fred didn't move or answer. He walked over to him, placed his head in the position he wanted it, and knew he was still alive.

"Fred, it's too bad you won't see your precious friends anymore. I so like the thought of smashing your head and pulling out your brains. When I leave here, you will have a closed casket funeral."

He started pacing back and forth, watching, making sure he didn't wake up on him. "What shall I do first? The better question is, what bone should I break first? Let's see your arm." It moved with no resistance. It snapped with ease and was left turned the wrong way.

"Pain isn't going to wake you up. That's fine. I have a solution to keep you asleep forever." He knelt to his knees and raised his fist beside his head. "It is time to die. Yes, Fred, it is time to die."

CPSIA information can be obtained
at www.ICGtesting.com
Printed in the USA
LVOW04s2054120816
500060LV00016B/192/P